About th

Sam Haysom is a writer and journalist covering culture and entertainment for *Mashable*. He wrote the bulk of *The Moor* during National Novel Writing Month in 2015. You can read all about his experience on *Mashable*'s website. He's also written a number of short stories, one of which won first prize in a monthly competition run by the dark fiction website *Spinetinglers*.

A graduate of Cardiff University, he grew up on the edge of the New Forest and now lives in London.

You can follow him on Twitter @samhaysom.

THE MOOR

THE MOOR

SAM HAYSOM

This edition first published in 2018

Unbound

6th Floor Mutual House, 70 Conduit Street, London W1S 2GF

www.unbound.com

All rights reserved

© Sam Haysom, 2018

The right of Sam Haysom to be identified as the author of this work has
been asserted in accordance with Section 77 of the Copyright, Designs and
Patents Act 1988. No part of this publication may be copied, reproduced,
stored in a retrieval system, or transmitted, in any form or by any means
without the prior permission of the publisher, nor be otherwise circulated in
any form of binding or cover other than that in which it is published and
without a similar condition being imposed on the subsequent purchaser.

ISBN (eBook): 978-1-912618-07-1

ISBN (Paperback): 978-1-912618-06-4

Design by Mecob

Cover image:
© Shutterstock.com/

Printed in Great Britain by Clays Ltd, St Ives Plc

For my mum, Clare Midgley,
The kindest person I knew.

Dear Reader,

The book you are holding came about in a rather different way to most others. It was funded directly by readers through a new website: Unbound.

Unbound is the creation of three writers. We started the company because we believed there had to be a better deal for both writers and readers. On the Unbound website, authors share the ideas for the books they want to write directly with readers. If enough of you support the book by pledging for it in advance, we produce a beautifully bound special subscribers' edition and distribute a regular edition and e-book wherever books are sold, in shops and online.

This new way of publishing is actually a very old idea (Samuel Johnson funded his dictionary this way). We're just using the internet to build each writer a network of patrons. Here, at the back of this book, you'll find the names of all the people who made it happen.

Publishing in this way means readers are no longer just passive consumers of the books they buy, and authors are free to write the books they really want. They get a much fairer return too – half the profits their books generate, rather than a tiny percentage of the cover price.

If you're not yet a subscriber, we hope that you'll want to join our publishing revolution and have your name listed in one of our books in the future. To get you started, here is a £5 discount on your first pledge. Just visit unbound.com, make your pledge and type MOOR18 in the promo code box when you check out.

Thank you for your support,

Dan, Justin and John
Founders, Unbound

Super Patrons

Jamie Anderson
Dominic Aquilina
Nicole Barbosa
Emily Bater
Henry Bell
Catherine Bowles
Steven Bristow
Jessica Bull
Rosie Caporn
David Carr
Declan Cashin
Nick Chen
Tim Chester
Adam Claessens
Sophie Claessens
Neil Claessens
Terry Claessens
Dani Claughton
Laurence Clayton
James Coleman
Clive Collison
Adam Crossman
Dan Dalton
Kate Davies
Lindsay Davis
Neil Dickson
Danielle Donnelly
TriumphoftheNow Dot Com
Simon Emmett
Hannah Evans
Martin Evans
Tony Field

Will Frampton
MJ Franklin
Jennie Gale
Jack Gillespie
Rebecca Greer
Nicola Gurney
Verónica Gutiérrez
Sarah Ham
Louise Harris
Katie Harrison
Elisha Hartwig
April Hautea
Charlotte Hawkins
Janel Hayley
Duncan Haysom
Pamela Haysom
Marcus Haysom
Jake Haysom
Maisie Haysom
Blathnaid Healy
Liza Hearon
Tom Hickish
Becks Hill
Mark Hillman
Susanna Holden-White
Tatjana Humphries
Carly Hunt
Alexandra Jeffries
Khali Joel
Marius Jooste
JSM
Tyler Kenyon
Dan Kieran
Anthony Lavea
Chloe Lockhart
Karen Lockhart

Neil Lockhart
Debby Lockhart
Keely Lockhart
Amy Lord
Robin Lutman
Alison Marlow
Kate Martin
Julie McQuaig
Charlie McWilliams
David Midgley
Clare Midgley
Phil Midgley
John Mitchinson
Tara Mulholland
Nikolay Nikolov
Maya Ninel
Mark O'Neill
Nadiyah Patel
Billy Picard
Justin Pollard
Eoin Purcell
James Roberts
Anna Robertson
Anja Robinson
Daniel Ross
Carlton Rowlands
Oliver & Lydia Rowlands
Alan Searl
Claire Shaw
Becca Snabel
Francesca Spence
David Spittle
Sam Stevenson
Helen Stevenson
James Tallant
Amanda Tanner

Rachel Thompson
Nancy Thompson
Gary Thompson
Anne-Marie Tomchak
Mark Vent
Emma Vince
Deborah Wade
Paul Ward
Miranda Whiting
Joshua Winning

News Cuttings (1951)

From the Devonshire Herald, 13 August 1951

Police appeal for information regarding missing schoolchildren

Anyone with any information on the whereabouts of two missing school children in the Rutmoor area has been asked to contact Devon and Cornwall police immediately.

Devon and Cornwall Police have issued an urgent appeal for information regarding two school children who were last seen on the evening of Friday, 10 August.

Paul Reece, 16, and Charles Gregson, 14, were reported missing on Saturday after wandering off from a school camping trip in Rutmoor National Park. Teachers and classmates, who camped in the north east of Rutmoor just south of Gorgon Tor, first noticed their absence after they failed to turn up for the register at 8am on Saturday morning. Upon inspecting their tent, trip leader and school PE teacher Mr Simon Matthews found it to be empty. Aside from two pairs of walking boots, the rest of their possessions were still in the tent. Police were contacted by Mr Matthews after a search of the surrounding area yielded no trace of the boys.

Reece is described as being an athletic, sensible young man with several years' hiking experience and a good knowledge of the surrounding area. He was in training for the 13 Peaks Challenge (Gold Award) – a competition in which groups of children from different schools aim to walk to the summit of 13 different tors in a weekend – after successfully completing the Silver Award last summer.

Gregson is described as sensible and intelligent, but an inexperienced walker. It was his first visit to Rutmoor National Park. The boy's mother, Mrs Sarah Gregson, has issued a passionate plea for information regarding her son's whereabouts.

'If anyone has seen my boy or has any information at all, no matter how small it seems, please contact the police immediately so we can

1

get him back safely,' she said. 'Charles doesn't know the area at all well and we're very, very worried about him. Please come forward so he can be safely returned to us.'

Chief Inspector Douglas Brown, who is heading up the investigation, said the public should not to hesitate to contact police.

'No matter what you think you may have seen or heard, no matter how small or insignificant you think it may be, we would like to hear about it,' he said. 'We're also interested in speaking to anyone who was out walking or camping on Rutmoor on the night of Friday, 10 August or at any time over the following weekend.'

From the Devonshire Herald, 15 August 1951

Boot of missing schoolchild sparks further police appeals

The discovery of a walking boot thought to belong to missing 14-year-old Charles Gregson has prompted fresh appeals by police and a £30 reward for information.

Devon and Cornwall Police have issued a further appeal for information after the discovery of a child's walking boot thought to belong to missing teenager Charles Gregson. The boot was found by a dog-walker on Tuesday, 14 August, 15 miles south of the area Gregson and fellow camper Paul Reece were initially reported missing. Police say the boot was discovered on the bank of Foxglove Stream, but have refused to give further details at this stage.

Charles Gregson and Paul Reece were on a school camping trip in the north east area of Rutmoor when they were reported missing on the morning of Saturday, 11 August.

Parents and teachers are said to be organising a search of the 15-mile area between the children's original campsite and the spot where the boot was found yesterday.

'We're following up a number of leads and speaking to various people,' said Chief Inspector Douglas Brown. 'At this stage, I'd urge anyone who may have seen or heard anything unusual in the Rutmoor area, at any time from Friday, 10 August until now, to come forward immediately.'

2015

This time it's the rain that gets him.

Every time he makes the journey out of London – starting on a train at Waterloo and winding away from the city, flashing past towns and villages and cutting back into the countryside of his childhood – every time there's something that triggers the memories.

Last time it was the sight of the sun catching a field of heather, peeking out from behind a cloud to turn the mass of purple into a lighter violet and making him squint as he stared out of the train window; this time it's the rain.

Only it's not really rain, is it?

Pissy fucking drizzle is what Gary would probably have called it, and Gary may have been wrong about a lot of things but he wouldn't have been wrong about that.

He stares out of the train window and the droplets seem to hang there in the air, blowing about in the wind like snow, and he knows it's the type of drizzle that'd soak you through to the skin in less than a minute if you were stupid enough to go outside without a decent rain coat.

It's the type of drizzle they used to get on Rutmoor.

He lays his head back against the red patterned seat of the train and stares out at the drizzle, and when he shuts his eyes a series of images pinwheel across his vision like a film reel.

It's funny, he thinks, how something as small as the sight of rain from a grimy window can invoke such strong memories.

He used to get it a lot in the years after leaving university and starting work – something would catch one of his senses and hit him hard enough to transport him briefly to another place, another time. He'd hear a snatch of MGMT's *Time to Pretend* and he'd be taken back to a summer festival, *any* summer festival, or he'd open a can of Grolsch and the smell would remind him of the house party in first year where he'd lost his virginity.

Small things that for some reason brought on strong memories. Little moments that could make you infinitely nostalgic.

Now, looking at the rain and cutting south away from London, he doesn't feel nostalgic.

The rain makes him think of Rutmoor, it makes him think of the summer of 2002, and in his mind he sees drizzle picked out in cones of light from their minivan as they carve their way through cracked country roads; he hears the sound of whispering and twigs breaking outside a tent; he tastes the cloudy purified water they drank from streams that were little more than trickles in the mud. Mostly, though, he remembers Tim and Mr Stevens. Mr Stevens looking up from his map and the sun reflecting off his glasses, turning his eyes into hard rectangles of silver light.

Thursday, Part Two

He's got a large bag that's shoved up in the luggage area above the seats; it's his walking bag, the big green one, and it's got most of his stuff in it. On the seat next to him is a smaller bag, a brown one he takes to work with him. It's full of paper. Cuttings, mostly, bits he's torn out and built up over the last few months, but there's something else in there too.

He glances around to check who else is in the carriage. It's a Thursday, midday and it's not very busy, but there's a couple across the aisle from him and an old lady a few rows in front. She's reading a book, though, and the couple are watching some film on an iPad.

He glances back into the bag, satisfied, and pulls out an old Polaroid. It's yellowed around the edge from being handled over the years, but the picture is still clear.

It's all of them, the six that went to Rutmoor together in 2002. All standing together outside a tent. Everyone in the photo is smiling, and he runs his finger from left to right checking them off: Gary, James, Tom, Matt, Tim, and Mr Stevens, tick, tick, tick, tick, tick, tick.

All present and accounted for.

He frowns to himself and flicks the photo with his finger, looking out at the drizzle-soaked scenery.

When he thinks about his friends – both the ones that died and the ones that are still alive, no matter how different the surviving few may look now – it's always this photo that he sees in his mind.

All of them lined up like that, smiling in front of a row of green tents, a small campfire on the ground in front of them and some water bubbling away in a saucepan. All frozen in time.

Who was it that took the photo? He can't remember now, and doesn't think it matters.

The whole nightmare started with the six of them, after all; they were the ones who mattered.

He glances at the pieces of paper stuffed in his bag, then shakes his head. The nightmare didn't start with the six of them; it would do him well to remember that. This was something that had been going on for more than half a century, probably even longer.

At the time – during that long weekend in Rutmoor in the summer of 2002 – it had seemed like it was just about the six of them, but when you're 13 years old everything feels as though it's just about you, doesn't it?

Now he knows better.

He's different from the boy smiling out of that Polaroid photo – maybe not that different physically, at least compared to the others – but he knows he's different nonetheless. He's a lot less tolerant, for one. A lot less forgiving, too.

If I'm going to put a stop to the whole thing once and for all, he thinks, *I'll have to be.*

For a while he goes back to staring out of the window, not really thinking anything at all. Eventually the drizzle eases up.

News Cuttings (1958–1998)

From the West Devon Gazette, 23 June 1958

Man's body found in Rutmoor National Park

Police are launching an investigation after the body of an 18-year-old man was discovered beside Collier Lake in south Rutmoor.

The body of 18-year-old Fred Phillips has been discovered on the shore of Collier Lake in Rutmoor National Park.

Phillips and his fiancée, Jude Peterson, were camping half a mile from the lake near the top of Collier Tor. Peterson woke Sunday morning to find her fiancé's sleeping bag empty. After searching the nearby area for approximately 30 minutes, she told police she came across his body on the southern shore of the lake.

The cause of death is thought to have been drowning.

Devon and Cornwall Police are appealing for information from anyone who may have been in the area in the early hours of Sunday, 22 June.

They say they are not treating the incident as a murder inquiry.

From the Plymouth Daily Herald, 22 June 1986

Teenagers drown in freak river crossing accident

George Perry, 18, and Paul Samuels, 19, died after falling into the Sully River in Rutmoor National Park on Saturday.

Two teenage boys have drowned while attempting to cross Rutmoor National Park's Sully River.

The bodies of the two boys were found by hikers a mile down the river from the place they attempted to make their crossing on the afternoon of Saturday, 21 June.

It is understood that the boys had tried to use fallen branches to cross the river at a narrow point at the base of Stallion Tor. Police say one of their packs was recovered from the bank next to the makeshift crossing.

'That river is fast, a lot faster than most people realise,' said Inspector Daniel Rodgers. 'It's likely that one of the boys fell in and the other went in after to try to rescue him, and the current swept them away. It's a real tragedy.'

Perry and Samuels were out camping in Rutmoor – a place they were familiar with after completing the 13 Peaks Challenge there together while at school at Plymouth Comprehensive – for a long weekend.

'I don't understand how it could have happened,' Perry's father Roger told the *Daily Herald*. 'Both of them knew the terrain well; they'd been all over that moor while they were at school training for their 13 Peaks event.

'I just don't understand why they would have tried to make such a dangerous crossing in the first place. They were taught about the dangers at school, they would have known what was safe and what wasn't.'

From the Yeovil Daily Post, 6 April 1998

Yeovil's 'cat serial killer' strikes again: decapitated Persian is latest victim in series of bizarre pet murders

The decapitated body of a 2-year-old Persian cat was left on its owner's doorstep in what local animal safety officers are calling 'a depraved and deliberate act of violence calculated to cause distress'.

The killing is the latest in a string of brutal cat murders that has left Yeovil residents locking their pets up indoors to keep them from wandering the streets at night.

72-year-old Mr Terry Patrick, the owner of the Persian and Yeovil resident for over 40 years, said he was 'devastated'.

'I opened the front door in the morning to let Jonesy in – I'd been meaning to put a cat flap in but he normally likes to wander at night and I hadn't gotten round to it yet – and when I walked out onto the front step I seen him lying there in front of me.'

'It was just his body and his head was missing but I knew it was him, he's got this little dark splodge of black on his left leg and I knew it was him.'

Mr Patrick said the discovery left him feeling 'ill for days'.

'I reported it to the police and I just hope they catch the person that did it, so no one else has to see what I saw,' he said. 'My wife passed away three years ago and I got Jonesy because the house felt too empty.'

'I'm devastated, to be completely honest with you.'

The Yeovil Animal Safety and Rescue Centre have issued a warning to residents, advising them to keep their pets locked up indoors at night.

'We've had reports of mutilated cats turning up for several weeks now,' said a spokesperson. 'We believe it could be the work of the same individual, or individuals, and we'd advise anyone in the Yeovil area to keep a close eye on their pets.'

Last week on Wednesday, the *Daily Post* reported on a 5-year-old cat that had been found with its stomach slit open and some of its organs removed. The week before, two more cats were found dead with their throats cut; one of them was missing a tail and the other was missing its front paw.

A spokesperson from Avon and Somerset Constabulary confirmed they are working with the RSPCA to investigate reports surrounding suspicious animal deaths in the area, and that an investigation is underway.

Dr Timothy Flagstaff, a lecturer in Criminology at the University of Bristol, said the evidence could suggest the work of a serial killer.

'These reports are very concerning,' he said. 'The extreme violence of the killings coupled with the missing body parts – which could be being kept as trophies – suggests an individual with a disturbing lack of empathy.'

'When we look into the cases of well-known serial killers or psychopaths, these individuals have often committed acts of violence towards animals in their teenage years,' he continued.

'What may start as a thrill for the individual in question gradually loses its effect over time, which often leads to the criminal taking greater risks to recreate their initial excitement.'

James (2002)

When James Tramper looked around the campfire, he had a brief moment of unreality. Unreality, was that the right word? Maybe not, but he couldn't think of a better one, and his gran always told him that if you didn't have the right words you had to make do.

They were sat in a circle around the fire. The area they were camped in was large and sprawling, with tents of various colours and shapes spread out across an open field. The light was just going out of the day, and James could see other people huddled around fires in the distance, drinking from cans or mugs as they sat on the grass or in fold-out green camping chairs. His own little group of six had finished eating not long before, and James could still feel the remains of his boil-in-the-bag chilli con carne sloshing around in his stomach. He'd only managed to eat half of it in the end – partly because he was nervous about the coming weekend and partly because it tasted disgusting – which had prompted a predictable dig from Gary.

'Finally going on a diet are you, Tramper?' he'd said, loud enough so the whole group could hear.

James had done his best not to look embarrassed.

In the half-hour since the food had been finished, a sleepy silence had fallen as his friends stretched out and shuffled closer to the fire. Gary was on his left, his long legs folded awkwardly beneath his body; Matt and Tom were to his right, laughing about something or other, their heads close together as they spoke in half-whispers. And across the fire, which was just catching and beginning to give off tendrils of smoke, were Tim and his father.

Tim.

The New Boy, as Gary still insisted on calling him.

Tim wasn't actually that new anymore – he'd joined Oaksmith Secondary School about halfway through Year 8, maybe just after Christmas – but they didn't often get new kids coming into their school during term time. James guessed that made Tim the new boy.

And besides, he still *felt* like the new boy.

There was something about Tim that was sort of absent – *stand-off-ish*, James' gran might have said – that made him hard to get to know.

With someone like Gary, he'd just come up and punch you on the arm or make some stupid joke and that would be that, *friends for fucking life* as Gary liked to put it, but Tim seemed to give off this aura that meant you couldn't joke around with him in the same way you could with the others.

James remembered a day earlier in the year – one of many school-days that seemed to meld together into a blur of forgettable lessons and too-short lunchtimes spent hanging around on the field or walking to the cafe to get chips – when Tim had wandered up to their little group during break.

At that point he wasn't someone James would have thought of as a friend (*not that he really is now, either*, a part of his mind added), but the new boy didn't know anyone else and James' gran had made a point of asking them to look out for him.

'Mr Stevens says his son's very shy,' she'd said one night over dinner. 'It might be nice if you kept an eye on him – it's no fun starting at a new place where you don't know anyone.'

She'd looked up at James and fixed him with her blue eyes as she said this, and James knew that when she said *It might be nice* what she really meant was *You'd just better get on and do it or I'll be cross.*

James' gran had met Mr Stevens at their local church. Like all of the parents, she had taken a shine to him. He was charming and polite, and seemed to have no trouble meeting new people.

His son was a different story.

He'd come up to them during that not-so-distant break, a tall and brittle boy with skin that looked like it had never seen the sun, and instead of saying anything he'd just stood there at the edge of their group and stared at them.

James and Matt had mumbled hello and Tom had nodded before going back to his bag of potato wedges. But Gary had stared at Tim with a curled smile on his face. He had that look in his eye he sometimes got before he dead-legged James out of the blue or called him a new nickname for the first time. A sort of hungry look.

'You alright, mate?' said Gary. He stared at Tim with false concern on his face, and then glanced around the circle at the rest of them. He shot a wink at Tom and then looked back at Tim, who was staring at him without saying anything.

'I said are you alright mate?'

For a few long seconds Tim still didn't say anything, and James had to stare down at the ground to stop from feeling awkward. Finally, Tim shrugged.

'I'm fine.'

'Really? Cuz you don't look fine. You look like you've just swallowed a mouthful of piss.'

Gary spluttered laughter. Matt rolled his eyes and Tom shook his head, smiling.

Gary was just warming up. He now had an eager half-grin on his face that James knew all too well: it was the look he got when he was really ripping into James over something, that slightly predatory smile that was half a joke and half something more serious.

'I mean you *really* don't look well, mate,' said Gary. 'Maybe you should visit the school nurse or something, have a little sit down. It's overwhelming coming to a new school, isn't it? All these new people.'

Gary made his face into an exaggerated pout and looked at Tim, who stared back without saying anything or dropping this gaze.

Gary's smile faltered slightly.

'Hey, what the fuck's your problem, anyway?' he said. 'Can't you talk?'

Tim regarded Gary through eyes that were a very light brown. *Almost orange*, James remembered thinking. 'What's your problem with me?' Tim said.

'Huh?'

'I said what's your problem with me?' Tim's face was a pale blank. His voice was steady.

Gary looked confused for a moment. James stole a quick glance at Tom and Matt, but Tom was concentrating on his potato wedges and Matt's eyes were fixed on something on the ground.

'No problem,' Gary muttered. 'It's just you wander over here and stand there without saying anything and it's sort of weird, mate.' Gary paused. With what looked to James like a real effort, he forced a grin back onto his face. 'It's like you're some kind of homo or something.'

This time no one laughed. Gary glanced round the circle for support, but everyone else was looking at the floor. Tim still hadn't dropped his gaze.

'How's that?' he said.

'How's what?'

'Well, how does coming over and standing here make me a homo, exactly?'

Gary met Tim's gaze for a moment longer and then he looked away and mumbled something at the floor. James felt a sudden wave of affection for the new boy. After a few seconds of silence Matt turned to Tim and asked him about where he'd been to school before Oaksmith, and Gary scowled and asked James about the slice of pizza he owed him.

And that had been that.

In his own strange, silent way, Tim had become a part of their group.

2

'Has everyone marked their maps?'

Mr Stevens' quiet, sharp voice rang out over the campfire and put a stop to the mumbled conversation.

He was sitting directly opposite James on one of those green folding chairs the campsite hired out for £5 a pop, putting him higher up than the rest of them.

The light from the growing fire shivered and jumped in front of his face as he glanced at each of them in turn.

Mr Stevens had a long, thin face framed by rectangular glasses. His hair was short, dark and always carefully combed and parted. James thought he looked like the most 'dad' dad in the world. With his neat haircut and pale, clean-shaven face he seemed to James like a nerdy embodiment of everything a typical middle-aged man should look like. His eyes, like his son's, were a pale brown, and like Tim's they also had a habit of lingering awkwardly when he looked at you.

Now Mr Stevens reached into the walking bag by the side of his chair and drew out a clear plastic pouch, which he unzipped to take out his map.

He reached his other hand down and placed it on Tim's shoulder who, without saying anything, opened his own bag and did the same.

James found himself picking out his own map without even realising he was doing it.

'Did we all need to mark our maps then?' asked Tom. He was sitting with one arm leaned casually on his raised left knee, his long right leg stretched out in front of him so his foot was near the fire.

'Yes, everyone should have the route marked out before we set off,' said Mr Stevens.

James heard Gary let out a sigh. It was quiet, almost under his breath, but Mr Stevens' head swivelled in his direction just the same.

'Did you say something, Gareth?'

Gary sighed again, louder this time. 'Nah, it's just that, well, do we really all need to mark it out? I mean we're not all going to be navigating, are we?'

'I hope you're not going to be navigating,' grinned Tom. 'We'd never get out of the car park.'

Gary scowled. 'We're only doing, what, 60 odd miles in three days? It's not like Rutmoor's the Amazon forest—'

'Rainforest,' muttered James, quiet enough so Gary wouldn't hear.

'And besides,' continued Gary, 'We'll probably never be more than a couple of miles from a path.'

He tilted his head back and rubbed his chin. It was a habit James noticed he'd copied from his father a while ago, and James found himself thinking *It's less impressive when you don't even have any stubble yet you idiot.* He knew if he ever said that Gary would come back at him with something worse, though, so he kept quiet.

There was silence for a few seconds, and then Mr Stevens cleared his throat. Tim shot a glance up at his father, then looked back into the fire.

'Timothy, pass Gareth your map,' he said.

Tim handed the map over to Gary, who took it with another, more audible sigh.

'If you look at the route, Gareth, you'll see that we're actually travelling to an area of the moor that's probably the furthest in the park from any roads. We're carving out west tomorrow and then heading up north, and by Saturday – assuming we're on course – we'll be a good 10 miles or so from the nearest bit of civilisation.'

James glanced over at Matt, who raised his eyebrows and gave James a half-guilty smile before looking away again.

It was Matt who'd convinced James to come on the trip.

James couldn't remember exactly where the idea had come from or who'd first suggested it, but one day it seemed to be all their parents were talking about. They thought it'd do the boys good, apparently, and they were keen for them all to go with Mr Stevens. Probably they just wanted them to take a break from sitting in a dark room at Gary's and playing *GTA III* on his PS2 all day, James thought.

Either way, he hadn't been at all keen at first.

He'd made the mistake of sharing his reluctance with Gary.

'For fuck's sake Tramps, how are you ever going to lose any weight if you don't do anything other than sitting round scratching your balls all day?' had been the response.

Gary wanted to go on the trip because he was keen to get into the 13 Peaks Challenge team next year at school. Year 9 was the first year kids could try out, but it was mainly the Year 11s that ended up getting selected.

'What's so great about walking all weekend, anyway?' James had asked, in a last ditch attempt to turn things around.

Gary rolled his eyes. 'I don't give a shit about the walking,' he said. 'What *I* care about – and you might be less interested in this than me, so sorry if I'm boring you – what I care about is a full weekend of walking behind Beth Jacobs in a tight little pair of walking trousers. Or maybe waiting for her at the top of a hill while she bounces up after me.'

Gary smiled and closed his eyes, as if picturing it.

'Yep, it's gonna be good,' he said. 'And then when it's time to set up camp for the night and everyone's asleep, I'll wander over and pay her tent a visit.'

'Sure, and then she'll start screaming.'

The words were out before James could stop himself, and Gary's eyes flashed open.

'Don't fucking start with me, Trumper,' he whispered. 'At least I've got a chance. She'd take one look at you and throw up in her pretty little mouth.'

Later that evening, Matt had called James on the phone.

'I'm thinking of going along on this walking trip,' he said. 'I know it's a bit random but my mum won't stop banging on about it – keeps saying how excited Mr Stevens is and how nice it'll be for his son to make some new friends – and I'm fed up with listening to her.'

James knew exactly what Matt meant. Ever since he'd made the mistake of mentioning to his gran that Tim had come up and spoke to them at school, she'd been like a dog with a bone.

'You really should spend some more time with him you know, James,' she'd said as soon as he told her. 'Tim's dad is always saying how shy his son is. You should invite him along to one of your video game nights.'

James thought about telling his gran that nobody called them video games anymore, but quickly decided against it. Comments like that never seemed to go down too well.

'I could do,' he mumbled. 'He seems nice enough, it's just—'

'Just what?'

'It's just he's a bit odd, I guess. He's sort of quiet.'

James' gran was sitting on a chair with a magazine open in her lap. Now she snapped it shut and scowled.

'He's not *odd*, James. He's new to the area, and he doesn't know anyone, that's all. He's just shy.' She was staring at him now, unblinking, and there was a hard tone creeping into her voice James didn't much like the sound of. He backtracked quickly.

'I didn't mean odd, exactly, it's just… well, he looks sort of unwell, doesn't he? Kind of tired and stuff, and he doesn't really say that much…'

He trailed off awkwardly and looked away from his grandmother's gaze. She didn't say anything for a few moments and James stared at the floor, bracing himself. But when she next spoke, her voice was softer.

'All I'm saying is it's hard to be the new boy. And I'm sure he'll come out of his shell once he gets to know you all.' She paused. 'If he's anything like his father, he'll be quite the charmer.'

James glanced up at that and his gran smiled at him. 'What do you mean, charmer?' he said.

'Oh, nothing.' She picked up her magazine, but the smile stayed on her lips. 'I just mean Tim's dad has been quite the hit with the ladies over at the church. He always has them giggling over coffee and biscuits after the Sunday service.'

She glanced up at James and winked, and in that moment he'd made the swift decision to end the conversation right then and there by agreeing to invite Tim round that very weekend. Having your gran smiling about someone's dad was bad enough, but James thought that wink had been downright uncalled for.

So sure enough, that Saturday, Tim had come over. He was just as quiet as before at first, but James' gran wasn't wrong – after a few rounds of multiplayer on TimeSplitters he was laughing along with the rest of them. He was *good*, too. Said he'd never played before, but after only a couple of games he had Gary convinced he knew some kind of cheat code that he wasn't telling them about. James chatted to him a bit on his own in the kitchen later when they went to get some squash, and although Tim could be a bit vague at times – he seemed to get awkward if you asked him too much about himself – James came away realising he was starting to like the kid. As James' gran might say, he had *potential*. He wasn't as much fun as Matt and Tom, exactly, but when he did talk he had this cool way about him that even Gary didn't seem to have an answer for, and—

'Oi James, you still there?' Matt's voice in the telephone cut through his thoughts. James realised he must have been doing what his gran liked to call 'space staring', and he blinked. For a moment he couldn't remember what Matt had called him about.

'Sorry, what were you saying?'

'I said I'm fed up with listening to Mum bang on about this walking trip. I think I'll head along.'

Right. The walking trip.

'I don't think I'll go,' James said quickly.

'How come?'

'Well, where do you want me to start? Mainly, I don't fancy the idea of having to put up with Gary for a whole four nights. And besides, I'm not even sure I *could* walk 60 miles. In case you hadn't noticed I'm not exactly as fit as the rest of you guys.'

The words came out sounding angrier than he'd meant them to, and Matt was silent for a moment before answering.

'Let me and Tom handle Gary,' he said. 'You know what he's like, he never means to be a dick. At least I don't think he does,' Matt paused, 'and think how cool it'd be if we start walking now and then we *do* end up making the team in a year or two? Then we'd all be ripped, I reckon.'

In spite of his annoyance, James found himself grinning.

'I know Mr Stevens is a bit of a nerd, but he seems like he'd be pretty organised about what we can and can't do,' Matt continued. 'If anyone's struggling too much I bet he wouldn't force them to do anything they didn't want to.'

James knew Matt was in persuasive mode – *That boy's gonna grow up to be a lawyer or a politician*, James' gran had said in the past, and James thought she might have a point – but he could feel himself being swayed nonetheless.

'I dunno.'

'It would make your gran happy though, right? She seems to love Mr Stevens.' Matt paused, and when he next spoke there was a smile in his voice. 'And besides, don't pretend you don't like the idea of sharing a tent with Beth Jacobs one day if we make the team. Christ, I know I do.'

And that had been that. Several weeks later and here he was, sat around a campfire watching as Gary and Tom marked routes on their maps with black marker pens, and starting to seriously wonder how he was going to walk 60 odd miles with a backpack triple the size of his school rucksack.

Gary stuffed his map in his pack and yawned. The light had seeped out of the sky, and the campsite was falling silent as families and couples around them headed into their tents, or lowered their voices to the hushed whispers that seemed appropriate in the huddled silence of the moor.

To his right, Matt fidgeted and changed position. Mr Stevens cleared his throat.

'You never know Gareth, you might be glad of that map over the weekend if we somehow get separated.'

He had a half-smile on his face and James knew he was joking – *making a dad joke*, as Matt sometimes said when one of the teachers at school tried to join in with their banter – but James suddenly found himself thinking about something Gary had whispered to him on the journey down, as they sat shoulder to shoulder in the backseat of Mr Stevens' minivan.

You'd better stick with me out on the moor, Tramper. You wouldn't want to end up like all those kids that went missing.

James had grinned and ignored him at the time, knowing what Gary was doing and that he wanted James to bite. But now the words drifted back to him.

'What should we do if we get separated?' he asked. Out of the corner of his eye he saw Gary grinning at him, but he kept his eyes on Mr Stevens.

'Oh, I shouldn't think we will, James,' Mr Stevens smiled across the fire, 'but it's always best to be prepared, don't you think?'

James nodded and Gary stifled laughter.

Mr Stevens frowned slightly.

'I know it sounds silly, boys – and let's be clear, the chances of anyone getting lost on this trip are almost non-existent – but it can happen and it does happen.' He paused and rearranged his glasses as he glanced at each of them in turn. 'I'd much rather everyone had a route marked down and knew the basics of navigation.'

James could see Gary fiddling with his shoe laces out of the corner of his eye, but Mr Stevens had the attention of both Matt and Tom now. James looked at him and noted the calm, serious expression on his face.

When he'd first met Mr Stevens he'd been reminded of someone he couldn't quite place, and it was only now – watching as Mr Stevens took a compass from his pocket and held it up so it caught the light from the fire – that James made the connection to a teacher he'd had back in junior school.

Mr Parker, he'd been called. He'd taught science.

Mr Parker had been one of those adults that had a strange command of the classroom which only became apparent when someone crossed him. He didn't look like Mr Stevens physically – he wore glasses but he was shorter and much fatter – but he'd had a similar presence that was hard to put your finger on until you got to know him.

James remembered that some of the boys had tried messing around in Mr Parker's class, and how quickly Mr Parker had straightened them out, pulling them into line with his firm voice and hard stare. He'd looked kind of nerdy on the outside – permanent sweat patches and a podgy build, someone Gary probably would have rinsed in the playground – but there was an edge to him hidden not too far below the surface.

James thought Mr Stevens was a bit like that.

'–and that's how you take a bearing boys, does that all make sense?' James blinked and realised he hadn't been listening to a thing Mr Stevens had said. The man's brown eyes flicked over to him, and James forced himself to smile and nod.

'Does that make sense, Gareth?'

Gary was halfway through muttering something inaudible when a sudden wind kicked up and shook the fabric of their tents. The fire spluttered. James heard a shriek from the other end of the campsite, and then distant laughter.

He glanced round at Matt, who gave him a reassuring smile.

'Isn't there a storm forecast for Saturday night?' said Gary. James turned to look at him and saw a smile on his face. He was looking at Mr Stevens but James knew he was directing the comment at him.

Mr Stevens frowned again. 'I'm not sure about a storm,' he said. 'There may be some wind and rain forecast, but I haven't seen anything to suggest it could be worse than that.'

Gary feigned concentration. 'I thought I read something about a storm,' he said. 'Wasn't there a storm the time that family went missing out on the moor?'

'Oh shut up Gary,' said Tom. But he had a grin on his face and James could tell the last thing he wanted Gary to do was shut up.

'No, I'm serious!' Gary raised his eyebrows. His eyes were wide with surprised innocence. 'My dad told me about it before we left. Something about a whole family getting lost out here back in the '50s or '60s or something. I think they got caught out in a storm.'

Gary looked around at them all. His eyes lingered on James for a moment but he didn't smile.

'That's not the only thing I heard, either,' he continued. 'After what Dad said I looked this place up on the internet, and there's all sorts. Teenagers turning up drowned. Kids coming out here and going missing. There's a whole forum talking about a witch that they say was burned at the top of one of the tors back in the olden days. Really bad stuff.'

James tried his hardest to remind himself what Gary was doing, but when he glanced over at Matt to share a grin or a roll of the eyes he saw his friend wasn't even looking at him. He was staring into the fire, listening, his face yellow in the flickering light.

Tom was still grinning.

'I heard some stuff about that too,' he said. 'My uncle used to come walking down here when he was younger, and he said there were stories the locals used to tell in pubs about people seeing a woman out on the moor at night.'

Gary nodded. 'That's right. They said in the forum that she'd appear on the moor to people that got lost, and that she'd be standing there in a white dress and waving and—'

'No, that's not quite right.' James felt relief at the sound of Mr Stevens' voice. Despite his best efforts to ignore Gary he was growing more and more aware of the chilly night air and the wailing rush of the wind flapping through the tents around them. He wanted Gary to shut up but he knew that if he said anything he wouldn't hear the end of it for the whole weekend. Although Gary had barely looked at him as he spoke, James knew this whole stupid speech was for his benefit. Gary was trying to scare him. Probably something he'd been planning for days before the trip as a way of keeping himself amused.

Mr Stevens cleared his throat in the silence. Gary stared at him expectantly. Mr Stevens took off his glasses, looked at them, and then placed them back on his face.

'You're not quite right there, I'm afraid,' he repeated. 'There is a story about a woman who they believed was a witch, but she wasn't burned at the top of any tor. She was murdered by someone local.'

The boys were silent now. The wind picked up again, moaning through the hills in the distance, and James shivered.

Mr Stevens glanced at his watch. 'Well, we've got an early start tomorrow morning, boys, and we should probably be thinking about—'

'Aren't you going to tell us about the woman?' That was Tom. He was staring at Mr Stevens with his lips slightly parted in expectation, and James could have kicked him.

Matt was still looking into the fire and didn't say anything, but Gary spoke up again. 'Yeah, come on, you can't start a story and then not tell us how it ends.' He still had the ghost of that predatory grin on his face, but now he looked genuinely interested, too.

James thought about just getting up and going to bed, but dismissed the idea.

Tim was looking up at his dad with an expectant expression on his face. Mr Stevens cleared his throat.

'Okay, well I suppose a quick story before bed wouldn't hurt.' He gave a small smile and looked around at them. 'It's a bit grim though, I warn you now, so you'll have to promise you won't get me in trouble with your parents if I tell it to you.'

He paused and looked on as Gary and Tom shook their heads. His eyes moved over to James for a second, and he smiled before adjusting his glasses and staring back into the fire.

'It's just a story, at the end of the day,' he said. 'But it's one quite a few locals around here enjoy telling of an evening, and I wouldn't be surprised if one or two of them believe it. The man I heard it from is a local historian. He works over at Plymouth University, and the moor's history is his area of expertise.

'It's a dark history, too. You were right about that Gareth. There have been disappearances over the years, and I believe I may have heard something about the family you mentioned, although I'm not sure that happened during a storm. I think they just vanished.'

He paused and readjusted his glasses.

'The woman you were talking about – the one some people say was a witch – was called Emily Brown, and she worked on a farm not too far from the moor in the 19th century. It must have been around the 1830s or 1840s, and although many of the laws relating to crimes associated with witchcraft had been repealed by then, there was still a lot of violence towards—'

'Dad.' Tim's voice was so sudden it actually made James jump. He'd been staring into the fire, focused on the sound of Mr Stevens' voice. The story, despite its grim subject matter, was strangely hypnotic. It reminded James of an audiobook called *Spooky Tales for Sleepovers* he'd stolen from the library when he was eight years old, one he'd kept under his pillow and brought out when his parents went downstairs to watch TV. That had been scary, too – it had given him nightmares for weeks, he remembered – but it had also had a strange pull that made it hard to turn off.

James blinked and pulled his gaze away from the fire. Tim was staring up at his father, a slight frown on his face. The others were staring at Tim, waiting to see what had caused the interruption.

'Dad, maybe we should be getting to sleep,' said Tim. 'It's late, and we'll need to get up at six tomorrow if we want to keep on schedule.'

Gary started to say something but Mr Stevens held up a hand and he fell silent.

'Timothy, when someone's telling a story, don't you know that it's very rude to interrupt them?' Mr Stevens didn't raise his voice – if anything it grew quieter – but there was a firmness to it that made James think once again of his junior school teacher Mr Parker.

'Dad, I—'

'No. I've started my story now and you'll be respectful enough to listen to it until I'm finished.'

Tim stared at his father for a moment longer before dropping his eyes. None of the boys said anything, but James thought he saw Gary grin out of the corner of his eye.

Mr Stevens frowned and went back to staring at the fire.

3

'Emily Brown worked on a farm, and she got into something with the wife of a man who owned a different farm on the other side of the village,' continued Mr Stevens. 'The woman hated her, apparently. There are different theories about how their feud started: some say Brown was having an affair with the woman's husband; others think it was nothing more complicated than a simple case of jealousy. Brown was young, after all – probably about 17 or 18 when this happened – and by all accounts she was beautiful. Long red hair, freckles. Green eyes.'

James stared into the fire and all of a sudden he could see her. A slim beauty with hair that flickered and jumped in the wind like flames, the type of girl he sometimes conjured up in his mind after everyone was in bed and he was sure his gran wouldn't come barging in on him.

'Whatever it was,' said Mr Stevens, 'this farmer's wife had a terrible grudge against her. And back then, if you had a problem with someone, sometimes the easiest thing to do was to start a rumour about them.'

He paused and glanced up from the fire, looking round at the boys.

'The thing is, with Emily Brown it wasn't even that hard. She was known in the village as something of a recluse – she never attended church or came out to the pub or village fetes, and she'd turned down several of the local men when they'd expressed an interest in her.

'There were already strange stories about her family, too. She'd moved to the village when she was about 12 or 13 to live with her uncle, who owned the farm she worked on, and some people said her parents had been killed in a house fire over in Somerset. Others said it was Dorset and they'd drowned at the beach. No one seemed to know the exact story.

'Anyway, this farmer's wife – for whatever reason – had it in for Emily. She'd lived in the village her whole life and she was well-known and well-liked, so one day she walked into the Horse and Hare – that was the local pub, if I've not got it wrong – and got chatting to some of the locals. Gossiping, really. She asked them what they thought about Emily, and then she said she was worried about her. Said she'd seen her wandering on her own, late at night. Said that one night she'd been woken up by a strange sound, and when she'd looked out of her window she'd seen Emily out in one of their fields, standing completely still and staring up at the house. As if she knew the farmer's wife was there and she was waiting for her to come to the window.

'Obviously most people were sceptical, but then the farmer's wife got some support from a local lad in his twenties – probably one of the men Emily had turned down, that would make the most sense – who said he'd seen her out wandering on her own at night, too. Out wandering with a cat following along at her heels. Said he'd seen her talking to the cat too, and although he knew a lot of people spoke to their pets it looked a whole lot stranger when it was the middle of the night and the girl was out on her own.

'He made a joke out of it, apparently, and a lot of the men had laughed, but not all of them. There were men in that pub who were suspicious by nature; ones who'd seen their crops fail after a bad run of weather, or come out in the morning and found sheep lying dead with their throats chewed out by animals. Religious men, and ones who knew stories about women like Emily Brown. Women from other villages who'd been caught in bizarre night-time rituals. Women singing and dancing around fires, or doing unnatural things with animals. Stories that were fine when they were told by men passing through from Cornwall or Hampshire, but not so fine when they were springing up in their own village. No, not fine at all.

'So anyway, what started off as a seed planted in a local pub and a bit of a joke quickly became more serious. The word "witch" started being mentioned. By eleven o'clock that night they had a group of about 15 or 20 people from the local area – scared and angry people who wanted to get to the bottom of what they'd heard. And that was when the farmer's wife made her second move. She'd lit the first match and then watched as a small flame grew and took hold, and now she came back in just as people were fired up and wanting to take some sort of action. And she played a very clever game.

"We can't just go out there and confront the poor girl without any proof," she said. "I wouldn't want to get her in trouble just because of something I saw." And she put on her best innocent face and the men patted her on the arm and told her not to worry, and then she retreated into the background again when someone else came forward and made a suggestion – the suggestion the farmer's wife had clearly been waiting for all along – that a few of them go up to the Brown girl's farm that very night and see what they could find. See if there was anything out of the ordinary going on.'

Mr Stevens paused and cleared his throat. He pulled a cup out of the holder in the arm of his chair, took a sip from it, and then put it back. None of the boys spoke. He readjusted his glasses and picked up where he'd left off.

'Now, the story gets a bit fuzzy at this point. The way the historian told it to me, the farmer's wife had played a very clever game and been over to the Brown girl's farm before she came down to the village that night. She'd prepared everything. But then I've heard the story from other people – local men who swear their great-great-great grandfathers were there at the time and they'd had the real version passed down – that say the farmer's wife had nothing to do with what happened next. They paint her as nothing more than a local gossip who only wanted to spread some rumours about a girl she didn't like, nothing more sinister than that. I'll let you make up your own minds.

'Either way, a group of five or six men left the pub and set out on the two mile walk through the countryside to the farm the Brown girl shared with her uncle. He owned a good few acres and the farm was large and old, and Emily had her own little side cottage away from the main farmhouse where she lived on her own.

'When the men got there they saw a light in one of her windows, a small candle flame, and they split up into two groups and circled the house to see if they could see anything through the windows. One group approached through the front field, and the other went around the back.

'It was the second group that made the discovery. Obviously, no one knows exactly what happened or what those men really found except the men themselves, and they're long dead. But the story goes that they discovered a circle of old stones in the field behind Miss Brown's cottage, and in the middle of those stones was a dead rabbit with its eyes removed. Apparently, the belly had been slit from the neck down, and its entrails were spread around inside the circle.

'Well anyway, a couple of the men wanted to break down the door and drag Miss Brown out right then and there, but they were outnumbered by the others. It's worth remembering that although all this happened a long time in the past it wasn't the 17th century anymore, and as I mentioned before many of the laws made against witchcraft had been repealed by the 1800s. Lynch mobs and vigilante crimes weren't brushed off in the same way as they had been a hundred or two hundred years before.

'So the men decided to play it safe. They came back to the village, back to the Horse and Hare where there were still a few people sitting around and drinking – although not the farmer's wife; she was long gone by then – and they reported what they'd found. After what the people had been hearing all evening about Brown and the state they'd worked themselves up into, no one questioned them.'

Mr Stevens paused. He reached under his glasses and rubbed his eyes, then repositioned them on his nose and stared around at the boys. He seemed to be measuring each of them in turn, as if making doubly sure they were ready to hear what he had to say next. James realised he could no longer hear anyone else talking around the campsite. The lights had all gone out in the surrounding tents, and the only sound left was the wind.

'It was her uncle that found her, in the end,' said Mr Stevens. 'The story goes he came out of his house early the next morning to see to his morning chores and, when he couldn't find Emily, he walked over to her cottage to wake her up. Only she wasn't in her cottage.

'The farmer had a key to the back door but he didn't need it because the door was standing open, and when he went from room to room calling her name she didn't answer. Eventually he came back out and stood in the doorway, and that's when he saw one of her shoes lying on the grass, partway down the garden.

'He went over to investigate and saw her other shoe further down, by the base of an oak tree. The bottom of her garden ended in a copse of trees that divided it from the next field over, and as he walked along the little path through the trees he found her stockings and her headband. Eventually he found her dress, hanging from the branch of an elm. It was torn and had blood on it. Then, a little way further in, he found her.'

Mr Stevens let out a sigh and shut his eyes, just for a second, before opening them again.

'She was hanging by her neck from a large oak at the back of the copse. She was naked, and someone had cut her throat and written the word "witch" in jagged red letters across her stomach. They'd written it in her own blood.'

Mr Stevens started to say something else, then stopped himself. James stared at him, his stomach suddenly feeling very heavy and full with the meal he'd eaten hours before, and although most of him wanted Mr Stevens to stop talking a small part of him wanted to hear more, to hear every detail Mr Stevens knew.

His gran had never told him a story like this before. The audiobook he'd swiped from the library had had nothing similar either, nothing quite so *real*. Even the sick stories Gary liked to tell in the playground weren't the same.

Mr Stevens suddenly looked unsure of himself. He took his glasses off, wiped the lenses and looked around at the boys. Then he cleared his throat and stood up.

'Right, it really is time we all got some sleep I'm afraid,' he said. 'It's past midnight. Very early start tomorrow.'

Gary groaned. 'But what happened after that? Did the men who did it get in trouble?'

Mr Stevens glanced down at him as he folded up his green chair. He suddenly looked distracted.

'No, no, they didn't catch anyone,' he said. 'No one in the village wanted to talk about it, and as no witnesses came forward there wasn't much they could do in those days. No forensics, no DNA – nothing like there is now. Anyway, it really is just a story, Gareth.' He glanced at James and then over at Matt, who looked pale. 'Don't take it to heart. I doubt any of it ever even happened, anyway.'

He smiled and gestured to Tim, who slowly got to his feet.

'Right, Timothy and I are sharing a tent, and I believe the rest of you have sorted out your sleeping arrangements, so I think we'll bid you all goodnight.'

'But I thought you said you heard the story from a historian?' said Gary. 'Someone who studies local history and knows about all this kind of stuff?'

Mr Stevens, who had turned away from the fire towards his tent, paused for a moment. For a second there was just the sound of the wind, and then he cleared his throat and carried on towards his tent without turning round.

'Alarms set for 5.30am and I'll see you all out here for a quick breakfast before we set off,' he said.

He unzipped his tent and disappeared through the entrance. Tim glanced back at them with an unreadable expression and then followed.

A gust of wind blew through the campsite and caused the slowly dying fire to gutter, making their shadows dance in the orange light.

4

James lay awake staring at the roof of his tent. He could hear the wind outside, howling like a dying animal, and the sound of a light rain that had begun not long after they climbed into their sleeping bags. It pattered against the canvas like thousands of tiny fingers.

He knew the minute he'd climbed into his sleeping bag and Gary had turned his torch off that he wouldn't be able to get to sleep.

His mind was still swirling with images from the story Mr Stevens had told. The slim, beautiful redhead with the green eyes. The farmer's wife twitching back her curtain to see a girl standing in a field, just standing there staring straight back at her in the dead of night while a cat wound its way around her legs. The same girl hanging from a tree with her throat cut.

This last one was the worst, because although it made James feel sick to his stomach there was also something else, something tied up with the girl's naked body that he felt deep down in the lowest part of his stomach. In his mind, the hanging girl's green eyes were still open, staring back at him as if she were accusing him of something.

After about an hour of checking his watch and listening to the wind mingling with the sound of Gary's heavy breathing, James had given up even trying to sleep.

At one point he thought he'd heard a whispered conversation coming from one of the other tents – his mind had shot back to the woman in Mr Stevens' story and his back had itched with fear before he realised it was probably just Matt and Tom, nothing more than that – but when he sat up in his sleeping bag and strained his ears the whispering stopped.

James thought about masturbating, anything to take his mind off the sound of the wind and the thought of the dark, empty moor opening up on either side of him like some black ocean, but he couldn't bring himself to in case Gary woke up.

James didn't even want to imagine how much ribbing he'd get if Gary heard him cracking one out in his sleeping bag. He'd never hear the end of it.

For a long time he lay completely still, staring up at the green canvas of the tent. He was finally starting to drift off, to feel sleep winning out over the whirling thoughts in his head, when he became aware of a subtle change in the sound around him and suddenly realised Gary was no longer breathing in the deep, steady way he had been before.

James rolled over onto his side and saw Gary's open eyes watching him in the dark.

'Struggling to get to sleep, Trumper?'

James couldn't see Gary's expression in the tent – there wasn't enough light – but he could tell from Gary's eyes that his friend was smiling.

'I'm fine,' muttered James. It didn't even sound convincing to him.

Gary blinked in the darkness. 'You don't need to worry about anything tonight, mate,' he said, and for a brief second James thought he was actually being genuine. Then Gary let out a quiet chuckle in the darkness. 'It's tomorrow night you want to worry about. Tomorrow and the night after, when we're out there in the middle of nowhere.'

'Why don't you just shut up?' James whispered.

'Yep, the next couple of nights will be the big ones,' Gary continued. 'Mr Stevens told a good story earlier, but he didn't even get to the best bit. All those stories the locals tell about Emily Brown nowadays, we didn't hear anything about that. I read them all in that online forum, though.'

James didn't say anything. He knew nothing he said would stop Gary now he was in mid-stride. It was easier just to lie there and let him say his piece.

'Some weird stories in that forum,' Gary continued. 'A lot of people link that Brown woman to all the disappearances there have been in the years since. Missing teenagers, missing kids. That whole family that vanished back in the '50s, or whenever it was. Some people think it was the Brown girl that did it, you see – that she wanders across the moor at night looking for all the people who hurt her, and the ones who didn't speak up against her killers after she was dead.

'She never finds them, of course – they're long gone now – but sometimes she finds others. And they're the ones that pay for what those villagers did to Emily all those years ago.'

James could feel the back of his neck itching and he badly wanted to scratch at it, but he forced himself to lie still and breathe normally.

'Yep, she always finds someone to pay the price in the end,' Gary said softly. 'All those disappearances. They said in the forum that compared to other national parks in the UK, Rutmoor has one of the highest instances of missing people. That can't just be a coincidence, can it?'

'I don't know,' James muttered.

'No, I don't think so. I think there's more to it. What *I* think is we'd best keep our eyes peeled when we're out on the moor tomorrow, that's all. Especially when it starts getting dark and that storm rolls in.'

Gary laughed in the darkness of the tent, and James suddenly felt like screaming. He didn't want to hear any more. For a second he thought he might hit Gary, just leap out of his sleeping bag and jump on the bigger boy before he knew what was happening, but then all at once Gary stopped laughing and rolled over onto his other side.

'Night night, Trumps,' he whispered. 'Sleep well.'

James turned over in his sleeping bag and lay listening to the wind.

2015

Thursday, Part Three

It's a funny thing, time.

He first noticed it when he started university and then suddenly found himself going into his final year – that strange elastic property that time has. How it can shoot by in a blur, and even though Freshers' week feels like a century ago when you're in your third year, the time in between is still one lightning fast streak, the days and memories running together like a film on fast-forward.

It's like that when he thinks about the moor, too. It's been almost exactly 13 years since that memorable trip with Mr Stevens – the trip that completely changed them forever – but in some ways it feels much more recent than that.

He can shut his eyes and picture their faces, their teenage faces lit up in the light from the campfire as they sit around and let Mr Stevens' words wash over them.

He's done some research into trauma and has heard it can be like that. Memories that won't fade; images that seem to actually get fresher in the mind as the years pass.

He's had counselling on and off over the years, and for a while he was on citalopram, but while it helps to talk about his symptoms to someone and the pills take the edge off his anxiety, it's never quite enough.

Although he can dance around the subject and talk cryptically about what's going on in his mind, it'll never be enough.

Because he can't tell anyone what really happened.

Thursday, Part Four

The train arrives at Southampton Central and stops for a minute while it divides in two. He stays in the front half, which is carrying on south, while the other half will travel off towards Portsmouth in the east.

The platform outside is quiet, almost empty. A pregnant woman is sat on one bench with a load of shopping bags next to her and a wailing little girl tugging at the leg of her trousers. A guard in a fluorescent jacket hovers near her, staring up and down the platform with an orange whistle clutched in one hand. Two teenage boys are hunched with their heads together further down. Their eyes are fixed on a phone screen while they wordlessly pass a bag of Maltesers back and forth. He watches them for a moment, then looks away.

It won't be long now before he gets in to Brockenhurst, and his mum will be there to meet him in the car with that half-worried smile she always seems to have whenever he comes home. It's like she's studying him the minute he walks out of the station, searching his face for any minute trace of how he might be feeling below the surface.

They're spooky sometimes, mothers. It's almost as if they can take one look at you and know exactly what you're feeling – like their bond to you allows them some kind of pseudo-telepathy.

He'll have to try extra hard this time to guard his face when he gets off the train.

If he gives away anything about how he's feeling this time – even just a hint of what he's planning to do – his mum will pick up on it and she won't stop pestering him with questions.

Maybe she'll recognise it's got something to do with the reunion – the trip to Rutmoor that he makes most years, and which she's never felt good about him going on – and then she might try to persuade him not to go.

But he needs to go, that's the thing.

He's got something important to do.

Thursday, Part Five

As he waits for the train to divide, his mind goes back to the Friday of that weekend in 2002. Their first day of walking. It's tricky to pinpoint exactly when things started to go wrong, but if he had to narrow it down – if he had to pick the point when everything began sliding away from them – he'd say it was the argument Tom and Gary had on the Friday afternoon.

The moment their little group started to split.

It wouldn't have changed anything if they hadn't argued, of course.

He knows that now; if it hadn't been that it would have been something else that triggered everything, and there was nothing any of them could have done to stop it.

As the train leaves Southampton and starts to cut through the countryside on its metal path towards the New Forest, he lies back against the headrest and stares out at the passing fields.

He remembers.

Gary (2002)

1

Gary Roberts lay fuming in his sleeping bag.

He'd been lying there for an hour now, barely noticing his aching thigh muscles or the blisters that had sprung up on both feet after a day's walking, focusing only on the anger.

He had a cut in his lip which he kept probing with his tongue.

Fucking Tom. Fucking Tramper. Fucking Tom.

The thought cycled through his mind like a mantra. He concentrated on it, focusing the anger on those names even though he knew it was only fuelling the sense of injustice he felt.

That fucker hit you, and you just stood there and took it.

That was his old man's voice, speaking up in his mind as if the bastard was lying there in the tent next to him.

You just stood there and took it, didn't you? You've always been weak, Gary. Just like your mother.

Gary gritted his teeth and squeezed his eyes shut. He made an effort to block the voice out and focus his attention on the two people that deserved it.

Fucking Tom. Fucking Tramper.

Lying in bed with the same thoughts going through his mind again and again, the same angry accusations, was nothing new to Gareth. He remembered doing it ever since he was little, after his dad shouted at him or hit him for doing something wrong. He'd learned from a young age that crying didn't do any good, and running to his mum for help did even less.

She'd always open her arms to him, but she never said anything while his dad stood there berating them both.

That's right, you go running to your mother. Can't even stand still and face me when I'm talking to you. It's you he gets it from, Laura, you know that, don't you?

Eventually, Gary learned to hold the tears in. He learned to ignore his mother and just stand still and try to go to another place while his father stood screaming in his face, his stale beer-breath pouring out in rank waves as he told his son exactly what a disappointment he was. Gary would stand there and in his mind, he'd be somewhere else, and any fear or anger he felt would be scrunched up and pushed down deep inside.

Then, when he got upstairs and everyone was in bed, he'd start his mantra.

Fuck you, Dad. Fuck you, Dad. Fuck you, you fat, worthless cunt.

It was better that way. It was better if he got it out quietly like that, without his dad knowing what he thought. The one time he'd slipped and told his dad to shut up – it must have been when he was 11 or 12, a good year or two ago now – the old man had slapped him hard around the face. It had hurt badly and left him with a black eye.

Being shouted at didn't hurt, there was that at least. Better to keep your mouth shut and go somewhere else, and then say your mantra every night like a prayer.

And if he sometimes found himself getting angry during the day at teachers or people in the playground he didn't even know? Well, that was a small price to pay, wasn't it?

Fucking Tom. Fucking Tramper. Fucking fat Tramper.

And really it *was* James Tramper that had started this all off, wasn't it? Just because he couldn't take a fucking joke. Just because he had to get all whiny and run off to Tom for protection.

It *was* just a joke, that was the thing. Gary might get into fights occasionally in the playground and Mrs Williams might call him a bully, but Gary always stood up for his friends.

Once, at the start of Year 8, some Year 10 kid had stuck out his leg and tripped James up in the hallway. Gary had been with him at the time and James had gone sprawling, his Scooby Doo lunchbox flying out of his hands and his crisps and sandwiches scattering across the floor. He'd got up with a red face and looked as though he was about to cry, and after picking up his stuff for him Gary had gone running back down the corridor and punched the Year 10 boy as hard as he could in the face. He'd got into trouble for that one, too. Big trouble. His parents had been called in for a meeting with the headmaster and although his mum had sat there looking as though she was about to cry, his dad had held in a smile and then put his hand on Gary's shoulder as they walked out into the school car park together.

He'd stuck up for Tramper and he'd do it again, he knew he would, and what thanks did he get? A sense of humour failure and a split lip from the kid who thought he was God's fucking gift, that was what thanks.

Gary turned over in his sleeping bag and looked at his watch. 11.00pm. He glanced over at the sleeping bag next to him, at Matt's huddled form. His new tent mate. They'd swapped the sleeping arrangements around tonight without even asking him if he was okay with it, of course. Just so poor old Tramper wouldn't feel scared and he could cosy up next to big, strong Tom. Fucking pathetic. Now Gary was stuck with Matt, who'd barely said a word since they finished dinner and climbed into their sleeping bags. And what was it that Matt had muttered to him earlier that afternoon, after Tom had split his lip?

You take it too far sometimes, Gary.

As if he was the one who'd punched someone.

Fucking Matt. Fucking Tramper. Fucking Tom.

All he'd done was wind James up a bit about that fucking Emily Brown story, that was all. He knew James had been spooked by the story, and all he'd wanted to do was have a bit of fun with him.

He'd kept it up throughout the day, walking alongside James and telling him a few details he'd thought up that morning while they were packing away their tents. Just stupid stuff. He told James to keep an eye out for a lady in a white dress – he said that was what people were reported to have seen when they were out on the moor at night – and to let Gary know if he saw any dead animals.

'Apparently that's what people see, before they go missing,' he'd said. 'Sometimes it's rabbits or crows, sometimes something bigger, like a fox.'

James had looked at him with wary eyes – they'd been walking for eight miles or so by that point and they'd already climbed two tors – and Gary could tell that even though he was tired he was scared, too. That was good. Gary'd come clean in the end and they'd all have a laugh about it – James always laughed at Gary's jokes, that was why Gary liked hanging out with him – but for now he wanted James to be scared so that he could pull off what he was planning.

'Yep, that's right,' Gary had continued. He did his best to keep his voice soft and serious. 'That's how it starts. You're walking across the moor and all of a sudden you see a foot or an ear in the bracken, and then it's a trail of intestines and you suddenly realise you're standing in the middle of a stone circle.

'You look down and you're in the middle of this ring of stones with this dead rabbit lying next to you, and then you've walked right into the trap. *Her* trap.'

'Gary,' James puffed. They were at the base of Duck Tor, their third of the day, and James was already out of breath. 'Do me a… favour… would you… and… fuck off.'

He said it without looking at Gary, without the usual smile he had on his face when Gary was winding him up, and Gary had to restrain the urge to shove him.

'Alright, fine.' Gary glanced up and looked around. Mr Stevens was walking with Tim not far behind them, bringing up the rear, and Matt and Tom were about 20 metres or so ahead, making their way up the start of Duck Tor. 'Don't get your fucking panties in a twist about it.'

James frowned. 'I'm just not in the mood for it, Gary.'

'Fine, walk on your own then.' Gary lengthened his stride, picking his way through the tussocks and accelerating away along the thin muddy path they'd been following. He could feel the anger welling up inside him.

I'm not in the mood for it, Gary.

What kind of a pissy thing to say was that, anyway? That was the sort of shit middle-aged women came out with, wasn't it? Gary picked up his pace and glanced back over his shoulder. There'd been a light drizzle falling all morning, and on the higher parts of the moor there was a thin fog that made it hard to see too far in front of you. James was already about 20 metres behind him, his chubby hands clutching the shoulder straps of his backpack and his head down as he picked his way slowly and carefully along the path. Gary squinted into the mist but could no longer see Mr Stevens or Tim.

Fuck you, Trumps, he thought. *You can walk with the nerd and his retarded fucking son.*

Gary picked up his pace even more, relishing the way his thighs burned and blinking away the mingled sweat and drizzle that ran down into his eyes. He could taste salt in his mouth, and he pulled the tube of his Platypus around to take a mouthful of water.

He squinted through the mist and saw Matt and Tom just ahead of him on the path, and put on a burst of speed to catch them up.

'Alright dickheads,' he said, pushing through the middle of them. 'You feeling tired or something?'

They glanced round at him, breathing heavily. Matt looked red in the face, but Tom managed a grin.

'Not a chance,' he said. 'Want me to race you to the top, do you?'

'Nah, you can babysit these two this time,' said Gary. 'I'm gonna scout ahead, but you might want to check on Trumps. Think he's got his period or something.'

Gary didn't really give a shit whether they checked on Tramper or not, but he wanted a bit of space to himself. He needed time to think through his plan.

'Oh dear, what have you said to him now?' said Tom.

'I didn't say anything to him! We were just having a laugh about that Emily Brown story Stevens was banging on about last night, then all of a sudden he got all pissy on me.'

'The two of you were having a laugh about Emily Brown,' puffed Matt, 'or you were winding him up about her again?'

Gary shrugged and laughed. 'Just trying to toughen him up a bit, that's all.'

Matt wiped sweat off his forehead and didn't say anything. Tom glanced at Matt and then looked down at the path.

'You didn't go too hard on him, did you Gary? He's already knackered as it is, mate.'

Mate.

There it was. Tom's favourite word. His little way of trying to sound casual and chummy when he was actually just talking down to you. A lot of people didn't think Gary was very bright – he knew Tom didn't think he was and he was pretty sure Tom and Matt joked about him when he wasn't there, he'd bet money on it – but the truth was he just hid it well.

'I know he's knackered, *mate*,' replied Gary. 'I was just having a little bit of fun with him, nothing else.'

He gave Tom his best fake smile, then started to pick up his pace again. 'Right, I'll see you dickheads at the top.'

He was expecting them to call out something after him but they didn't, and when he looked back over his shoulder 30 seconds later he saw the two of them standing still and looking back down the path into the mist, waiting for Tramper.

Gary felt another flare of anger. Of *course* they were waiting for Tramper. He wiped sweat off his forehead and hoisted his pack higher on his back, then turned around and continued up the path. He could see scattered rocks on either side of the muddy trail now, emerging out of the mist and then disappearing back into it as he strode past them. The drizzle coated his face and he closed his eyes and held out his tongue, catching the droplets.

Tom could be such a two-faced prick sometimes. He always laughed and grinned when Gary was winding James up, and then all of a sudden he'd switch and say *mate* and make Gary feel as if he'd done something wrong. As if he was the leader of the group, and it was him who decided when something was funny and when it wasn't.

Tom Carpenter, with his long legs and wide shoulders and his easy way of joking around with people and making them laugh. Mr Fucking Popularity. Tom sat two rows in front of Gary in their English class, sat right in between Sarah Harding and Emma Timpson – the two most popular girls in the year – and just a couple of weeks ago he'd seen Tom laughing with Emma as she giggled and ran her fingers through his curly fucking hair. Gary had seen that and he'd remembered the way Emma had rolled her eyes at him in the corridor when she'd seen him giving the wanker sign to Matt and James as they walked past, and in that moment he'd wanted nothing more than to strangle Tom.

Because it wasn't fucking fair, was it? Gary was tall and he was just as good at football and running as Tom was, but girls like Emma Timpson rolled their eyes at him and they giggled when Tom did nothing more than glance in their direction.

'Fucking bitches.' Gary spat the words out into the drizzle. Saying them felt good. 'Fucking sluts.'

He suddenly remembered something his dad had told him one night, years ago now. Gary must have been about eight at the time. It was late at night but Gary was still wide awake in his bed, because he was listening to the sounds of his mum and dad arguing in the other room. This wasn't uncommon, but it always kept him awake and even though he didn't really want to listen to it he couldn't help himself.

Shouts. Screaming. Crying sometimes, too. The sound of his mum sobbing through the walls of the house as his dad berated her.

That time had been worse than the other times. He couldn't remember what they'd been shouting at each other, but he remembered it had gone on for a long time and that he'd heard a crashing sound from the other room that made him sit up straight in his bed, eyes wide with fear as he strained his ears and wondered if he should see what was wrong or go and get help. But that was stupid, wasn't it? Who would he go and get help from? Your parents were the ones you were meant to go to when you were scared. Who did you go to when it was them you were scared about?

Eight-year-old Gary had sat there in the dark, his bladder suddenly feeling very full, clutching his Winnie-the-Pooh teddy bear tightly to his chest and straining his ears for a sound from his parents' room. He thought he could hear sobbing, but couldn't be sure. He thought about getting up and leaving his room, but he was too scared. He sat still in the dark and held his breath.

It was about five or ten minutes before he heard his father's footsteps approaching. Gary lay back down on his pillow and squeezed his eyes shut as the door to his room creaked open.

'Son? Are you awake?'

Gary held his breath as the footsteps came across the room. He felt the bed creak and sag as his father sat down near the foot of it.

'It's alright lad, I know you're awake.' Gary opened his eyes and saw his father looking down at him. His eyes were red and Gary could see the veins standing out in his cheeks.

'You okay, boy?' Gary's father shifted closer along the bed and leaned forward to look down at him. Gary restrained the urge to cringe away. His father's breath smelled of whisky and cigarettes.

'Did you hear any of that?'

Gary stared up at his father and shook his head slowly, and his father sighed. 'Yes, of course you did. That bloody woman, she—'

His father paused and looked down at him. He shifted his gaze and glanced around the room, not focusing on anything in particular. Without seeming to realise he was doing so, he reached over and pulled Gary's Winnie-the-Pooh bear out of his grasp.

'You're getting too old for things like this,' he said mildly, staring out across the room and squeezing the bear in his large hands. Gary noticed his knuckles were red.

'The thing you've got to remember, Gary, is that women aren't like us.' He was still staring out across the room. 'With men, it's simple. We get angry, sometimes we shout at each other or have it out, and then we move on. Women aren't like that. You can't have it out with a woman, because if you do they just cry and then *you're* the bad guy.'

He paused, then looked down at Gary. Fixed him with his stony blue eyes.

'Take it from me, son, you're best off having nothing to do with those scheming bitches at all. They bring out the worst in us.'

He leaned down and kissed Gary on the forehead, then stood up and went to leave the room. Before he got to the door he glanced at the Pooh bear still in his hands, then tossed it into the corner where it lay next to Gary's tennis racket and his school P.E. kit. Then he left. Even after the door was closed and his father's footsteps had receded down the hallway Gary still didn't dare to go over and pick it up, afraid it was all a test and that if he moved to get the bear his father would know and come back to teach him a lesson.

2

Gary's father wasn't a really big guy like Tom's dad, but he was strong. *Wiry* was what he called himself. When Gary was a little kid he used to think that was because his dad fixed the wires in people's homes for his job, but when he got older he realised it was what Mrs Francis in his English class called a *metaphor*. Like his dad was made of wires.

Gary didn't much care for metaphors, but he thought that was a good one. His dad may have lost most of his hair (he shaved his head with an electric razor once a week) and he may have a pot belly, but Gary thought wiry was a good way to describe him just the same.

Every now and then when Gary was little his dad would take him along on his weekend jobs, and Gary would sit there on the floor watching his father as he worked. Watching the cords and muscles stand out in his forearms as he unscrewed plug sockets and tinkered with circuit boards. Watching in awe.

As Gary got older, these work trips grew less and less frequent. Partly because Gary's dad was working less, and partly because Gary began finding excuses not to go along. The thing was, the trips scared him. It was alright if the people whose houses they were in were at home – that meant Gary's dad was on his best behaviour. If they were out and the house was empty, though, things were different. When Gary's dad was stuck with a tricky bit of circuitry he'd shout and swear. Sometimes he'd throw his tools. Once, when Gary was slow handing him a screwdriver, he'd cuffed Gary around the head.

Don't mind your father, Gary's mum would sometimes say when he got back from one of these trips and told her what had happened. *He's just got a temper, that's all.*

Got a temper was one of a handful of descriptions Gary increasingly heard people using about his dad as he got older. Another was *bitter*.

You should have seen your father when he was younger, Gary's mum once told him when the two of them were alone together. *We used to think he was going to make it as a professional footballer. He had trials for Tottenham under 21s when he was a teenager.*

Gary had stared at her, amazed, and asked her what had happened. He hadn't even known his dad played football.

Oh, he never made it in the end, his mum replied. Her face was hard and cold, her eyes distant. *He got a knee injury and couldn't play for a year, and after that it was game over. I sometimes think that's why he's so bitter.*

Gary hadn't known what she meant at the time, but *bitter* was a word that stayed with him for a long while after.

Bitter. Got a temper. They were like pieces of a puzzle. Gary thought if he could just figure out how the puzzle worked, things might get better.

The third piece of the puzzle had fallen into place one day in junior school. Gary had turned up to his first class with a cut above one eye, and when his teacher Mr Simons asked him about it Gary had done something he didn't usually do where his dad was concerned: he'd told the truth. He was tired and upset and before he could stop himself he was telling Mr Simons exactly what happened: how his dad had got angry with him for refusing to fetch him a beer, and how he'd slipped and cut his head on the kitchen cupboard after his father jumped up out of his armchair to chase him.

Mr Simons took Gary to the school nurse to get a plaster, and as he was waiting in the corridor outside after the nurse had stuck it on, he heard her and Mr Simons talking in low voices. Gary crept over to the door and pressed his ear against the wood to listen. He didn't hear everything they were saying, but there was one phrase Mr Simons muttered that stood out and stayed with him: *bit of a drinker.* This time Gary *did* know what it meant, too, because he'd heard someone saying it in an episode of *EastEnders* once. It meant that you liked beer and whisky too much. Like his dad.

He's bitter. Got a temper. Bit of a drinker.

Like pieces in a puzzle.

Temper. Bitter. Drinker.

Gary had wasted a good few years trying to solve that puzzle, and it had taken him a long time to realise one very important fact: there was no answer to it. Or even if there was, he'd given up trying to find it.

Now, lying on his back and staring into the darkness of the tent as these memories whirred and crashed through his mind, Gary thought maybe things weren't so bad after all. His old man might be a bastard, but at least he'd shown Gary how the world worked. He'd done Gary a favour, really, because he'd taught him how unfair everything was nice and early. He'd stopped Gary from getting his hopes up.

The world was full of people like Tom Carpenter, who went along with your jokes and then changed their personalities at the last minute, just switched like fucking chameleons so they always came out of things okay and you looked like the bad guy. The type of people that girls like Emma Timpson went for.

Best off having nothing to do with people like that at all, thought Gary, turning over in his sleeping bag to check the time on his watch. 11.30pm. *They bring out the worst in me.*

He was better when he was on his own, that was true. He could have walked the full 60 miles in a couple of days if he'd been on his own, he knew he could've, and he wouldn't have had people like Tramper distracting him and Tom and Matt looking down their noses at him.

Gary had made the top of Duck Tor way before everyone else earlier that day, pushing himself hard to try to work out his frustration and not looking back after he left Tom and Matt waiting on the path for James.

The sweat had run down his forehead and mingled with the drizzle and he'd welcomed the way it stung his eyes; he'd savoured the salty taste in his mouth and gritted his teeth as he climbed. Duck Tor was a big one, much higher than the first two they'd done that day, and the mist thickened the higher up he went.

The path kept getting steeper, too. Gary hunched lower and lower the higher he got, pushing down on the tops of his legs with each stride and willing himself to keep going. A couple of times he had to scramble over rocks and use his hands to pull himself up and once he slipped and scraped his knee, but he didn't slow.

Eventually, the ground began to flatten. There was some thin grass at the top of Duck Tor and he bent down and used his hand to scoop up a fine layer of dew, which he wiped over his sweaty face. A rocky outcrop – another of the bulky formations found at the top of every tor – emerged through the mist as he walked across the grass. Gary took his rucksack off and dropped it to the ground by the rocks. He paused and listened for the sound of the others approaching, but he couldn't hear anything.

The mist really was thick up here. It was more of a fog, actually, and when Gary looked around he couldn't see more than 10 metres in any direction.

He wandered over to the far side of the rocky outcrop, looking around. He suddenly had the urge to pee. He'd barely needed to stop for a piss all day – probably hadn't been drinking enough, like Mr Stevens kept telling them to do – but now that he'd stopped walking he could feel a heaviness in his bladder.

He walked further away from the rocky outcrop and saw a tree standing on its own in the mist. It was tall and thin and the branches were bare. As Gary got closer he saw that the upper part of the tree was black and twisted on one side. Lightning, probably. It was a wonder things could grow up here in the first place, he thought. Although people like Mr Stevens banged on about the beauty of Rutmoor, Gary secretly thought the whole place was a bit of a shithole. It was all well and good saying the scenery was great, but what good was scenery when you could never see more than 10 fucking paces in front of you because of the fog?

Gary unzipped his fly and started pissing against the base of the tree, his eyes closed. He finished and shook himself off, and it was only as he was zipping himself up and getting ready to walk back that he noticed a shape lying in the grass on his left. It was partway down the slope of the hill, half-hidden in the mist. Something large and white.

Gary felt his heartbeat quicken for just a second, his mind suddenly whirring with the stories he'd been telling Tramper half an hour before. He did his best to ignore any feelings of unease and took a step towards the shape.

Probably just a rock or something, he thought, but as he got closer he knew he was wrong.

The shape in the grass was a skull.

Gary walked nearer to investigate, ignoring the sudden hollow feeling in his stomach, and stopped when he was standing right over the thing.

It was a goat or possibly a sheep, he thought. Too small to be a cow, too big to be a rabbit. The thing was lying on its side, one empty eye socket staring up at Gary from the grass. Hairline cracks ran in a web over the thing's bony surface. Its bottom edge was lined with a thin row of teeth. As Gary stared at it with mingled disgust and fascination, an earwig squirmed out of its dark socket and fell down onto the grass at his feet.

Gary was about to turn away and walk back to the rocky outcrop where he'd left his bag when a thought popped into his head.

It was too good an opportunity to pass up, wasn't it? Gary had been planning to launch a big surprise on Tramper later that night after it got dark and they'd set up camp, but looking down at the skull he thought this might be the best chance he'd get.

This'll teach him for telling me to shut up.

He paused and listened again for the sound of his friends' voices. Nothing but the wind. That was just fine.

I could've been down the other side of this tor and halfway to the next one by now, thought Gary, as he started to look around in the grass for rocks. *And fuck Mr Stevens' precious navigation. You just follow the fucking path, how hard can that be?*

Gary found a few small stones lying around which he gathered into a pile. He looked about once more, scouring the grass, then turned and jogged back to the rocky outcrop where he'd left his bag. If he was going to have everything ready by the time the others got up here, he'd have to move fast. They were slow, but they weren't *that* slow, and he'd been up here five minutes already.

Gary looked around the base of the outcrop and found a few larger rocks scattered about in the grass. He scooped up an armful and carried them back to the skull, dumping them next to the stones he'd already collected. Then he dashed back and repeated the process.

After a couple of trips, Gary thought he had all that he could risk. The others couldn't be far off now. Moving quickly, he gathered up the stones and rocks two at a time and began positioning them in a loose circle around the skull. Every now and then he'd pause to listen, but the only thing he could hear was the wind. Gary shifted the stones for another minute or two, and he was just stepping back to admire his handiwork when he heard laughter drifting up from the far side of the tor. Tom's laughter.

Gary turned and sprinted back to the rocky outcrop. He found his bag on the far side, wiped an armful of sweat from his forehead, and sat down against a rock. He unzipped one of the front pockets of his bag, fished out a cereal bar, then leaned back against the rocks and did his best to look casual.

In his head, he pictured how the finished stone circle had looked. Would the thing actually have the desired effect? Gary thought it just might. If he'd tried the trick on Tom or Matt they probably wouldn't be all that fazed, it was true, but Tramper was a different story. He was way more gullible than the others, for one, and he was already on edge. Gary had made sure of it.

A few moments later, Tom and Matt emerged from the mist. They were grinning to each other and talking about something, but when they saw Gary they broke off and fell silent.

They're talking about you, whispered his dad's voice. *They're gossiping about you and laughing at you behind your back, son.*

Gary ignored the voice and held up a hand in greeting. Tom returned the wave and the two boys wandered over to him. By the time they reached him James had also emerged from the fog, followed by Tim and then Mr Stevens bringing up the rear.

'Finally thought you'd join me, did you?' Gary grinned at Tom and Matt. 'I almost drifted off up here waiting for you.'

'Yeah, yeah,' said Matt. 'Slow and steady wins the race. We'll see if you're so energetic by the time we get to Sunday.'

'Don't you worry about me, mate,' said Gary. 'Bags of energy. How you getting on Tom?'

'Can't complain,' smiled Tom. 'Be nice if I could actually see where I was walking, though.'

'Ah, that'd take away half the fun,' said Gary.

By this point James had reached the group. He stopped a foot or two away from them and bent down, hands on his knees as he pulled in deep, ragged breaths. After a moment or two he stood up straight and put his hands on his hips, staring past them into the mist. His face was bright red and Gary was struck by just how much his head looked like a giant tomato. He held in the urge to laugh.

'How you getting on, James?' he said.

James glanced over at him wearily, a slight frown of confusion on his face. *It's because I called him James and not Trumps or Tramper*, thought Gary. *He's not used to it*. He gave Tramper what he hoped was his most genuine grin and flashed him the thumbs up as Mr Stevens and Tim joined them.

'How's everyone feeling?' asked Mr Stevens. He looked round at them all in turn, a tired smile on his face. Gary thought he looked almost done in. The boys all muttered in response, and Mr Stevens forced his smile to go a bit wider. 'If it makes anyone feel any better, that was the biggest climb we'll be doing today. There are a couple more small tors before we set up camp, but it's mostly downhill from here.'

Mr Stevens unshouldered his pack, and Tim followed his lead.

'Right, let's take five, boys. Have a drink and something to eat and we'll get moving again in a minute.'

Mr Stevens sat down on the grass and started rummaging through his backpack. Tim sat down next to him without saying anything. Tom and Matt slipped their rucksacks off and slung them next to Gary's against the rocky outcrop, and James was just moving over to do the same when Gary caught his eye. He pushed himself off the rock and walked over to where James was standing.

'Have you got a second, mate?'

'Why, what's up?' James' face was filled with suspicion, and Gary realised he'd have to tread carefully.

'It's a bit of a weird one,' he said. 'Sort of embarrassing, actually.'

James frowned at him, but Gary could tell he'd caught his interest. 'Come round the other side of the rock with me for a second and I'll explain, I don't want those guys to hear and take the piss.'

Gary nodded to Tom and Matt, who were sat with their backs against the rock, talking.

James looked as though he was about to protest, but Gary kept his face as serious as he could and finally James shrugged.

'What's up?' he said again.

'Come over here and I'll tell you.' Before James could say anything else, Gary turned around and spoke to Tom and Matt. 'We're just gonna see if we can see anything from the other side of the tor.'

He turned and started walking around the rocky outcrop before the boys could react, sure that James would follow.

When he got to the other side he stopped and turned around. Sure enough, James was right behind him.

'Look, if this is another wind up, I don't—'

'Calm the fuck down, would you, there's no wind up. I just need to take a shit and I've forgotten my toilet roll.'

He grinned at James and shrugged. James frowned at him for a second or two longer, and then eventually he smiled too. He slung his rucksack off his shoulder and put it on the ground.

'You mean to say you didn't read the equipment list Mr Stevens sent round last week?' He grinned, bending to rummage in the rucksack. 'Wet wipes were pretty high up there.'

Gary forced out a chuckle. 'I must have missed that one.'

'Yeah, well that's the one benefit of having a gran like mine.' James fished a plastic packet out of his bag. 'She gets all that shit sorted for me.'

He grinned and handed Gary the packet. 'Keep those. I've got a couple more packs somewhere.'

'You're a lifesaver.'

'No worries.' James bent to pick up his backpack and was turning away when Gary touched him on the shoulder. 'Hey, what the fuck's up with that tree?'

James turned and followed Gary's gaze to the tall, blackened tree Gary had spotted earlier. Its upper branches were half-obscured by the mist, but from where they were standing Gary could still make out part of their charred, twisted shape.

'Come on,' said Gary. Before James could respond he began striding towards it.

'Hey, wait a minute.' Gary could hear James protesting, but he was confident his friend would follow if he just kept walking. Hadn't James always followed him, in the end?

Gary reached the base of the tree and stopped. From the corner of his left eye he could just make out the white shape of the skull and the stones he'd arranged around it in a circle, but he forced himself not to turn his head and looked up into the tree's canopy instead. A few seconds later, he felt James by his side.

'It probably got hit by lightning, that's all,' James muttered. Gary was pleased to hear a hint of unease in his voice.

'Weird, though, isn't it?'

They stood looking up at the tree for a while, not saying anything. After waiting for as long as he could, Gary lowered his head and stared out into the mist.

'Not much of a view, is there?' he said. 'At least if all this mist cleared we'd be able to—'

'What's that?'

James' voice sounded dull and hollow. Gary didn't even have to turn to look at his friend to know he'd caught sight of the stones.

'What the fuck is that, Gary?'

Making a big effort to keep his expression neutral, Gary turned slowly to face James. 'What's what?'

James was staring off down the hill in the direction of the skull and the stone circle. His face was pale. He was rubbing his left shoulder with his right hand, something he did when he was nervous. Gary stifled a grin.

'What are you looking at?'

James raised a hand and pointed in the direction of the skull, and Gary was pleased to see his finger shaking slightly.

'That,' he mumbled. 'What the fuck is that?'

He took a slow step forward, as if in a trance. 'Oh Jesus, Gary,' he whispered. 'Oh Jesus fucking Christ, what the hell *is* that?'

His voice had taken on a whiny, high-pitched tone now. It was a tone Gary recognised well, the same one Tramper used when they'd done something they shouldn't have and he was worried how his gran would react, or when they had a test at school and he didn't think he'd done enough revision.

James took a few more steps forward and Gary stayed where he was, struggling to hold in the laughter that was threatening to bubble up to the surface. There was something about the image of Tramper tottering along, his hand still outstretched and pointing towards the stone circle as his lips moved soundlessly in his tubby, pale face that was almost too much to handle. Gary stuffed his fist in his mouth and bit down.

'Oh Jesus Gary, I think you need to come see this.' He was babbling now, the words spilling out in a panicked jumble. 'I really think you need to come see this.'

James took another tottery step forward and stopped just outside the circle of stone. He stared down for a moment, and although Gary couldn't see his expression from where he was standing he could picture it perfectly: the pale face, the wide open piggy eyes, the gaping mouth.

He started laughing silently, helpless to stop himself, his fist still clamped between his teeth as his whole body shook.

'It's her, Gary,' said James suddenly. 'Oh my God, I think it's *her*.'

He ended the sentence with a high-pitched squeak and turned around to face Gary, and the look on his pudgy face – exactly the same look as the one Gary had pictured a moment before – was too much.

Gary gave up trying to hold it in and let out a bray of wild laughter. He could feel tears running from his eyes.

'Oh man, your face.' He croaked the words out between deep, whooping breaths. 'Your fucking *face*.'

When he remembered that moment later as he lay fuming in his sleeping bag, Gary thought that Tramper had stood watching him laugh for an age. He felt as though that moment, as James' wide-eyed expression had slowly changed to one of frowning confusion and then finally to a red-faced, angry realisation, had lasted for several minutes. In reality, though, it could only have been a few seconds at most.

Gary was still doubled over with laughter when James charged at him.

It took him completely by surprise. One moment Tramper was standing there gaping, the next he was rushing across the grass with his face twisted into a furious snarl, and before Gary could move or react in any way James' full weight was barrelling into him.

James struck him low, his shoulder catching Gary in the ribs, and

Gary went down, winded. His shoulder caught the trunk of the tree and flared briefly with pain. James stumbled and went down on one knee, then regained his balance and stood over Gary, breathing heavily.

'*Fuck* you,' he shouted. His face was red and he looked as though he was about to cry. 'Fucking *bastard*.'

Gary sucked in deep breaths and rolled over onto his side. He felt the cold dew of the grass pressing against his cheek. Shutting his eyes and gritting his teeth against the pain, he got a hand under himself and pushed up onto one knee.

He still felt shock and pain, but they were quickly being replaced by anger.

'What the fuck was that?'

The words came out in a wheeze. Gary wiped his eyes and looked up at James, who was still standing over him. He still looked like he was about to cry, but he seemed unsure what to do next.

'Why me, Gary? Why is it always *me*?' James looked down at him and then his face seemed to sag and then he *did* start to cry, and there was something about his reddening features that made Gary more furious than ever. With his round cheeks and blotchy skin he looked like a giant, wailing baby. He looked *pathetic*. Gary climbed slowly to his feet and straightened up, still clutching his ribs. Standing directly in front of James, he was almost half a foot taller.

'It's because you're a fat, whiny, useless shit.' Gary put a special emphasis on every word, spitting them out into Tramper's blubbering face one at a time. 'You're a fucking fat dickhead and you can't even take a *joke*.'

He lashed out with his right hand and shoved James in the chest as he shouted the last word. James stumbled back, startled, and Gary was moving forward to push him again when he heard someone yelling his name.

He turned and saw Tom racing towards him through the mist, with Matt just a bit further behind him.

'What the fuck are you doing, leave him alone!' Tom shouted the words as he ran towards them, and Gary felt a flash of fear when he saw the look on Tom's face.

Gary stood still, frozen to the spot while confusion and adrenalin surged through him, and all of a sudden Tom was standing directly in front of him and gripping the front of his coat in one large hand.

'What the fuck is your problem, can't you see he's upset?'

'He's not, I didn't...' Gary tried to find the words to explain what had just happened, to explain that he'd just been defending himself, but nothing came. 'It was just a joke.'

'It's always just a joke with you, Gary,' said Matt. He was standing behind Tom, staring at Gary wearily. 'It's not a joke when you've made someone cry, is it?'

'Oh fuck you,' Gary yelled. 'You're always on his fucking side, aren't you, always pandering to that fat, whiny dickhead even when he—'

Gary didn't even see Tom swing. One minute he was shouting at Matt, and the next he caught a brief flash of movement and felt something thump hard into his mouth. At the same time he felt Tom's hand let go of its hold on his shirt, and he stumbled back a pace and sat down heavily on the grass. He moved his hand over to touch his lip. When he took his fingers away he could see blood on the tips.

Tom stood by the tree, breathing heavily. The anger had gone from his face and he looked unsure now, almost afraid.

'You hit me.' Gary mumbled the words stupidly, staring from Tom to the blood on his fingers and back again. Out of the corner of his eye he saw Matt walking over to James and putting a hand on his shoulder, asking him if he was okay. Then the three boys just stood there, staring down at Gary. Later he'd remember the looks on their faces, and the fact that none of them came over and offered to help him up. He'd remember that time the Year 10 boy had tripped James up in the corridor, and how he'd chased after him and punched the boy in the face. The way James had hugged him afterwards in thanks. Mostly, though, he remembered their eyes staring down at him. The mingled expressions of confusion, pity and fear.

Then Mr Stevens' voice was floating through the mist, and a few seconds later him and Tim emerged to stand behind Tom. Mr Stevens took off his glasses and wiped them on his sleeve, then put them back on and looked at each of the boys in turn.

'What's going on?' he said.

Gary wiped his mouth on the back of his sleeve and climbed up onto his knees. Tom moved forward suddenly and held out a hand to help him, but Gary knocked it to one side and stood up on his own.

'Mate, I—'

'Just forget about it,' Gary muttered.

Without looking back at them, he turned and began striding back to the rocky outcrop to pick up his bag.

3

He'd barely spoken a word for the rest of the day.

Matt had tried to speak to him a couple of times and he'd mumbled one-word responses, but when Tom offered him a cereal bar later in the afternoon he hadn't even looked at him.

Matt and Tom had spent the afternoon walking together, occasionally muttering to each other in low voices. James had tagged along by their side, his head down, not saying much.

Mr Stevens and Tim had carried on pretty much as normal; they obviously knew something had happened, but Mr Stevens appeared to know better than to ask. Tim was his usual, quiet self. When they'd finally stopped to set up camp, Gary sat a few metres apart from the rest of them, eating his Wayfarer meal on his own.

He chewed every mouthful hard, not really tasting what he was eating, concentrating instead on the anger and sense of injustice that was pulsing through his head like a migraine.

They'd all gone to bed early that night, and Matt had wandered over to Gary as he was about to climb into the tent.

'Mind if I bunk with you?' Matt said. He grinned uncertainly, and Gary could tell he was testing the waters to see if Gary was still angry.

Well, let him fucking test.

'Whatever,' Gary muttered. He climbed into the tent and unrolled his sleeping bag without making eye contact with Matt. Five minutes later, when Matt had crawled in after him, he hadn't said anything.

Now it was God knew what fucking time, and Gary was still too angry to even feel tired.

Fucking Tom. Fucking Matt. Fucking Tramper.

He thought of the way Tramper had charged him and knocked him down, just because he couldn't take a prank. Gary had reacted as any normal person would do, defending himself, only to get punched by another one of his so-called friends. He remembered how they'd all huddled together that afternoon after it had happened, the three fucking musketeers, talking about Gary behind his back and shooting sneaky glances at him that they didn't think he'd notice.

But he did notice. He noticed and he was going to get them back.

Saying your mantra before bed was okay, that was fine, but getting revenge was an even better way to get rid of anger. Gary had learned that lesson as a little kid. Whenever his dad had done something really bad to him – hitting him or making him cry, for instance – Gary had filed the memory away. And every one of those times he'd paid the old man back in some secretive way.

Sometimes it was something small, like hiding his cigarettes or pouring some of his whisky down the sink – normally when the old bastard had gotten drunk and passed out, that way he never remembered how much he'd actually drunk and Gary never got caught. Other times it was something more creative.

One time he'd gone into the bathroom, locked the door and then run the bristles of his dad's toothbrush under the rim of the toilet, making sure there were no visible lumps of shit when he put the thing back. Another time, when his dad was out, he'd pissed against the side of his car.

They were small victories; nothing his dad would ever find out about. But that didn't matter.

Gary knew about them.

Gary leaned over and checked his watch once more, pressing one of the buttons on the side to light up the digital display in a yellow glow. 01:38. Even later than the fucking witching hour, ha-ha.

Gary lay back against his shitty inflatable pillow – God knew why he'd ever even agreed to come camping in the first place, everyone knew camping was a fucking nightmare – and thought about how he could get them. Images of revenge swam in front of his eyes. He saw himself silently unzipping his tent and creeping over to the tent Tom and Tramper were sharing, then carefully opening the flap at the front, being sure not to wake them. He'd slip in barefoot, not making any noise, then find their bags and take out the most important stuff. All the things they really couldn't do without. Maybe their coats or their food. Shit, maybe he'd even pick up their shoes. He'd gather it all together and then take it outside of the tent – maybe go for a little walk with the stuff so he was a safe distance from the camp – and then he'd set fire to the lot. Burn, baby, burn.

Gary saw fire dancing in the darkness in front of his closed eyes, flames licking against the night sky as Tramper's North Face coat twisted and crumpled into a black ball. He saw the whole lot go up. The flames spread in front of him and he could actually hear them, he could hear them starting to whisper.

Gary smiled, finally drifting towards sleep.

He was standing in front of a huge bonfire, watching his friends' possessions burn and listening to the flames murmur. It was cold, even by the fire, and he was moving closer to try to get some heat into his skin, he was stepping closer and the whispering of the flames was growing louder, an insistent mutter that sounded like low voices, and—

Gary jerked awake in his sleeping bag. He'd been on the edge of sleep, drifting through that limbo between thinking and dreaming, but something had brought him back. Some noise. Gary lay in the dark and strained his ears.

For a second, so brief he thought he might have imagined it, he heard whispered voices below the sound of the wind.

Gary held his breath and sat up in his sleeping bag. He glanced over at Matt, but he was nothing but a bulky shape curled up in the darkness. It hadn't been him that had made the noise.

Gary was pretty sure it had come from outside.

Was that what I was hearing just now, as I was drifting off? he thought. *People speaking outside the tent?*

For the second time on the trip, Gary felt a faint hint of unease. He shut his eyes and strained his ears once more, but now there was definitely nothing. Just the wind.

Jumping at ghosts, sunshine, whispered his dad's voice. *First you let a*

boy hit you, and now you're getting scared of old wives' tales. Maybe you're
turning into your fat little friend.

Gary shook the thought off and lay back down. Stupid. There was
no one outside the tent, of course there wasn't. He'd just drifted off
and started dreaming, that was all, and the dream had stayed with him
after he'd woken up.

Or maybe you did hear something, and it was just one of the others, he
thought to himself. But then if it had been one of the others, what
were they doing awake and chatting at this time in the morning?

Maybe it's your fat friend and Tom, talking about you again, whispered
his dad. *Maybe they're lying in their tent right now laughing about the way
you went down like a sack of shit after Tom hit you. Big tough Gary's not
so tough after all, is he?*

Gary felt another small flare of anger, but this time it was dampened
by the unease that had settled into his stomach like a bad meal.

He closed his eyes and tried to remember which direction the whispering sound had seemed to be coming from. He thought it might
have been behind him slightly, somewhere outside the little camp
ground they'd set up, but he really couldn't be sure. If it had been
behind him, though, then it definitely wasn't coming from one of the
other tents; James and Tom's two-man was over to his left and in
front of him, and Mr Stevens and Tim were set up over to his right.

Gary suddenly realised he needed to pee.

He lay still for a while, trying to work out how bad the urge was
and if he could hold off until morning, but he quickly realised it was a
losing battle. He was wide awake, and now that he'd started thinking
about it he wasn't going to be able to put the thought out of his mind.
It was going to keep bugging him.

The thing was, he didn't want to leave the tent.

It was stupid of course, and he was sure it was mostly just the
thought of how chilly it would be outside his sleeping bag – between
the fog, the wind and the near-constant fucking drizzle, summer
didn't seem to have touched Rutmoor. But whatever the reason, the
idea of unzipping his tent flap and stepping out into the night suddenly felt like a very bad idea.

Matt grunted and turned over in his sleep. Gary thought about waking him up, but dismissed the idea. He wasn't going to show weakness in front of that fucker.

Gritting his teeth, he reached a hand out and eased the zip on the side of his sleeping bag down. Outside the tent the wind gusted, and Gary heard tree branches rustling against each other in the distance. They'd set up camp in a slight valley between two tors, and there was a small copse of pine trees not far from their campsite; they were a good 50 metres or so away, but in the silence of the night the sound carried easily.

I'll just step out of the flap and piss straight in front of the tent, Gary thought as he pushed aside the material of his sleeping bag and lifted himself up into a crouch. *I'll make it nice and quick, and I'll be back inside in less than a minute.*

He was barefoot, dressed in just his boxer shorts and his black Helly Hansen under-layer, and he thought briefly about putting something else on but then decided against it. If he messed around putting on trousers, socks and shoes he'd only have to take them all off again. As an afterthought, he grabbed his digital watch – his dad had bought it for him specially for this weekend, probably because the bastard was feeling guilty for some shout or slap Gary couldn't even remember, and it had a torch function on the side. The light was weak and it only came in short bursts, but it should be just enough to see by.

Gary worked his way over to the flap of the tent on his knees, glancing once over at Matt's sleeping form before he unzipped the inner lining of the tent.

Beyond the light netting was a small bit of space – Matt always called it 'the porch' because it was where they left their shoes and stuff – and then the outer tent layer with the main flap leading outside.

Gary stepped through the first bit of netting, still in a crouch, and felt the temperature drop as he neared the outer surface of the tent. He could see drops of dew glistening on the canvas. In the distance, the wind howled.

In and out, that's all, in and out.

Despite the fact that he was doing his best to ignore it, Gary felt the unease in his stomach grow as he reached out for the tent's main zip.

You'll open that zip up and the first thing you'll see will be an eye staring back at you through the gap, whispered an alien voice in his mind. *Then she'll reach in and grab you.*

Gary shook his head. That was stupid stuff, fucking kids' stuff. He gritted his teeth and pulled the zip across the arching flap of the tent in one quick, fluid motion. Then he reached out a hand and snatched back the canvas.

Damp night air flooded in through the gap, but nothing else. Gary let out a breath he hadn't even realised he'd been holding, put one foot out through the gap (he winced slightly at the cold feel of the dew against his toes) and then stood up straight through the tent flap.

Without the light from a fire, the darkness was almost total. The night sky above Gary was like a yawning black throat. Thin light filtered down from the patches of stars which weren't covered by cloud, but the moon was nowhere to be seen. Gary thought the stars in those hollow patches of sky were impossibly dense, like hundreds of tiny, winking cats' eyes. Looking around the camp, Gary could just make out the shape of the other tents – one in front of him and over to the left, the other on his right – but apart from that the world was nothing but blackness.

Somewhere out in front of him he heard the pine trees whispering to each other. Gary felt a light chill against his back.

Not wanting to waste any time, he lifted his other foot out of the tent and stood with his legs apart. He pushed down the front of his boxers with the hand that was still clutching the watch, then reached down and pulled out his cock.

As an afterthought, he thumbed the button on the side of the watch to make the torch light up so he could see where he was pissing, and it was as he shifted the watch into position that he saw the rabbit's foot illuminated on the grass in front of him.

Gary froze.

The foot was small and grey, and a tiny sliver of white bone was jutting out from the place where it had been severed. The bone winked and sparkled in the yellow light from the watch. Next to the foot Gary saw a few beads of blood, still wet and clinging to the dewy grass.

The light from his watch flicked off automatically, and without thinking Gary thumbed the button again to turn it back on. He found himself staring down at the foot as if in some kind of trance, his mind blank for now as he took in the matted fur and the tiny droplets of blood.

He slowly adjusted his boxers and went to take a step backwards, but his right foot struck the edge of the tent and he wobbled, fighting to retain his balance. The light from the watch flicked off again, and this time it jolted Gary out of his shock.

He steadied himself and stood still in the darkness, breathing heavily and listening. Nothing. The wind was still groaning and in the distance the trees were rustling, but that was it.

A part of his mind tried to persuade him that the foot was already there when he went to bed – in his anger he could just have missed it, after all – but although he badly wanted to believe that was true he just couldn't do it.

If the foot had been there when he climbed into the tent, he would have seen it. Or Matt would have seen it.

Unless…

Gary cast his mind back to the brief exchange he'd had with Matt before he'd climbed into the tent. He'd brushed Matt off, climbed in, and then Matt had followed him in not long after. But – and here was the real kicker – he hadn't followed Gary in straight away.

It had been at least a couple of minutes between Gary getting into the tent and Matt joining him; plenty of time to go for a piss, clean your teeth, or maybe – just maybe – leave a nice little surprise for your old friend Gary to find the next morning.

But that was stupid, wasn't it? Matt wasn't the type of person to do something like that, and even if he was, where the fuck would he have suddenly found a rabbit's foot?

What about if he had an ally? whispered the voice in Gary's head. *What if it's all part of one big plan to make you look like stupid?*

Gary thought back to the way Tom and Matt had behaved that afternoon. The talking among themselves. The quick glances. The whispering.

The whispering.

Gary glanced at Tom and James' tent, over to his left, for any signs of movement. Was it possible that it *had* been them out there whispering earlier? Maybe the two of them were in on it together, and they'd just planted the foot now. Maybe all *three* of them were in on it.

Gary swept his eyes in a careful semi-circle around him, peering into the darkness for any slight sign of movement. There was nothing there.

They've got you good and spooked anyway, whispered his dad's voice. *You're so fucking paranoid you don't know what to do with yourself.*

For a brief, horrible moment, Gary thought he might cry. He was standing out in the cold in the middle of fucking Rutmoor, no one was on his side, and even though he was over a hundred miles away from his father he could still hear the old bastard's voice in his head.

Fuck this, he thought suddenly. *If they're looking for a reaction from me, they'll get one.*

Gary thumbed the light from his watch and held the thing up like a torch in front of him. He pointed it in the direction of Tom and James' tent, then took a big step forward over the rabbit's foot and started walking across the grass.

We'll see what they've got to say about it when I wake them up and fucking ask them.

He was halfway between his tent and theirs when he stepped on something soft. Gary froze once more, fighting the urge to scream, and slowly moved his foot off the thing beneath it. He felt it unfurl as his weight came off it, like rubber. His hands were trembling as he moved the watch into position and thumbed the button.

It was a rabbit's ear. Gary stared down at it with a dumb, rising horror before the watch light flicked off again. The ear was small and light grey, and he didn't need to look again to know it had come from the same unfortunate creature that the foot outside his tent belonged to.

He was shaking now, and it wasn't just from the cold. Without thinking he thumbed the watch once more and began moving forward, scanning the light across the grass in sweeping arcs ahead of him.

The yellow light was weak, and it only reached a metre or so in front of him before it stopped dead against the inky wall of darkness that coated the moor.

Gary almost didn't see the next piece. He'd been continuing in the direction of Tom and James' tent and it was lying on the grass to his right, just on the edge of the arc of light cast by his watch. He caught it out of the corner of his eye, a grey shape against the green. Gary walked over to it without thinking, needing to see what it was, vaguely aware that he was now pointing in the direction of the distant copse of pine trees.

Gary moved over the grass and the wind urged him on, whispering in his ear like a hungry voice. When he reached the shape and aimed his watch down at it, he saw it was another paw.

If this is you, Tom, I really have to hand it to you, thought Gary. *You've certainly been fucking thorough.*

He looked away and stepped over the severed paw, suddenly feeling in real danger of throwing up. And there was a part of his mind, a faint voice in the back of his head that was telling him to go, just turn and run back to the tent and wake Matt up, but it was smothered by a stronger voice – not quite his dad's voice, but close – that told him he couldn't.

Because what if they were watching him now? What if Tom and James were crouched in the darkness somewhere, giggling and whispering, just waiting for big tough Gary to show his true colours? He knew they'd never have the balls to actually *kill* a rabbit, there was no fucking way, but maybe they'd found this one already dead somewhere and decided to use the opportunity to have some fun with him?

If he gave them the satisfaction of seeing him scared, he'd never hear the end of it. Shit, he'd fucking die first.

With this thought in mind, Gary kept moving forward across the grass. Whenever the light from his watch went out he'd thumb the button and start moving forward again, sweeping it from left to right. He passed the tents and left the campsite without even realising it.

Ten paces on from the severed foot Gary found a tail, and a further ten paces on from that he found another foot.

The game can't go on much longer, he thought hysterically, *we're going to run out of pieces soon.*

A wild urge to laugh swept over him, and then quickly disappeared five paces later when he found the next item.

This time it was an eye.

Gary stared down at the thing with sick fascination, taking in the red gore and matted hair that still clung to the back of it, the way the wide blank pupil stared up at the stars.

That faraway part of his mind was back again, shouting at him to just turn around and get out of there, that none of his friends would ever cut out a rabbit's fucking *eye* just to teach him a lesson, but now he barely even heard it.

He stepped over the eye and moved forward again, his legs seeming to move independently from his brain.

All his jumbled emotions – the uncertainty; the anger; most of all the fear – felt distant as he moved across the grass. It was like they belonged to someone else.

Just got to keep following the trail, he thought. *Like Hansel and Gretel, lost in the woods.*

Gary's feet were numb from the dew. Every now and then he'd step on something – a couple of thin twigs, once a small and pointy stone – but he hardly even felt it.

He heard a whispering sound, much closer this time, and suddenly realised the copse of pine trees was now directly in front of him. They stood tall and clustered around him like ancient wooden sentries. The darkness between them seemed almost solid.

Just on the border of the trees Gary found another foot, and then as he stepped over it and into the copse his light fell on a larger shape. It was 10 paces into the trees, and before he'd even reached it he knew what it was.

The rabbit's body was a mangled pulp of flesh, bone and hair. Its eyeless, earless face stared up at him from the grass. Patches of drying blood lay on the grass around it.

From somewhere behind Gary, a tree branch snapped.

The sound jolted through him like an electric shock, and the strange blanket dampening his emotions was suddenly whisked away. Gary realised with terror where he was, and what was lying on the grass in front of him.

He spun around in the darkness, certain he was going to see a woman standing there in a white dress, but there was no one behind him. He peered back the way he'd come, straining his eyes to see the campsite, but it was lost in the gloom.

Gary felt freezing cold, and his whole body was shaking. He could no longer feel his feet.

Swept in a wave of fear and no longer caring if anyone could see him or what his dad would think, he sprinted out of the copse and headed back in the direction he'd come from.

The wind rushed past his bare arms, scraping his skin like fingernails. The frame of his watch dug into his clenched palm. Blood pounded in his ears, a quick thud-thud-thud that sounded like a second set of footsteps chasing him.

For one sweet, brief moment as Gary flew across the grass away from the copse, he thought he was going to make it. He could just see the shapes of the tents beginning to emerge in the gloom, and it was as he put on an extra burst of speed that he lost his footing.

He went down hard in a heap, scraping his side and winding himself. The thudding in his ears grew louder, more insistent.

Gary struggled to pick himself up, numb feet slipping on the grass.

He was up on his knees when he heard something move behind him.

2015

Thursday, Part Six

Sure enough, his mum had been worried about him. Almost as soon as he'd climbed into her purple Clio at Brockenhurst train station and kissed her hello on the cheek, the interrogation had started. Was he feeding himself properly up in London? Getting enough sleep? Was he worried about anything? Why was he so quiet?

Yes, no, yes, and no comment, he'd thought in his head. But of course he'd reassured her that everything was okay, and kept a smile fixed firmly on his face during the drive home.

Now that he's back in his old room and he's said goodnight to his mum, he starts unpacking his bag. Not the walking bag – that one's all ready for the weekend, and he leaves it standing in the corner by his old desk – but the briefcase containing all the folders.

All his work.

The ceiling light is on in his room and he spreads everything out over the bed, so it's nice and well-lit. His bedroom hasn't changed much since he left it for good after his third year at uni. It's like it's frozen in time. There's a *Pulp Fiction* poster on the wall next to his wardrobe. His old PC, which he used to sit in front of for hours playing strategy games like Red Alert, sits dusty and unused on his desk.

Looking down at the documents spread out across his duvet, he moves the folder marked 'News Cuttings (1951–1998)' over to the left, and places a slightly smaller folder – this one marked 'News Cuttings (1998–2015)' – over on the right.

He takes the Polaroid photo of them all together at the campsite and puts it in the middle and slightly above everything else, thinking of the way detectives always map out crimes in the TV series he likes to watch.

It's getting late now, and he needs to get a decent night's sleep – he's got a big day ahead tomorrow, and he's getting picked up early – but he can't turn in just yet.

His hand hovers over the bed, then moves to pick up the folder marked 'News Cuttings (1998–2015)'.

He'll get to bed in a few hours. His adrenalin will be up tomorrow, anyway, so he should be fine.

For now he has some reading to do.

Tom (2002)

Tom Carpenter opened his eyes and turned over onto his back.

Judging by the faint greyish light shining through the material of the tent and creating a swampy glow, it was the morning. Tom rolled onto his side, checked his watch, and saw it was just after seven.

He glanced over at Tramper and saw him sprawled on his back with his mouth wide open, snoring lightly. He'd half-kicked his sleeping bag off in the night and it lay partly off him, exposing one bare, meaty thigh. As Tom watched, James muttered in his sleep and twitched, before falling back into a regular breathing rhythm again.

Bad dreams, thought Tom.

Tom had had a couple of bad ones himself, but he could barely remember them now. He thought one had been a replay of the fairly dramatic events of yesterday morning – 'the fight', as James had started calling it – but Tom knew he'd had other dreams too. Nightmares, really.

At one point he'd woken up sweating, sure that he'd heard something or someone screaming, and when he looked at his watch he'd seen it was after 02:00.

What had that dream been about? Tom thought hard, summoning up images that were now like shadows disappearing as the sun goes in. For a second he almost had something – a faint sensation of running along a dark corridor – but then it was gone again.

Tom sat up and reached for his bottle. He took a swig of water that was flavoured with the sharp tang of purification tablets, resisted the urge to spit, and swallowed it down. Mr Stevens might be annoying, but his constant comments about the importance of staying hydrated had clearly had some effect.

Tom wondered if the others were up yet. Mr Stevens and Tim struck him as the early riser types, but Matt liked his sleep, and Gary...

Gary.

For a blissful few seconds Tom had forgotten about everything, but the thought of his so-called friend's name brought all the worries – which had been nagging at him pretty much constantly ever since he'd punched Gary in the face the day before – back to the front of his mind.

He knew guys like Gary – there were more than a few on the football team at school and at the Sunday five-a-side club Tom was a part of – and he knew they could be incredibly stubborn. Gary was arrogant, jealous and bitter, and Tom thought it would be a long time before he came around.

Tom had tried talking to him yesterday afternoon, and Gary had blanked him.

But he hadn't done anything wrong, had he?

James had thanked him afterwards and Matt, although he hadn't said much about it, had nodded when Tramper told Tom he'd done the right thing. He'd been sticking up for a friend, after all, stopping a bully who'd been allowed to get away with things for too long.

So why did he feel so shit about himself?

Tom unzipped his sleeping bag and sat up. He decided he'd go outside and get some fresh air, maybe take a short walk around the campsite. That'd help clear his head. Being as quiet as he possibly could and stealing the occasional glance at Tramper to make sure he wasn't disturbing him, Tom slipped on his walking trousers and a t-shirt and then laced up his boots.

He unzipped the tent flaps and stepped outside.

The first thing that struck him was how nice a morning it was. The fog and drizzle that had hung over Rutmoor since they arrived had vanished and been replaced by a mostly clear sky; there were still clumps of grey cloud on the horizon, but the patch directly above their campsite was a bright blue.

Tom closed his eyes and stretched. The light breeze felt nice on his skin.

Glancing around the campsite, he saw no sign of anyone else. The tents looked quiet and undisturbed, and their little campfire was exactly as it had been left the night before.

Tom did a slow 180-degree turn, taking in his surroundings. They were in a rock-strewn valley between two tors, and aside from a small copse of trees about 50 metres ahead of him, there wasn't very much to look at.

New day, thought Tom. *I'll make a special effort with Gary, maybe take him to one side and say I'm sorry and I was being a dick. Things will work out.*

He smiled and began walking in the direction of the trees. He thought he'd head over there, do a quick lap of the little copse to stretch his legs and then head back. Although Tom's thigh muscles were aching from yesterday's walking and he could feel a small blister on the little toe of his right foot, he didn't think he was in such bad shape. In fact, he thought he might—

The thought snapped off as Tom heard a rustling sound behind him. For some reason he felt a momentary lurch of fear in his stomach and he spun round towards the source of the sound, then let out a breath when he saw Matt's head emerging from the flap of the other tent.

Matt was rubbing his eyes and blinking, and when he saw Tom he raised one hand in a wave. Tom grinned and waved back.

'Hey!' yelled Matt with a grin, but he paused when Tom put a finger to his lips and nodded his head in the direction of his own tent. Tom mimed a sleeping gesture and then jogged over to join Matt, who had pulled back the flap of his tent and was kneeling in the morning light.

'What time is it?' mumbled Matt. He wiped the sleep from his eyes again and ran a hand through his messy brown hair.

'Not sure exactly, maybe 7ish?'

Matt groaned. 'Jesus, I thought it was much later than that. I saw Gary had already packed up his stuff and I thought you lot might be getting ready to leave without me.'

'Eh?'

'I said I thought you guys might have already eaten and be getting ready to go.'

'No, what did you say about Gary's stuff?' Somewhere deep down in his stomach, Tom felt something like unease beginning to stir.

'His stuff's not in the tent,' said Matt. He looked past Tom at the empty camp ground. 'Where is everyone, anyway.'

Despite the morning chill, the skin on Tom's back had started to prickle. He resisted the urge to push past Matt and look inside the tent, and instead took a deep breath.

'Matt, what the hell do you mean his stuff's gone? I haven't seen him this morning, I thought he was still in the tent with you.'

Matt stared back at Tom for a few seconds, frowning. He started to say something and then stopped, staring out across the campsite. Tom recognised his expression – the furrowed brow, the slight squint – as Matt's thinking face; he'd seen it plenty of times during the maths classes they shared at school.

'Last night...' Matt glanced at Tom and then looked away again, biting his lower lip.

'Last night what?'

'I don't know, I just thought...'

'*What*, for fuck's sake?' Tom's tone, which had come out a little sharper than he'd meant it to, caused Matt to jump.

'Nothing, I don't know. I was just trying to remember a dream I had last night, but...' He trailed off again, but this time Tom forced himself not to interrupt. If there was one thing he'd learned from sitting next to Matt in maths, it was that his friend always got to the answer in the end, but only if he had time to think.

'I think I may have woken up at one point last night,' Matt said carefully. He looked around at Tom, still biting his lip. 'I'm not sure if it was part of a dream or not, though.'

'What happened?'

'I... Well, I think I heard someone scream. But it might have been part of the dream I was having. I can't remember exactly what it was, but I think it was a nightmare. I might have woken up for a few seconds at one point – I sort of remember opening my eyes in the tent, although I'm not sure – and then I guess I went back to sleep again. But I heard this high-pitched sound, like a scream. I think I thought it was an animal.'

Tom nodded slowly. He suddenly felt very cold all over, and he wished he'd put on his coat before stepping out of his tent. In fact, a small part of him was starting to wish he hadn't stepped out of the tent at all.

'I think I dreamed something like that, too,' he muttered. 'Something about being in the dark, and hearing someone scream in the distance.'

He glanced around the empty campsite again, then looked down at Matt.

'So are you sure all his stuff's gone?'

Matt turned and disappeared back into the tent, then reappeared a few seconds later. He looked pale.

'Absolutely everything's gone,' he said. 'Come and have a look if you want.'

Tom shook his head and stood up straight. He turned in a full circle, scanning the horizon. He could only see a short way in one direction down the valley before the curve of the tor obscured his view, but in the other direction he could see quite far. There was nothing over there but grass that petered out into purple heather.

Tom glanced back up the tor they'd come down yesterday evening to make camp; he could see the footpath they'd followed winding up the side of the tor into the distance, but there was no sign of any movement on it.

Finally he looked the other way, craning his head to the top of the tor they would be climbing later that morning. His eye travelled from the top down, eventually finding a windy brown footpath halfway up. Tom traced this path down the side of the tor, all the way to where it eventually ended in the little copse of trees he'd spotted earlier.

The trees were dark and huddled close together. Thick shadows between the trunks made it hard to see into the copse. Tom looked up at the branches of the pines, which swayed and whispered against one another in the early morning breeze, and made a decision.

'Right, I'm gonna do a quick check around the area,' he said. 'He might just have wandered off for a piss or something.' He glanced down at Matt. 'You stay here.'

'Fuck that, I'm coming with you.' Matt disappeared back into the flap of the tent before Tom could object. 'Give me two minutes.'

'Don't hang about.' Tom's feeling of unease was getting worse. His stomach was now churning like it sometimes did before a big football game or a test at school, but it was nastier than that somehow, it was nastier because it wasn't just the nerves that were making Tom keen to get moving. It was the guilt, too.

He's gone and run off because of you, whispered a voice in Tom's head. *Because of what you did. You'll go into those trees but you won't find him there. Oh no. The next time you see Gary will be two tors down the line at the bottom of some ravine.*

Tom shook the thought off. It was all ridiculous, of course. He knew that. Gary would probably come wandering out of those trees or round the corner of the tor any minute now; he'd have been taking a shit or maybe he'd have wandered off with the intention of leaving and then come back after realising what a stupid idea going off on his own would be. Either way, it wouldn't matter. Tom would run up to him and tell him he was sorry and that he'd been a dick and that would be that.

A gust of wind blew through the camp and Tom rubbed his arms to keep warm, trying to ignore the part of him – the big part of him, actually – that didn't believe Gary was going to come walking back at all. If his friend had bothered packing up all his stuff and taking it with him, then he was obviously determined and more stubborn than Tom had given him credit for.

And what about that scream you heard? whispered the voice. *Don't forget about that. Maybe he fell down in the dark and cracked his skull open on a rock. Maybe he's lying out there on the moor somewhere even now, bleeding and semi-conscious and unable to talk. Or maybe – and here's a really good one – maybe something else got to him. Maybe he left his tent last night and—*

'Are we going then, or what?' Tom was jerked out of his daydream. He turned to see Matt climbing out of the tent, now dressed in a fleece, walking trousers and boots.

Tom nodded and turned towards the copse to lead the way. He glanced back at his own tent and then over at Mr Stevens' tent as they left the campsite, but there was no sign of any life from either of them. *Just a quick look*, thought Tom. *I'll just have a quick look around nearby, make sure he's not hiding or pissing around, then if we still can't find him we'll wake Tim's dad up straight away.* The tops of the pine trees were swaying gently in the distance, and Tom set his sights on them.

He marched across the grass, taking long strides, and he was almost annoyed when Matt shouted 'Hey!' before they'd even gone 20 paces.

Tom turned, ready to say something, but stopped when he saw Matt's expression. His friend was standing a few paces behind him with both feet rooted to the ground. His mouth was open slightly, and his gaze was fixed on something just beyond Tom.

'What's that?' he muttered.

Tom turned around and followed Matt's line of sight to a patch of grass ahead of him and just over to his left. He swallowed. Matt was looking at an area about six feet long that had been partially flattened. Tom thought it looked like those patches of grass you got in cow fields, after the cows had lain down and squashed the turf flat beneath their bodies. Sort of like that, only the wrong shape; this shape was about the same length but narrower, as if—

Tom's thoughts broke off as he noticed something darker in the grass. He took a few steps closer and saw that there was more than one of these dark shapes, and that what he was actually looking at were patches of grass that had been stained a different colour. They were darker, like rust.

He heard breathing and felt Matt beside him.

'Is that blood?' Matt's voice sounded high and weak, the voice of a small child. Tom got down on his knees by the patch of flattened grass without saying anything. He bent low towards one of the marked patches and plucked a stem of the rust-coloured grass out of the earth. He stood up and held it out to Matt.

Matt took it and squinted down at it, frowning. His face was still pale, but now two tiny round patches of red had sprung up on his cheeks.

'I'm not sure,' he said, offering the grass back to Tom. 'I don't know what else it could be, but it doesn't really *look* like blood, does it?'

Tom shrugged and tossed the stem away. He turned his attention back to the patch of flattened grass, looking to see if there was anything else that they'd missed.

'Something lay here at some point recently,' he muttered. 'It could have been a person, but I don't know.'

Tom got down on his knees and then lay flat on his back next to the shape.

'Is it the same size as me?'

'Yep, pretty much,' said Matt. 'Maybe a tiny bit shorter.'

Tom stood up. 'Gary's a tiny bit shorter.'

'Hey, what's going on?' This time both Tom and Matt jumped as a new voice spoke behind them. They turned to see James rubbing sleep out of his eyes and staring at them, a frown on his face.

'Morning mate,' said Tom, trying to keep his voice even. The last thing he wanted was for Tramper to start panicking and fly off the handle. 'It's nothing to worry about, we were just looking at this weird patch of grass.'

James wiped his eyes again and walked over to stand with them. He peered down at the grass, frowning.

'It looks like an animal lay down here to die,' he muttered.

'Why do you say that?' Tom's voice was still normal, at least to his own ears, but it was a big struggle to stop it from shaking.

'Well the grass is flattened and there's blood, and—' James broke off for a moment and walked past them, studying the ground. 'That's strange, there are drag marks over here, too. Like whatever was lying in the grass got dragged a few metres. Then they stop.'

Tom and Matt glanced at each other, and Tom could see the fear on his friend's face. He looked up and saw Tramper watching them.

'Hey, what's going on?' he said. 'Why are you guys looking at each other like that?'

Tom glanced again at Matt, but his friend was staring down at the ground and biting his lip.

'It's probably nothing,' he said. 'It's just that, well—'

'Gary's not here,' muttered Matt.

'What?' said James.

'I said Gary's not here.'

Tramper's frown deepened. 'What do you mean he's not here?'

'I mean his stuff was fucking gone from his tent when I woke up this morning, okay?' Matt spoke in an angry whisper, and James' eyes widened as if he'd been slapped. He looked from Matt to Tom, and then down at the patch of flattened ground in front of them.

'You don't think…'

'No,' Tom said quickly. 'We don't think anything at the moment. We were just going over to those trees to have a look for him, see if he's wandered off, or… or something…' Tom trailed off and the boys stood in silence for a few seconds, staring at each other.

'I think we should wake up Mr Stevens,' said James. He looked to each of them in turn, his face white. 'We need to go and wake him up right now.'

Tom glanced at Matt, who nodded his head.

'Okay, just a minute,' said Tom. 'I think you're right, but let me just run over to those trees quickly to make sure he's not wandered off for a shit, or… I dunno… or he's hiding there to play some stupid joke on us.'

As soon as he'd spoken the words, his mind jumped on the suggestion. He offered Matt and James a weak smile.

'You know, that's probably it,' he said. 'We're going to look pretty stupid if we raise the alarm and then he comes jogging out from behind a tree a few minutes later.'

Matt and James glanced at each other, but didn't say anything. Tom told them to wait there and started off for the trees again at a jog, keeping his eyes on the grass for any more signs as he went.

And it *was* possible, wasn't it? Surely it was more likely that Gary would just be getting a bit of revenge and playing a prank on them than actually running off on his own. People like him needed a way to salvage some pride when they felt like someone had got one over on them, and it'd be just like Gary to pull a stupid stunt like this so he could feel like he was back in control again.

Fucking let him, thought Tom. *If I get to those trees and find him there now I'll kiss him, and even if he starts banging on about how stupid we all looked I'll just grin and shut my mouth and be glad he's back.*

When he got within 10 metres of the copse, Tom slowed his pace to a fast walk. The branches rustled together above him, shushing each other like people locked in some permanent vow of secrecy. Tom peered between the trunks into the gloom, but couldn't see anything. He carried on walking, a light litter of twigs crunching beneath his boots, but when he reached the edge of the entrance to the copse he paused again, frowning.

For some reason he couldn't place, that feeling of unease was back. Tom peered into the grey-green gloom and all of a sudden the last thing he wanted to do was walk between the trees.

'Gary?' The sound of his own voice nearly made him jump. It was too loud somehow, almost out of place. The trees whispered and muttered above him, and Tom's skin prickled. As stupid as it sounded, he suddenly knew what people meant in those naff horror films when they said they thought they were being watched. If pressed he wouldn't have been able to explain *why* he felt this, exactly, but when he peered into the shadows of the copse he just had the feeling of being... well, *observed*.

He stole a glance back over his shoulder and saw Matt and James in the distance, watching him. He turned and looked back into the copse, casting his eyes in a 180-degree arc, and was just about to turn around and walk back when something on the ground caught his eye. Some dark shape that he'd almost missed, 10 metres or so into the trees.

Tom felt his stomach lurch. With an enormous effort, he took a breath and walked over to the shape. It was small and grey, and ringed by some sort of pattern that Tom couldn't make out in the gloom.

When he was five paces away from it he stopped. His stomach gave another lurch and he swallowed, forcing himself not turn away.

It was a rabbit's ear. It lay on a bed of pine needles that were stained a dark rust colour – *the same colour as that patch of grass*, Tom's mind whispered – and there was no sign of the body it had once been attached to.

'That's too much blood for one ear,' Tom muttered, crouching down. It looked to him as though something had killed the rabbit – maybe a fox or a bird of prey – and then other animals had been at it, tearing the body to shreds and leaving almost nothing behind.

Nothing except an ear.

Tom felt another chill run up his back. He glanced back over his shoulder, making sure there was nothing behind him, and then quickly looked in a full circle to be sure he was still alone. That strange prickly feeling on his skin hadn't gone away.

With an effort Tom tore himself away from the rabbit's ear. He turned away from it and began walking back through the trees, and it was as he glanced up and saw Matt and James in the distance that he suddenly remembered the dream he'd had the night before.

Tom stopped.

In his mind he saw another figure in the distance, a different one, and heard a piercing scream.

That was it, wasn't it? In his dream he'd been running down a long corridor, surrounded by darkness on all sides. At first there hadn't been any sound. Tom had heard his own ragged breathing, but that was all.

He'd stared around himself in the darkness, looking down and up, but there had been nothing to see. Then he'd glanced back, over his shoulder, and it had been as he looked around again that he'd seen the figure in the distance.

The woman in the white dress.

She was a pinpoint of light at the end of the dark corridor and although Tom couldn't make out her face he could see that she had long red hair and that she was waving at him, slowly. She could see him there in the dark, and she was beckoning him to come closer. And despite all the girls he'd run to in his dreams before – the girls from school; a couple of teachers; some of his mum's friends – Tom had a very bad feeling as he ran towards this one. From a distance she looked young and her hair was beautiful, like the hair of the women in adverts on TV, but the sight of her filled Tom with nothing but a kind of hollow, heavy dread.

Because it was *her,* wasn't it? Even though Tom couldn't see her face, he knew it was her.

He tried to slow down but he couldn't. It was the exact opposite of the nightmares you got where you were being chased by something and couldn't run; this time Tom wanted to *stop* moving but he couldn't. It was as though his legs didn't really belong to him.

So he'd kept running and the woman kept up her slow wave, and just as Tom was getting close enough to pick out her smile and her unblinking green eyes a scream had ripped through the darkness, an almost inhuman, animal sound, and Tom had turned his head and then he'd been falling through blackness, tumbling over and over until—

Until he'd woken up.

Tom stood still in the copse of trees, remembering the dream. He felt cold all over. He blinked and saw Matt and James still standing there, staring back at him, and with an effort he began to walk towards them again. As he left the copse his neck and back started to prickle once more, and without thinking he started to jog.

'Well?' said Matt when he reached them. 'Did you see anything?'

Tom shook his head. 'Nope, nothing.'

James looked white and uncertain, and Matt bit his lip and stared down at his feet.

Without saying anything Tom turned and led the way to Mr Stevens' tent.

2

The tent Mr Stevens shared with his son was slightly larger than the two-man pop ups they had. It was the same square shape with a domed top but it was wider and deeper, and the porch area stuck out slightly from the main bit to create more room.

Tom stopped outside the tent and shivered. He really should have gone to his own tent to fetch a coat, but he kept forgetting. He glanced round and saw Matt and James standing behind him, staring at him expectantly, and he knew it was up to him to lead the way.

'Mr Stevens,' he called. 'Mr Stevens, are you awake?'

Tom listened but could hear nothing from within the tent. After a few seconds, he reached out a hand and struck the material over the porch a few times, making the tent shake.

'Mr Stevens, we really need to speak to you.'

After a few more seconds of silence they heard a rustling sound from within the tent, and a moment later the zip was pulled back. Tim poked his head out and blinked blearily into the sunlight. His dark hair was standing on end and there were greyish-yellow bags under his eyes.

He stared up at them without saying anything.

'Hey Tim,' said Tom. 'Is your dad up yet? We really need to speak to him about something.'

Tim glanced from Tom to the others, and then back to Tom again. 'What time is it?' he croaked.

'I don't know, maybe eight,' said Tom. 'Listen, we need to speak to your dad now. Gary's gone missing.'

Tim studied Tom for a moment or two longer, not saying anything. His face was a tired mask.

'What do you mean he's missing?' he said slowly. 'You mean he went off for a walk or something?'

Tom could feel his impatience growing.

'No, his stuff's gone. This is serious, we don't know where he is.'

'His stuff's gone,' repeated Tim. He looked past Tom and out across the moor, his eyes distant and glassy. After a few seconds he wiped his eyes and looked at Tom, not saying anything. He looked pale and faintly concerned, but not nearly concerned enough. Tom was beginning to find his dopiness annoying.

'Tim, you really need to wake up,' he snapped. 'Gary's fucking missing, okay? He didn't just go for a wander on his own, he hasn't gone off to take a piss – his stuff's gone, all of it. Now can you wake your dad up so we can work out what to do?'

Tim recoiled and blinked. He glanced around himself nervously, chewing his lower lip, then looked back at Tom.

'My dad, he's not...' He broke off and looked round himself once more. 'He's already up, I think, he...'

Tim trailed off again, and Tom felt a sudden urge to reach out and shake him. 'Is he in the tent or not?'

Tim looked up at Tom with wide eyes and an expression of confusion. He was normally quiet and calm, and Tom had never seen him looking this rattled before. *At least I'm getting through to him*, he thought.

'No, he's not in the tent,' said Tim. 'I think he's gone and... I think maybe he's out collecting firewood?'

Tom frowned. They'd built campfires on both the last two nights, but they hadn't had one yesterday morning and Mr Stevens had made no mention of having one this morning. Yesterday it had just been a case of getting up, packing the stuff away and grabbing a cereal bar or two before setting off.

'Firewood? Are you sure?'

'I don't know! I don't know where he is, I've just woken up. Maybe he went off to the toilet, or maybe he…'

'What?'

'I don't fucking know alright!'

There was a flash of something in Tim's eyes, only briefly, but Tom saw it and it nearly made him take a step back. Then it was gone and Tim just looked pale and tired again.

'Look,' said Matt. 'It's fine, he'll be back in a minute and then we'll work out what to do. We just need to—'

'Morning boys!'

The sound of Mr Stevens' voice made them all jump. Tom turned to his right and saw Mr Stevens striding across the grass towards the tents, a CamelBak and two water bottles in his hands. He was sweating slightly and red in the cheeks despite the chill. There were bags under his eyes but he had a smile on his face as he waved to them.

'I've just been down to the stream to top up the water,' he said. He gestured behind him to where the curve of the tor blocked off the view further down the valley. 'Lovely little stream round there. What's the matter, everything okay?'

He entered the campsite and walked over to the tent where they were all standing. He was already in his walking kit, Tom noticed, including a new light blue fleece that he hadn't been wearing the day before. As he drew closer to them his smile faded.

'What's the matter?' His eyes flicking from Tom to Matt and James, then down to his son and back up to Tom.

Tom stepped forward. 'Mr Stevens, we're worried about Gary,' he said. 'When Matt woke up this morning all his stuff was gone, and we can't find him anywhere. Have you seen him?'

Mr Stevens eyes widened. 'Have I? No, I've just woken up and been straight down to the stream, I…' His eyes drifted past Tom, in the direction of the copse of trees, and then he turned his head and stared around the campsite as if seeing it for the first time. 'Did you say all his things are gone?'

'Yep,' said Matt. 'There's nothing in the tent.'

'And no one's seen him?'

Everyone shook their heads, and Tom felt James nudge him in the leg with his foot. He sighed.

'There's something else,' he said, glancing down at Tim and then back up to Mr Stevens. 'Matt and I thought we heard a scream in the night, we can't be sure because we might have just dreamed it but we think we did, and... well...' He glanced round at Matt and James for help. It was Matt that spoke.

'There's something over here you should see,' he said. His face had lost most of its colour but he turned around and led the way across the grass.

Tom glanced at Mr Stevens' worried face, nodded his head, and then turned to follow Matt. James and Mr Stevens came with him. Tim clambered out of the tent and walked after them, his eyes wide in his pale face.

They reached the flattened patch of grass with the rust-coloured stains and formed a ring around it. The shape in the grass was slightly less distinct than it had been earlier, but it was there.

'Well, what's this?' said Mr Stevens. He'd placed his CamelBak and water bottles at his feet and now he was frowning down at the ground.

'We don't know,' said Tom. 'I found it this morning when I got up to go for a walk. It looks like something was lying here, though. And we think that stuff could be blood.'

They stared down at the ground in silence for a while. Tim glanced round at the boys and then stared up at his dad, looking nervous. Mr Stevens crouched down and studied the grass without saying anything, his face serious.

After a few moments he got up and walked around the patch of flattened ground, his head down.

'No other tracks,' he muttered to himself. 'It's probably been quite a few hours now, though.'

He paced once around the patch of grass, paused to look back at the tents, and then stopped to scratch his head.

'Did you say you looked all around the campsite?' he asked Tom.

'Well, sort of. I went over to those trees for a quick look.'

'And you didn't see anything?'

Mr Stevens' eyes were fixed on Tom's, and for one guilty second he thought Mr Stevens knew about the rabbit. Tom still felt funny when he thought about that ear, just lying there in its little nest of rust-coloured pine needles. It clearly didn't have anything to do with Gary, though, so why bother spooking the others by even mentioning it? Tom shook his head and Mr Stevens' face relaxed. He thought for a second, then looked at Tom again.

'Gareth seemed very withdrawn yesterday afternoon and evening,' he said. 'I could tell something happened with you all at the top of Duck Tor.' He paused and looked at each of the boys in turn. 'I didn't say anything yesterday because I didn't want to pry, but I think it might be time to tell me about it now.'

He stared back at Tom, and Tom could tell from the set of his mouth that he wasn't asking.

Tom stared at the ground, feeling a guilty warmth flood into his cheeks. He was about to will himself to say something when James spoke.

'He'd been winding me up all weekend, and Tom stood up for me,' he said. Tom glanced over at him and James smiled nervously back.

'It's true, Tom didn't do anything wrong,' said Matt. 'Gary was the one that shoved James. He's always messing with him, and Tom was just defending him.'

Then Tom began to explain what had happened between him and Gary, and James told Mr Stevens about the prank Gary had played, and before long they'd covered everything – from the build-up right through to Gary's sullen aftermath and their failed attempts to talk to him.

Mr Stevens listened to the whole story without saying anything, his head cocked slightly to one side. When they'd finished he took off his glasses, wiped the lenses, and put them back on.

'Okay,' he said. 'Well first of all I don't want any of you boys worrying or thinking that any of this is your fault.' He glanced at James and Matt and then his eyes returned to Tom's face, where they lingered. 'What's happened is no one's fault, and if we all work together I'm sure we'll find Gary in no time and get this all sorted out.'

He paused, glanced over at the copse of pine trees, and then looked up at the tor they would be walking up next. He cleared his throat.

'Now, my guess is Gareth decided to go on up ahead of us – he's taken all of his things, which suggests he was planning this yesterday afternoon and didn't just wander off on a whim – and that he'll be aiming to stick to the route but beat us back to the finish. Sort of a wounded pride thing, I reckon; he's probably thinking he wants to show us all—' his eyes flicked over to Tom as he said this '–show us all that he's better than us. That's one possibility, anyway. The other is that he's out to play some sort of joke on us, and he's somewhere up there—' Mr Stevens gestured to the tor that rose up beyond the copse of trees '–waiting for us. I hope that *is* the case, if I'm honest, but I've got a feeling it might not be. Either way, we'll have to prepare for the former just in case.

'Now, turning back for help at this point won't do us any good because we'd have to walk almost as far back in the direction we've come,' he continued. 'Carrying on with our route, however, will eventually take us to a road, and we should be able to flag down a car or get some phone signal.' He smiled reassuringly and glanced at the tor in front of them. 'But you know what? I'm just betting we'll find Gary at the top of Hayworth Tor, fed up and waiting for us to catch up with him. Teenagers can only stay stubborn for so long.'

'You don't know Gary, then,' muttered Tom. The words were out before he could stop them, and he thought he caught a brief shadow – something like annoyance – slip over Mr Stevens' face. Then it was gone again, like a cloud passing over the face of the sun.

'You may be right about that, Mr Carpenter,' he replied. 'Had I known him better I would certainly have intervened yesterday after the two of you had your argument. Do you have another suggestion?'

Tom looked down at his shoes, felt his neck reddening even more, and then made himself look up and meet Mr Stevens' gaze. 'I don't know, shouldn't we look around here some more first?' His eyes travelled back to the patch of flattened grass. 'What if he's still around here somewhere, or...'

Tom trailed off and Mr Stevens smiled. He looked down at the patch of grass again and shook his head.

'Oh dear,' he said. 'You boys really have got yourselves worked up, haven't you?' He crouched down and patted the flattened grass with one hand, then smiled up at them.

'I've been walking on this moor for years, and you'd be surprised how common this sort of thing is,' he said. 'It'll be a sheep, most likely, or a calf. There is no shortage of those wandering around the moor, and they'll often bed down for the night like this. Their bodies protect the patch of grass under them from getting wet, you see, so they've got something of a dry surface to sleep on.'

The boys looked down at the ground.

'But what about the red stains?' asked Matt.

Mr Stevens raised his eyebrows. 'That could be any number of different things. It could be that a cow came here to give birth last night, or it might be nothing more than a sheep that nicked itself against a barbed wire fence.' He pointed at the shape and traced an outline of it with his finger. Tom saw that Matt looked slightly doubtful, but James was following Mr Stevens' gesture with wide, hopeful eyes.

'The thing is, the grass won't stay like this for long,' he continued. 'I'll bet it's already lost its shape a bit in the time since you discovered it this morning.' He looked over at Tom and smiled. 'That's what will have happened to the tracks. They'll have disappeared already. The sheep or cow, or whatever it is, will probably be long gone by now.'

Tom stared down at the grass again. It *had* lost its shape since earlier, Mr Stevens was right about that. But a sheep or a cow? It looked like the wrong shape, for one thing, and Tom thought that there were too many of those rust-coloured stains to account for a simple barbed wire nick. But then again, Mr Stevens *had* spent a lot of time on the moor, so maybe he was right. He certainly knew more about this sort of stuff than the rest of them.

Now Mr Stevens was dusting his hands and smiling once more, as if he'd settled everything, and saying something about them getting packed up as quickly as they could so they could catch Gary up. Matt looked less doubtful, and James was practically smiling again. Tom glanced over at Tim, and for just a second before Tim caught his eye and smiled back, Tom thought he saw his own concerns reflected in the boy's face. Tim still looked very pale, and the bags beneath his eyes were the colour of a light bruise in the morning light.

Tom had a sudden memory of the confused, almost fearful look that had passed over Tim's face when they went to his tent that morning. *Maybe he heard something in the night too, and he doesn't want to say.*

Tom was deep in thought when Matt clapped him on the shoulder, and he realised the others were already moving across the grass in the direction of the tents. He waited until Tim and James and Mr Stevens were out of earshot, and then he slowed Matt down with a hand on his shoulder.

'What do you reckon?' he whispered.

Matt turned to him and shrugged. He looked tired and confused. 'I think Mr Stevens is probably right,' he muttered. 'Knowing Gary, he probably just got pissed off and decided to go on without us. We'll probably catch up with him over the next tor or something.'

'Do you really think so?'

Matt nodded his head in response, but his eyes didn't meet Tom's.

'What about the screams we heard in the night?' said Tom. 'What about that weird patch of grass and the blood? No fucking way that was just a sheep, Matt.'

Matt looked after the others, who were now moving over to their respective tents. Mr Stevens said something to his son, then ducked down and disappeared through the flap of their two-man. 'Mr Stevens is the adult,' he said slowly. 'My mum said we should do what he tells us out here and not make a fuss. She told me before the trip that he was in charge, and that I'd be in trouble if she found out we'd been playing up.'

He turned to look at Tom and forced a smile. 'Besides, what else can have happened to Gary? People don't just disappear with all their stuff in the middle of the night.'

He clapped Tom on the shoulder and moved off across the grass. Tom stared after him, listening to the wind rustle the trees of the distance copse.

The heavy feeling in his stomach was back again.

3

They didn't find Gary at the top of Hayworth Tor.

The conversation had been fairly stunted after they'd packed up their tents and set off across the grass, and it fizzled out entirely as they started to climb Hayworth. Tom was worried they'd have to walk through the copse of pine trees and everyone would see the rabbit's ear, but in the end Mr Stevens led them along a path that wound around the trees rather than through them.

As the muddy trail they were walking along began to ascend, Tom felt the wind pick up. It bit into his skin and he had to stop to put on another layer. Clouds moved overhead.

By the time they were halfway up the tor, a fine drizzle had started. 'It's going to be bad weather today,' Mr Stevens said cheerfully. 'Best to get your waterproofs on sooner rather than later I think, boys.'

The drizzle turned into a light rain as they neared the top of the tor. Coats were dug out of packs and hoods were pulled up, and everyone walked the rest of the climb in silence. Mr Stevens was out front this time, with Tom and Matt not far behind him. James was a little way behind them, puffing along, and Tim brought up the rear. He hadn't spoken since they'd packed up their stuff that morning.

They reached the top of the tor around 10am. The light rain was holding steady, but when Tom looked out across the moor he could see thick black clouds in the distance. The sky below those clouds smeared down to touch the earth, as though a giant hand had smudged the horizon.

Tom wiped the rain from his forehead and stared out at the clouds. As soon as he'd reached the top of the tor he'd walked in a circle around the stone outcrop in the middle, looking in all directions, but he'd seen no sign of Gary. There were no distant figures on the horizon, no dropped food wrappers to suggest someone had been at the top of the tor before them, and no fresh muddy footprints on the ground.

As Tom scanned the view from his vantage point he felt someone come up alongside him. He glanced to his right and saw Tim. The boy had taken his hood down and his dark hair was soaking wet, his fringe plastered against his pale forehead in thick strands. He stared out over the moor without saying anything, and the two of them stood there in silence for a while.

'Did you see any sign of him?' Tom said eventually.

Tim jerked and looked round in surprise, as if he hadn't even realised Tom was standing there. He glanced down at the ground before looking out across the moor again.

'No,' he muttered. The wind gusted against the hillside, making him squint.

'I dunno,' said Tom. 'I just had this feeling as we were coming up the tor. This feeling that he wouldn't be up here. I mean I looked and everything and a bit of me was hoping we'd see him, but the biggest part of me didn't really believe it. You know what I mean?'

Tom glanced sideways at Tim, but the boy didn't say anything.

In the distance the sky was a patchwork quilt of colours: whites, blues, greys and roiling black. Although most places looked like they'd see rain, there were one or two areas – over to the south and a small patch in the west – that showed signs of better weather. The clouds there were less threatening, and occasional breaks allowed rays of bright sunshine to spotlight sections of the moor in light yellow. Tom thought there must be a rainbow about somewhere, but he couldn't see one from where he was standing.

'They're beautiful, these moors,' Tim said suddenly. He was staring into the south, his eyes tracing the patterns of green fields, purple hills and blue streams. 'When the sun comes out, they're beautiful.'

'Yeah, it's better up here now that the fog's cleared,' said Tom. He glanced sideways at Tim again and saw the boy wiping his eyes, and for one alarming moment he thought he was crying. Then he realised it was just the rain.

'My dad used to take me up here now and then when I was younger,' said Tim. 'Just the two of us. We'd get a map and go all over the place, and he'd teach me about navigation and stuff.' Tim paused, and then turned and stared at Tom. 'I don't think we're going to find Gary.' He said it softly, almost in a whisper, and the wind nearly carried his words away.

Despite the rain, Tom's throat felt dry. 'Why do you say that?'

Tim looked out over the moor, squinting into the rain and wind, and didn't say anything. After a few moments he shrugged, and Tom thought that this time he *did* look as though he might cry.

'Tim, did you hear anything last night?' said Tom. 'Anything weird or strange at all? Did you see anything?'

Tim moved his head and turned to look at Tom. His eyes were distant. He opened his mouth, seemed about saying something, then closed it again. Tom resisted an urge to reach out and shake him.

After a few moments, Tim looked down and tried again. 'I... well, I...'

He broke off when they heard footsteps crunching through the heather behind them. Both boys turned and saw Mr Stevens, smiling down at them. There was something clutched in his right hand that fluttered in the wind.

'I was sat on the rocks just now and I found this shoved down into one of the cracks,' Mr Stevens said. He opened his clenched fist to reveal a Nature Valley Granola bar wrapper, which he pinched between his forefinger and thumb. 'Gary had some of these, didn't he?'

Tom studied the bar, frowning. Gary *had* had those, it was true, but the wrapper looked old to him. Like it might have been stuck between those rocks for a good few months. Maybe longer. Then again, the wrapper was so covered in mud it was hard to tell. For a moment Tom felt a faint flicker of something like hope.

'Yeah, he did have those. It was stuffed down in the rocks, did you say?'

Mr Stevens smiled and nodded.

He reached out and patted Tom's arm with one thin hand. 'We're going to catch up with him, son,' he said. 'He can't be much further ahead now.'

4

They made camp at midday at the base of Garrett Tor, which was the next one along from Hayworth.

The going from Hayworth hadn't been pleasant, and although they'd only covered around six miles, it had taken them most of the morning. After they'd descended from the summit the path had disappeared and the ground had turned into a sea of tussocks – knobbly little mounds that Matt dubbed 'ankle twisters'. Tom almost did twist his ankle a couple of times, too, and the second time he'd actually fallen over and landed awkwardly on his side. He'd put out his right hand to cushion the fall and it had sunk into the boggy moss, causing brown water to ooze over his fingers. Lying there in the mud as the rain pattered down on his face, a low-level churning of nerves and guilt in his stomach because they still hadn't found Gary, Tom found himself wondering why he'd agreed to come on this weekend in the first place.

Matt's mum and James' gran had wanted them to go; they'd met Mr Stevens and thought he was a nice man, and they wanted the boys to make friends with Tim to help him feel welcome in his new school. But Tom's parents didn't give a shit. They might have said hello to Mr Stevens once or twice when picking Tom up from Gary's or Matt's, but they weren't the sort to stay over for a coffee and a gossip while the boys played GTA in the other room. Tom's father was a lawyer – a large, serious man who always seemed to be off working somewhere – and his mum's main group of friends were from her riding club in the New Forest. They kept themselves to themselves.

No, Tom supposed he'd just gone along because his friends were going, and as the athletic one of the group he was expected to take things like this in his stride. Big Tom, the captain of the Year 8 football team and the first pick for the 100-metre sprint on sports day; he could handle himself.

Only he wasn't handling himself now, was he?

Lying there in the mud, Tom had closed his eyes and felt the rain beating against his skin and in his mind he'd heard that scream again, he'd listened to that scream and seen the red-haired woman in the white dress as she waved at him down a long dark corridor.

You lost Gary, and now you'll never find him again, whispered a voice in his mind.

At that point Tom had felt a hand on his shoulder and opened his eyes to see Matt and James standing over him, looking concerned. Matt had offered him his hand and Tom accepted it, and when Tramper said, 'Jesus, I thought I was going to have to put you on my back or something!' Tom laughed in spite of himself.

He'd laughed in spite of the rain and the mud, and that anxious feeling gnawing in his gut like a rat chewing at the inside of a box.

They'd carried on through the tussocks until the ground finally levelled off into a sea of rainbow-coloured heather. After a mile or two of big, awkward steps and grit in their shoes, they'd finally found a path again.

Now they were a few miles on, eating lunch at the base of Garrett. They'd dumped their bags on a flat bit of ground away from the footpath, and were sat around on a relatively grassy patch of earth. Tom had a pasta and tuna meal that he dug out of his pack and tore the foil off to dig in to; the others had similar meals apart from Tramper, who brought out some cling film-wrapped Marmite sandwiches and a Snickers bar. Tim didn't eat anything.

Mr Stevens looked disapprovingly at the Snickers James had balanced on his knee.

'Those things aren't very good for walking, you know,' he said. 'Sugary foods like that go right through you; you get a five-minute burst and then you feel more tired than you did before you ate the thing.'

You're one to talk about being tired, thought Tom, looking at Mr Stevens. The man was perched on his backpack with his thin hands clasped in front of him, and although he had looked practically energetic that morning, Tom thought he now looked pale and ill. The bags under his eyes weren't quite as bad as his son's, but they weren't far off.

'Don't worry,' said Tramper, fishing out a Nutri Grain from his coat pocket. 'I've got the fast burn *and* the slow burn options. So I'm covered both ways.'

He grinned and Matt let out a little laugh. Tom wanted to ask them what they were laughing about, exactly; Gary was still missing, and since the granola bar wrapper on the top of Hayworth they hadn't seen any sign of him at all.

'How do we know we're still on the same route as Gary?' Tom asked suddenly.

They all looked round at him. Matt's grin faded, and Mr Stevens cleared his throat.

'Well, Gary had a map and I made sure before we started that he knew the basics of navigation,' he said.

Tom looked from Mr Stevens to the unreadable expressions on the faces of his friends, and he felt his temper rise.

'Yes, but there wasn't even a bloody *path* for a while back there,' he snapped. He heard James draw in a breath, but he ignored him and kept his eyes on Mr Stevens. 'What if Gary's lost, or hurt or something, and we've just left him behind?'

Tom heard the desperation in his own voice and Mr Stevens obviously heard it too, because when he next spoke his voice was gentler.

'Tom, I know this sounds like a horribly blunt thing to say, but if he's wandered off or decided to go on a different route then we're still doing the right thing. We've stuck to our route and we're making our way for the nearest road, which means we'll be able to get help as soon as we can.'

Tim stood up and mumbled something about going to fetch some water from the river. He grabbed his pack and wandered off away from the group. Mr Stevens ignored him, keeping his brown eyes fixed on Tom.

'Now personally,' he continued, 'I *do* happen to think we'll find Gareth. We know he was at the top of Hayworth, and even though the terrain hasn't exactly been plain sailing – you were right about that, Thomas – the visibility's not as bad as it was and we've been able to see Garrett Tor all morning. Even if Gary got confused with his compass, all he'd have to do would be to head in the direction of the tor.'

He smiled, and Tom looked down at his shoes. All at once he felt embarrassed for overreacting. And Mr Stevens *was* right, wasn't he? If you thought about it logically – something his dad was always telling him to do – if you thought about it and looked at the *facts*, what they were doing made the most sense.

Because Gary's stuff had been gone, and in real life people didn't just get abducted by aliens or stolen away by witches; in real life they just got pissed off and decided to wander away.

Is that what happened to all those children that went missing on Rut-moor? That family, too?

Tom didn't know about that, but he felt sure there was a decent explanation. His dad said there was an explanation for everything, no matter how weird it seemed.

Tom went to take a sip from his CamelBak and realised it was nearly empty.

'Is there a place near here where I can fill up?' he mumbled. All of a sudden he wanted to be away from the group for a bit, to have his own space for five minutes.

'Head along that way through those bushes,' Mr Stevens said, pointing in the direction Tim had gone. 'There's a little river nearby, and if you follow the path downhill you should find a point where you can fill up safely. Do you want me to come with you?'

'No, that's okay, thanks. Tim left a couple of minutes ago so I'm sure I'll catch him up.' Tom thought that he'd actually do his best to avoid Tim and find a different part of the river to fill his CamelBak, but he wasn't going to tell Mr Stevens that.

He stood up and shouldered his bag.

5

Tom followed a tiny brown trail that weaved its way between gorse bushes and ran roughly parallel to the river. He'd only been walking for a couple of minutes before he heard it, gurgling along off to his right somewhere. The wind had quietened down a bit and his foot-steps were loud and heavy.

At one point he paused, straining his ears to see if he could hear his friends back along the path, but there was nothing.

That was good.

Tom's dad had been in the TA when he was younger. Tom couldn't remember the exact name of the division or section he'd been a part of – he wanted to say reconnaissance, but that didn't sound quite right – but he'd told Tom all sorts of stories about the things he'd done. Nothing really scary, of course – he'd never been abroad to do any fighting – but the training could be pretty intense. Often, Tom's dad said, they'd go out somewhere and dig themselves in so they could observe something – an enemy camp, maybe, or a building – and they had to spend the whole weekend squashed together in this tiny little trench they'd dug out. Eating, sleeping and spending every minute in a muddy hole being as quiet as possible with hardly any room to move. Once, Tom's dad had whispered (when he was sure Tom's mum wasn't around to hear him say it), he'd woken up to see one of his army buddies taking a shit about a yard away from his head.

No matter how good the guys in your unit were, you went stir crazy eventually, he said. People losing their tempers. Snapping at each other. Guys just straight up quitting and deciding they'd had enough.

Tom was starting to feel like he could understand that. Okay, so he'd had sleepovers with his friends before a bunch of times, and once or twice they'd even turned into double sleepovers that lasted the whole weekend, but this was different. This time they weren't just playing Gary's PS2. This time they were out in the mud and the rain. This time they were with two people they hardly fucking knew, for Christ's sake.

And Gary had disappeared.

Yes, don't forget that one, whispered the voice. *And who's fault was that again, exactly?*

Tom shook the thought off and concentrated on the sound of his footfalls. How far had he gone now, anyway? The path had widened out slightly but apart from that it looked exactly the same. He stopped and listened for the sound of the river. Yes, it was closer now. It sounded as though it was just on the other side of the gorse bushes to his right.

Tom started walking again. He picked up his pace and as he rounded a bend in the path he saw the bushes starting to thin. He could hear the gurgling, louder now, but the grass was so thick and high there was still no sign of the river. He carried on down the path as the bushes continued to thin, rounded another slight bend, and then stopped.

Tim's pack was on the path up ahead.

It was about 10 feet in front of him, lying on its side just off the muddy track. Tom started to move towards it and then stopped himself. The feeling in the bottom of his stomach – that gnawing guilt and anxiety that had been there in the background ever since Gary left – had suddenly stirred at the sight of the pack. Tom hesitated, listening for any sound of Tim. There was nothing but the wind and the gurgling of the river. Why was his bag just lying abandoned on the path like that?

Tom looked at the pack again and had a clear, nightmarish image of going to pick it up. He'd get right up close and reach out a hand, and the second he touched one of those straps he'd feel something reach out and touch *him*, something behind him that he wouldn't even hear coming.

It was ridiculous, of course, but he couldn't shake the feeling.

So what are you going to do, just stand here staring at it all day long?

Tom took a breath, then took a slow step towards the pack. He paused again, listened, and took another step, then another. It was on the fourth step that he caught movement out of the corner of his eye.

Tom tensed, feeling heat bloom through his cold skin. He bit his lip in an effort to stop himself crying out and turned his head slowly, preparing to turn and run.

To his right there was a gap in the bushes, and beyond the gorse there was an open area of smaller bushes and thick grass. The ground sloped down there, and although Tom couldn't see the river he could hear it clearly and knew it must be there in that dip.

Tim was standing in the dip, facing away from Tom. He was bending down, and as Tom watched him he straightened up and looked at something in his hands that Tom couldn't see.

Tom let out a slow breath and felt the heat drain away from the surface of his skin. It was Tim, filling up his water bottle like he'd said he was going to do. That was all. That was why his pack was on the path in front of Tom – because he'd tossed it down when he'd found a suitable spot to access the river.

And what exactly had Tom been so worried about anyway, for Christ's sake?

You're losing it, that's all, he thought to himself. *You're going mad out here.*

Tom walked off the path and though a gap between two gorse bushes, heading towards Tim. The boy had his back to him, still staring at the thing in his hands, and Tom was about to call his name when he saw a glint of light bounce off whatever Tim was holding. Tim twisted it one way and then the other and the glare of light winked off its surface like a signal. Tom squinted. The thing was too small to be a water bottle.

He took another couple of steps forward across the grass. Now he could see down into the dip. Tim was standing on the bank of what looked more like a large stream than a river. As Tom watched he crouched down by the water again, lowering his hands to the surface.

Tom took another step forward and a stick snapped beneath his boot.

Tim jumped up and whirled round, almost losing his balance. His left hand shot inside his front coat pocket and he looked at Tom with wide eyes and a slightly open mouth. For a second they stared at each other, and then Tim let out a shaky laugh and shook his head.

'Jesus Tom, you made me jump.'

Tom looked back at him without saying anything. He noticed Tim's hand was still inside his coat pocket. The boy's greasy dark hair was plastered down over his pale forehead, and his light brown eyes stared out from twin hollows in his face. Tom thought he looked ill.

'Yeah, you really jumped there,' he said. He saw the way Tim was looking at him and forced himself to smile. 'I guess we're all a bit jumpy at the moment.'

Tim nodded and smiled back. It looked incredibly forced to Tom, the type of smile teachers sometimes put on when they were trying not to scream at you.

'What are you doing out here, anyway?' Tom asked. He tried to keep the question light and casual.

Tim stared back at him for a moment, then looked at the ground. 'Just came down to fill up my bottle,' he said. 'I'm running low on water.'

'Ah yeah, I remember you saying.' Tom held up the tube of his CamelBak and waved it at Tim. 'I'll come and join you if that's alright.'

He walked steadily down the bank. He kept his eyes on the ground as he moved, being careful where he was putting his feet, and he could feel Tim's eyes on him the whole time. When he reached the bank he looked up and smiled at Tim again. He smiled despite the gnawing in his stomach, which was suddenly so bad it was starting to make him feel sick. Tom went to take his pack off and then paused.

'Hey, do you have a water purification tablet or two I could borrow?' he asked. 'Think I'm all out.'

Tim stared at him for a couple of seconds and then nodded.

'Yeah, I think I might have some back in my bag,' he said. 'It's just up there on the path.'

'Don't you purify the water you get from the stream?'

'Yeah, but I was just going to do it all in one go when I got back to camp.'

'Ah, got you.' Tom paused. 'Are your bottles and your CamelBak all back by your bag too, then?'

Tim stared at him, then gave a sharp nod.

'I thought I saw you filling something else up when I was coming over,' Tom said carefully. 'You were bending down by the stream and you had something in your hands.'

Tim continued to stare at Tom, his expression unreadable. After a few seconds, that glassy smile returned.

'I was just splashing some water on my face,' he said. 'Trying to get some of the sweat and dirt off, you know?'

Tom nodded. He stared out across the stream, listening to its gentle lapping and burbling. He could hear the wind, faintly, but it was muted down here. He looked back at Tim.

'No,' he said.

'Huh?'

'No, you weren't washing your face,' Tom said. 'It's dry.'

Tim's mouth opened, then closed again. His eyes never left Tom's face. After a moment Tom grinned.

'Come on man, what's the big secret? You can tell me.'

Tim said nothing. He continued staring at Tom, and his right hand moved in his coat pocket. He shook his head slowly back and forth.

Tom took a step towards him.

He hadn't meant it to be threatening – at least he didn't think so; he had no plan in his head when he started moving – but Tim flinched and took a step back, raising both hands in front of him. As he did so a small object went tumbling from his coat pocket onto the grass between them.

Tom paused and looked down, then bent to pick it up.

'That's... that's not...' spluttered Tim. 'That's just mine.'

Tom stared at the watch in his hand. It was bulky and black; one of those digital ones with two metal buttons on either side of the face. For a second he felt only confusion, but then a sudden realisation hit him and the feeling in his stomach went from a background gnawing to a horrible, wave-like lurch.

The watch was Gary's.

Tom turned it over in his hand, held it close to his face, and saw two small stains on the black strap. Dark maroon splotches. They were faded, almost washed clean by the water, but they were there. Tom felt something hot rising inside him, a sharper version of the angry adrenalin he sometimes felt on the football pitch.

He held the watch out to Tim. His hands were shaking.

'What the fuck is this?'

Tim still had his hands up in front of him. He took another step back away from Tom.

'Listen, I can explain,' he said. 'I was trying to clean it off, and—'

'I can see you were trying to clean it off!' Tom shouted. 'But where the fuck did you get it?'

'I...no, I...'

Tim's eyes were wide. His normally calm voice was a panicked, stuttering mess. He took another step back and shook his head.

'Back at the tent, I knew I saw something,' Tom continued. 'I saw something in your eyes when we said Gary was missing. I thought maybe you'd heard something in the night. Then up on Hayworth Tor this morning you were about to say something to me, but your dad interrupted us. Now there's this, and—'

'I found it,' Tim said suddenly. His eyes flicked from Tom's face to the watch held in his hands.

Tom, who'd been on the verge of taking another step forward towards Tim, paused and stared at him. Tim started nodding his head.

'Yeah, I found it on the grass this morning,' Tim said. 'By our campsite. I was going to tell you, but I didn't want to scare anyone.'

Tom stared at the nodding boy in front of him. His eyes were wide and desperate, and in that moment Tom was sure he was lying.

Tom grimaced and took another step forward, and as he did so Tim's eyes flicked up and over his left shoulder. Then they shot back to Tom.

'No!' Tim yelled as Tom took another step forward, and Tom thought he was yelling at him until he heard heavy footsteps crunching across the ground behind him.

Tom's years on the football pitch and the many times he'd spent crouched on the school field waiting for the starting gun had given him quick reactions. At the sound of the footsteps he whirled to his left, spinning quickly away from Tim, but just as he was turning something that felt like a steel rod smashed into his left shoulder. Tom was thrown backwards. His legs caught against a tussock and he fell, landing on his back. His landing was cushioned by the grass, but his right thigh slammed into a rock and sent a sharp pain shooting up his leg. His left shoulder throbbed and burned.

Mr Stevens was standing a few feet away from Tom, looking down at him. He held a walking pole in his left hand. There was no discernible expression on his face. As Tom watched he took two quick steps across the grass.

'Dad, no.' Tom heard Tim's voice up and over to his left. It sounded thin and scared.

Mr Stevens lowered himself to a crouch. Tom heard his knees pop. He looked at Tom for a moment, then smiled and removed his glasses.

'What are you doing to my son?' He asked the question pleasantly, as if they were still sat around the campfire and talking about the weather.

For one horrible moment Tom didn't think he'd be able to get any words out – he felt dazed, as if none of this was really happening – but he swallowed and licked his lips and they finally came.

'Tim's got… Tim's got Gary's watch,' he said.

Mr Stevens frowned, then turned and looked up at his son.

'Is that true?' he asked.

'Dad, I—'

'Answer my question.'

'Yes, I've got it.'

Mr Stevens' frown deepened. Tom thought for a moment he looked angry. Then the frown broke and he sighed and shook his head. 'And you let him see you with it just now?'

Tim didn't say anything. Mr Stevens sighed once more, then looked back at Tom.

'I want you to know, Timothy, that you did this,' he muttered.

Tom heard Tim scream, and as his head turned automatically towards the sound Mr Stevens reached down with his right hand and clamped it around Tom's throat.

Tom gasped in shock and managed to pull in a half-breath. He kicked his feet and pushed himself back across the grass, feeling the rock beneath his right thigh tear across his skin. He could taste sweat in his mouth. In the background, the stream gurgled.

Moving with the speed of a much younger man, Mr Stevens scampered forward and dodged Tom's kicking legs. Keeping his right hand on Tom's throat he jumped to one side, then moved his left leg over Tom's waist so he was straddling Tom's stomach. Tom bucked and thrashed from side to side, but Mr Stevens was much too strong. He shifted his weight, dropped the walking pole, then brought his left hand down and fastened it around Tom's throat along with his right.

Tom tried to breathe in again, couldn't, and squeezed his eyes shut. He opened them again and saw Mr Stevens' red face straining above him. The hands around his neck felt like a metal collar. His vision was starting to swim. Tom closed his eyes, desperately trying to pull in breath, but it was like trying to breathe through a straw. His chest throbbed and his eyes stung with tears and he tried to drag some air into his lungs, anything, but Mr Stevens was crouched on his stomach like some giant bird and his hands were metal talons, and surely all of this was just some sick dream anyway? Surely it wasn't happening?

A distant image of them all sat around the campfire on Thursday night flashed across Tom's racing mind and he saw Mr Stevens smiling and adjusting his glasses with a map balanced on his lap, and in that moment Tom knew that this wasn't real, of course it wasn't, he must be hallucinating or still trapped in a nightmare because it just couldn't be. Blood thumped in his head. Fingernails dug rivets into the flesh beneath his chin. Somewhere deep in his mind, Tom felt something fragile starting to give.

When he opened his eyes again he saw that Mr Stevens' face had changed.

His mouth was hanging open slightly to reveal sharp needle-like teeth, and his cheeks were slack around his face. The skin was loose around his jaw like a badly fitting mask. Spittle fell from his mouth in thin streams.

The thing Tom noticed most, though – the lasting image that stayed burned into his retina and followed him into the darkness – was Mr Stevens' eyes.

They'd been brown before, like his son's, but now they were a muddy yellow. They looked sharp and ancient, like the eyes of an old cat. He was in a nightmare, of course he was. None of this could be real.

Mr Stevens' grip tightened.

Blood pounded through Tom's head in hard, thudding heartbeats. He could taste sweat in his mouth.

Somewhere, way off in the distance, he heard Tim continuing to shout and scream.

Tom reached out with his mind, looking for something to hold on to, anything else, and he found the gurgling noise of the stream. He could no longer move his head but he shifted his eyes to the left, away from Mr Stevens' sagging face and in the direction of the water.

The gurgling of the stream was still there; it would always be there. The world started to blur and his eyes drifted shut.

News Cuttings (1998–2015)

From the Southampton Daily Star, 8 October 2007

Dog found DECAPITATED in suspected satanic ritual

The gruesome discovery was made by an elderly couple out on their morning walk.

The decapitated and mutilated corpse of a dog was found on Sunday morning in a field beside Southampton's River Itchen, leading police to look into the possibility of a Satanic cult.

Marla Francis, 73, and Sam Francis, 79, said they made the discovery while going for their weekly stroll along the banks of the river.

'We were just out walking when Marla saw something lying in the grass a little way off the path,' Mr Francis told the *Daily Star*. 'We thought it was a rabbit or something at first. When Marla walked over to it she dropped her bag and screamed. That's when I knew something was wrong.'

The dog, which police report was a black labrador, was found with its head missing. Police later recovered the head from a neighbouring field after conducting a search of the area.

At this stage little information is being made publicly available, but an inside source told the *Daily Star* that there are even more disturbing details to the case.

'The head was lying in the middle of a stone circle,' said the source. 'Its eyes and tongue had been removed.'

The *Daily Star* understands that police are now investigating the possible involvement of 'devil worshippers'.

No collar was found on the dog, but the owners are believed to have been located and informed.

Police are appealing for anyone who lives on Woodmill Lane and who may have seen or heard anything suspicious on the night of Saturday 6 October, or early Sunday 7 October, to come forward.

When asked about the case, a spokesperson from Hampshire Constabulary said they are pursuing a number of lines of inquiry, and it would not be appropriate to go into more detail at this stage.

From the Bournemouth Herald, 6 August 2008

Police hunt for suspect after failed abduction attempt

Dorset police are looking for a man, described as being tall and of slender build, who attempted to snatch an 8-year-old boy from Christchurch Quay on Tuesday.

A manhunt is underway after an unidentified man attempted to abduct an 8-year-old boy from Christchurch Quay on Tuesday afternoon.

The man, who was wearing a dark blue tracksuit and a green baseball cap, has been described as 'tall and slender'. The boy did not get a good look at his face.

Dorset police say the child was cycling along Christchurch Quay when he was approached by the man, who asked him if he'd like to see a puppy he'd just bought. When the little boy asked where the puppy was, the man responded by saying that it was in his car, which he said was parked nearby.

'He's a bit scared and he needs someone to give him a stroke,' the man reportedly said.

When the boy tried to ride off on his bike the man reached out and grabbed his arm, but after the boy screamed he panicked and fled.

The boy then cycled home and his parents contacted police.

Dorset police are asking anyone who was in the Christchurch Quay area on the afternoon of Tuesday 5 August to come forward with any information.

'This type of thing is unusual, and we take it very seriously indeed,' said Chief Inspector Marcus Porter. 'If someone is approaching children in broad daylight it implies that they're either very unwell or very desperate. I'd advise parents in the area to make sure their children are accompanied, both at night or during the day, when they leave the house.

'Anyone who may have seen a man matching the description given by the boy should contact us as soon as possible.'

From the Southampton Echo, 16 March 2010

Missing twin girls: have you seen Samantha and Marie Plumber?

Samantha and Marie Plumber, two 6-year-old twins, have been missing since last Sunday evening.

Hampshire Constabulary have issued an urgent appeal to anyone who may have information regarding the whereabouts of two 6-year-old twin girls who have been missing since Sunday, 14 March.

The girls were last seen by their mother, Sally Plumber, at around 5.30pm on Sunday afternoon at their family home on Cemetery Road.

Miss Plumber told police she let the girls out to play in front of the house while she prepared dinner, but when she called them half an hour later they didn't respond.

'I shouted for them to come in because dinner was ready,' Miss Plumber explained at a press conference on Monday afternoon. 'When they didn't come in or reply, I looked out the lounge window and saw that they weren't in the front garden. They'd been out there playing with their Barbie dolls; I saw the dolls lying in the grass near the front gate but there was no sign of the girls.'

After searching the house and the surrounding area, Miss Plumber contacted the police. They are currently conducting a thorough search and appealing for anyone who may have been out walking on Southampton Common on Sunday afternoon to come forward.

'We're speaking to neighbours and asking anyone who may have been around the Southampton Common area at the time to come forward urgently,' said Detective Inspector Bill Timber. 'Cemetery Road leads on to the common, so it's possible the girls wandered out of the garden to go and explore. We're carrying out a search of the area and doing everything we can to ensure they're returned safely to their mother.'

'I just want them to come home,' Miss Plumber said. 'I just really, really want them home safe with me. They're only little, and I keep thinking about how scared they must be. I feel totally powerless.'

Anyone with any information regarding the whereabouts of Samantha and Marie Plumber can contact Hampshire Police or speak anonymously to Crimestoppers.

From the Southampton Echo, 18 March 2010

Police find the bodies of two girls in the River Itchen

Hampshire Constabulary have released a statement saying the bodies of two young girls were found in the early hours of Thursday morning.

Police searching for missing twin girls Samantha and Marie Plumber have found two bodies on the bank of the River Itchen, near the train track south of the A335.

At this stage, the bodies have yet to be identified. Police say no one has been charged with any crime, but a 58-year-old man has been taken in for questioning.

'We can't give any more details at this stage,' said Detective Inspector Bill Timber. 'We're currently following up on a number of different lines of inquiry and we're speaking to several people who may have information relating to the bodies.'

When asked if he could confirm if the bodies were those of missing twin girls Samantha and Marie Plumber, Detective Inspector Timber said he couldn't comment.

'As soon as we have more details a press conference will be called,' he said.

From the Southampton Echo, 19 March 2010

Mother of murdered twin girls said to be 'devastated'

Miss Sally Plumber has released an emotional statement following yesterday's discovery of two bodies, now confirmed to be those of missing 6-year-old twins Samantha and Marie Plumber.

The 32-year-old mother of murdered twin girls Samantha and Marie Plumber has said she's 'devastated' by what has happened and urges anyone with any information to come forward.

'I sent my girls out to the front garden to play while I cooked dinner,' she said in an emotional press conference on Thursday afternoon. 'They were just two little girls, playing with their dolls, who'd never dream of hurting anyone. For someone to do this to them…

'Please, please, can anyone who may have seen or heard anything, no matter how small it may seem, come forward to the police so we can find the person or people responsible and I can get justice for my girls.'

Hampshire Constabulary led a four-day search after Samantha and Marie went missing from their front garden on Cemetery Road last Sunday. On Thursday they discovered two bodies on the bank of the River Itchen south of the A335, which were later confirmed to be the bodies of the missing twins.

The cause of death hasn't been released, but police say the deaths have been classed as suspicious and they're following up various lines of inquiry.

'We're speaking to a number of people and following up on various leads,' said Detective Inspector Bill Timber. 'But we'd urge anyone who knows anything or saw or heard anything suspicious in the Southampton Common area last Sunday, to come forward immediately. This is now a murder investigation.'

On Friday morning police released a 58-year-old man, who'd been taken in for questioning, without charge.

From the Plymouth Daily Herald, 29 September 2014

Teenage boy reported missing on Rutmoor camping trip

Devon and Cornwall Police are searching Rutmoor after a 13-year-old boy was reported missing by his family on Sunday.

A teenage boy has been reported missing after his family woke to find his sleeping bag empty on Sunday morning.

Thirteen-year-old Philip Railman was on a weekend camping trip with his mother Jenny Railman, his step-father Paul Simons, and his younger brother Seth Railman when he went missing.

According to Devon and Cornwall Police, Philip was sharing a tent with his brother Seth on Saturday night, but when Seth woke at around 7am on Sunday his brother's sleeping bag was empty.

'This is obviously an unusual case,' said Chief Inspector George Boering. 'The younger brother didn't see or hear anything in the night, and at this moment in time we're working on the assumption that Philip may have wandered off on his own. The moor is a big place but we're putting together search teams made up of police, family and local volunteers.'

The family were camping at the base of Hayworth Tor on the night of Philip's disappearance. Anyone who was in that area of the moor on Sunday who may have any information is urged to come forward immediately.

Tim (2002)

He couldn't look away.

Tim stood on the grass, unmoving, as the sound of Tom's desperate gasps for breath gradually faded and became nothing more than horse whispers.

His father was straddling Tom's waist, silent and intent on his task, and Tim couldn't bring himself to look at his dad's face. He knew what he'd see if he did; he'd seen that face before.

Blood roared inside his head. He felt a nasty mixture of fear, horror and – just a little bit, deep down – exhilaration.

Tom's face had gone from red to purple. His eyes bulged outwards, large white eyes splintered with thousands of red capillaries. A line of snot ran from his nose down to his bruised lips. Tim felt his penis stiffening in his pants. He bit the inside of his cheek, hard, and looked down at the ground. There was a large flat rock by his left foot, and Tim prodded it with his toe.

After a few moments his dad let out a long, ragged breath. Tom was completely silent now, and Tim knew it was done.

He glanced back up and saw his dad in the same position, looking down at Tom. His father's face was back to normal again. The skin of his cheeks had tightened, and his eyes were their usual light brown colour. They stared down at Tom's lifeless body with something like love, and Tim felt a wave of hate pulse through his mind.

He glanced down at the large rock by his left foot again.

Would he have time, if he moved quickly? He imagined himself bending slowly and grasping the rock, then springing forward and bringing it down against his dad's head with both hands. His dad's startled gasp. The thick crunching sound as his skull broke open. The blood.

Tim looked up and saw his dad watching him.

His eyes were fixed on Tim's face, and for one horrible moment Tim thought his dad knew exactly what he was thinking.

Could he do that? Tim didn't know, and didn't want to know. The wave of hate in his mind was being taken over by fear, the way it always was in the end. He looked once more at Tom's bloated face and glassy eyes, and fought the urge to throw up.

'Don't worry, you'll get the taste for it.'

Mr Stevens was smiling at his son; it was a thin smile that Tim also knew well. He'd seen it countless times when he was growing up, after all.

As Tim watched, his dad glanced around himself at the grass, said 'Ah!' and then reached out and picked something up. He put his glasses back on and smiled at Tim once more.

'It's always good to keep up appearances,' he said.

2

Tim's earliest memories of his father were of the stories his dad used to tell him before bed.

Like many of the memories he had from that age – walking the dog with his mum; playing in the sandpit at nursery school with a red-haired boy whose name he could no longer recall; drawing with coloured crayons over the wallpaper of his bedroom after his mum sent him there for being naughty – Tim couldn't remember the build-up or what happened after. It was as though his life from the time he was born until the age of around seven was a dark landscape, with only the occasional spotlight to shine down and light up random memories.

Brief, bright islands of time.

His first memories of his dad were like that.

Tim would be lying in his semi-dark bedroom, looking up at the glow-in-the-dark stars and planets his mum had stuck to his ceiling, and his dad would be sat at the end of his bed adjusting his glasses. In these memories his father looked exactly the same as he did now, as if he hadn't aged. His dad would be perched at the end of his bed, sitting completely still like some large, skinny vulture, and Tim would know it was story time.

Tim's dad never carried a book, because the stories were all in his mind. They were lessons, really.

In one – Tim thought of this one as *The Boy Who Didn't Fight Back* – his father explained what happened to little boys who never stood up for themselves. As with most of the early memories he had of his father, Tim didn't remember the build-up to this one, but he *did* remember having a slightly swollen, split lip that he probed with his tongue while his dad talked. It could easily have been a detail his mind had added later, but Tim didn't think so.

In *The Boy Who Didn't Fight Back*, Tim's dad told him about a skinny little kid he'd known when he was younger who let the other children push him around at nursery school. The kid in the story didn't have a name, but he was a lightweight and the other children used to take advantage – stealing his toys, pushing him over if he got in their way, that sort of thing.

And because the little boy never stood up for himself or pushed them back, they just did it more and more. Pretty soon the boy was at junior school, and the big kids were taking his football cards away from him in the playground and tripping him up when he came out to break. The boy never said anything back to them, though, he just let it happen, and the children in his own year laughed at him when they saw it because they were afraid of the big kids and they didn't want it to happen to them. Some of them even joined in, to try to make themselves more popular with the big kids.

And all the time, the little boy never said anything. He felt hurt and ashamed, but he was afraid to fight back so he just bottled up the feelings inside himself.

Then all of a sudden, he wasn't a little boy anymore. He was at secondary school, and the same things were happening only this time it was much worse. The same big kids that had tormented him at junior school were even bigger, and now they didn't just want to trip him over in the playground. Now they wanted to take the money he had for the canteen, and they wanted to punch him in the stomach when no teachers were looking. Sometimes they cornered him in the boys' toilets and beat him up. One time they even held him so that the biggest boy could piss on his trousers.

And the boy in the story never fought back. He had all that shame and hurt crammed down inside himself like a bin that's full to bursting with decades-old rubbish, only now as well as shame and hurt he also had anger rammed down in there too. Rage, really.

The more it happened and the more humiliated he felt at school, the more that impotent anger filled him up.

At this point in the story Tim remembered how his dad had paused, and how his brown eyes had flicked down to Tim's split lip. 'If only he'd had the courage to stick up for himself that first time at nursery school, when that other little boy had hit him,' Tim's dad said. His mouth curled up at the corners, but there was no smile in his eyes. 'If he'd hit the other little boy back, harder, everything else could have been different.'

Tim wanted the story to be different. He wanted the story to be one of his old favourites that his mum read to him about *The Famous Five* or *Hairy Maclary from Donaldson's Dairy*. He didn't like this story.

But his dad hadn't stopped. As Tim lay there beneath his Donald Duck duvet in the dim yellow light from his bedside lamp, his dad told him how, one day, the boy in the story had gone home and rummaged through his mum's cutlery draw. How he'd found the biggest, sharpest knife he could and hidden it in his school bag. He'd only meant to scare them off, of course. He hadn't meant to do anything, not really.

But then when the big boys found him the next day out on the school field and he'd pulled the knife out of his bag, that rubbish bin inside him had finally burst. He'd felt powerful standing there with the knife, he'd felt *better*, and all the shame and hurt and anger had spilled out of him in one big wave.

Some of the big boys had been shocked by the knife, but the tallest one – the same one who'd stood there in the toilets, laughing as he pissed all over the boy's school trousers – had made the mistake of stepping forward to take the knife away from the boy. The boy had panicked, lunged forward, and before they all knew what was happening the big boy's stomach had sprouted a wooden hilt. He was screaming and pawing at that hilt, trying to get it out, and the blood was pumping out around it in sticky red torrents. Kids were screaming. Teachers were running over. Eventually, there was the sound of sirens. And the boy in the story just stood there looking at the knife, his eyes glassed over, with nothing but this big emptiness inside him.

Tim didn't remember all the stories his dad had told him when he was younger, but he remembered that one well. What he remembered most about it, though, was how his dad had looked at the end of it. The light sheen of sweat on his skin. The way his mouth hung open, almost hungrily, making the skin of his cheeks look strangely slack and loose. How the light from Tim's beside lamp made his eyes appear yellow in the gloom.

There were other stories, too. Other islands of bright time on the dark landscape of Tim's childhood. He knew now that some of them had been variations of regular stories – a twist on *Jack and the Beanstalk* in which Jack gets thrown from the top by the giant and breaks his neck, dying in a pool of his own blood; a version of *Sleeping Beauty* in which the Prince decides to smother the girl in her sleep rather than saving her; a particularly nasty take on *Hansel and Gretel*, in which the children never escape from the witch's hut and Gretel is forced to watch Hansel get cooked and eaten in front of her.

But most of the stories Tim's dad told him were really lessons. Most of them were rooted in things that happened in Tim's life.

Then there was the story that Tim remembered most clearly of all. That one was rare, because he could remember some of the build-up as well as the story itself. He couldn't remember why or what had prompted it, but he knew he'd spoken back to his dad earlier that day. Maybe told him to shut up or go away, something like that. Probably the only time he'd ever spoken back to his father.

His dad had obviously noted its significance too, because later that night he was perched in his usual position at the foot of Tim's bed telling him about *The Boy Who Wouldn't Listen.*

Tim remembered this story extra well, because it had given him bad nightmares at the time. Nightmares that continued intermittently for years afterwards, and which even now as a teenager he found himself having every once in a while.

'Can you see up there?' Tim's dad had said, pointing to the middle of Tim's ceiling. Tim looked and saw he was pointing to the hatch that led up to the attic. Tim had never been up there before, partly because it was impossible to clamber up to, and partly because his mum told him there was nothing up there but dust and perhaps mice, anyway.

'Have you ever been up there?' Tim's dad asked. When Tim shook his head, he smiled. 'Good. That's a good idea. Because there's something that lives up there, you know. A monster.'

At this point he'd taken off his glasses and put them in his lap. Tim noticed once again how yellow his eyes were in the light.

'This monster only wakes up once or twice a decade,' he said. 'And when it does wake up, it's normally hungry. Very, *very*, hungry.'

Tim felt the usual cold fear go through him that he felt whenever his dad was telling a story, but this time it was worse. He glanced up at the hatch in his ceiling and shivered.

'Is it awake now?' he mumbled.

'Don't interrupt me.'

Tim's dad leaned forward on the bed and peered down at Tim with his yellow eyes. His mouth was hanging open, and Tim could see the white points of his teeth gleaming in the darkness.

'Now this particular monster happens to like the taste of children,' his dad continued. 'Small ones, teenagers... anything it can get its teeth into, really.'

He smiled, showing more teeth, and Tim resisted the urge to pull his Donald Duck covers up over his eyes.

'The thing is, though, the monster only really likes the taste of children who don't behave themselves. Children who don't *listen*.

'The last time it was awake, it got two teenage boys who thought they were too clever to listen to their parents. Not too long before that it got a whole *family*. The children in that family weren't very well behaved at all, and to punish them it gobbled up their parents in front of them before it went to work on them, too.'

Tim could feel his whole body shaking. There was a whimper caught in his throat that was doing its best to escape, and it was taking Tim all his effort and concentration to make sure it didn't. His dad wouldn't like that.

Tim swallowed and his eyes shot across to the hatch in his ceiling once more. His father followed his gaze, then smiled again. It was wide and unpleasant, that smile, the same one the bad crocodile from Tim's storybook had; the type of smile adults did when they weren't really smiling at all.

'I know, you're wondering how this monster could have got to all those children if it lives up there, above your room,' said Tim's dad. 'And the thing is, you're right. But it has to come down every now and then, doesn't it?'

He shifted closer to Tim on the bed and leaned forward until Tim could smell his breath. It was faintly unpleasant, half-minty and half-rotten, like toothpaste that hasn't quite covered up the smell of pork.

'Just keep your ears open,' his dad whispered. 'And if you ever hear something moving about up there, or that hatch starting to creak open, you'll know it's getting ready to come down.'

Tim's dad's eyes were wide, yellow discs. Tim wanted to shut his own eyes, but he couldn't.

'You'd just better behave yourself, Timothy, or it'll be coming down for you one of these days.'

3

They were standing side by side, looking down at Tom's body. Mr Stevens was humming lightly under his breath, drumming his fingers against his thighs as he crouched to study the purple-faced corpse.

'Now, you know what you did with the watch, so I'm not going to tell you about that,' he said. 'That was your mistake, and this is your fault, but we fixed it and I don't think it's going to be an issue.'

His tone was light and airy, as if they were discussing the best route to navigate to the next tor.

'Hmm?' Mr Stevens glanced down at his son, eyebrows raised, and Tim nodded his head.

'Yes, Dad.'

'Great. Well, ideally, I'd have liked to have got them all tonight after some stories around the fire, but that can't be helped. I was feeling tired before anyway, so maybe this is actually a good thing.'

Tim nodded his head without saying anything. He still felt nauseous and was concentrating most of his energy on not throwing up.

His dad wouldn't like that, and the last thing Tim wanted to do was spoil his father's good mood.

'I'm not worried about the fat one,' Tim's dad muttered, almost to himself. 'The fat one should be fine, but the other one might take some more convincing.'

He stopped drumming his fingers and looked down at Tim. 'Right,' he said. 'This is your chance to prove yourself. I can forget what's happened so far – all the mistakes you've made – if you can get this next bit right. We don't need anyone getting panicky, after all.'

'Yes, Dad.'

Tim's father placed both hands on his son's shoulders. He lowered himself down to eye level, and Tim watched as the eyes behind his glasses shimmered from brown to yellow, and back to brown again.

As he was telling his son the plan, Mr Stevens' mouth started to hang open. The skin around his cheeks grew looser, flabbier, like the face of an overweight older man. Tim didn't say anything while his dad talked. He tried to stop his nose from wrinkling at the smell of his dad's breath. He stood still and didn't fidget, and he listened.

He'd learned a long time ago what happened to boys who didn't listen to their parents.

Finally, Tim's father straightened up and smiled. This time the smile looked more genuine.

'Excellent,' he said. 'Now I'm just going to take care of this one here, first, and then we'll be heading back.'

He turned his back on Tim and walked over to Tom's body. He lowered himself to the ground so he was down on his knees, his head positioned by Tom's feet. Tim watched in sick horror as his father's body started to tremble. Tim couldn't see his face from this angle, but he knew what would be happening; his father's cheeks would be drooping and growing even more saggy, and his mouth would be opening to show his thin, white teeth. Then his mouth would start to open even wider, and—

Tim felt his stomach lurch.

At least he wouldn't have to watch this bit. His dad wouldn't know if he was looking or not. Plus, when it was over, he wouldn't have to see Tom's bloated face ever again. There'd be no trace left. His father had a big appetite, after all.

I'll still see his face in my mind, though, Tim thought. *There's no getting rid of that.*

He turned around and focused his gaze on the river, listening to it gurgle and trying to blot out the sounds coming from behind him.

4

For long periods of time when Tim was younger, his father hadn't been around. He'd been there for his bedtime stories when he was little, and he'd been there for a longer, memorable patch when Tim was around nine years old, but for many years he was nothing more than an absence.

During these patches it was just Tim and his mum.

Anne Stevens was a small woman with blonde hair and permanently red cheeks. She had a friendly, tired look about her and she didn't speak much. When Tim was younger her hair was always bright blonde, but as he got older he noticed that patches of grey had started to come through where she wasn't dyeing it as much as she used to.

The three of them shared a small house in Yeovil until Tim was 12, when they made the move across to the New Forest and Tim started his new school.

Tim had asked his mum before the move why they were doing it – why couldn't they just stay in Yeovil? – and his mum had looked tired and told him that his father wanted them to move.

'But he's not even here!' Tim had said, and his mother had turned around and gripped Tim's shoulder so tightly that he'd been scared. Even though they were in an empty house, Tim's mum spoke to him in a whisper.

'He'll be coming back soon,' she said. Tim remembered how red her cheeks had been, and how wide her eyes were as she spoke. 'He'll be coming to live with us in our new house, and you know how he gets when people disobey him.' She'd obviously seen the fear in Tim's eyes at that point, because her voice had suddenly softened and Tim thought she looked as though she might cry.

Don't cry, Mum, he wanted to say. He was suddenly remembering another of his dad's bedtime stories from all those years ago – one about a little boy who cried so much his eyes had dried up and stopped working. *Please don't cry*.

Anne hadn't cried, though; she hardly ever did. She was one of those people who always looked like they were close, but who usually managed to hold it in.

5

Tim and Mr Stevens walked back along the footpath together.

When they rounded the final bend, Tim saw Tramper and Matt sat on the grass together talking, and he felt a wild urge to scream at them to run, just RUN and get away while they still could. Instead of doing that he forced a smile onto his face and raised his hand in greeting.

'Hey guys,' he said. 'Anyone need a drink? We're fully stocked up, probably got enough to last the rest of the weekend.'

He felt his dad's eyes on him, and told himself to reign it in a bit. *Don't overdo it*, he thought. *Just keep things light and normal, like we discussed.*

'Yeah, I wouldn't mind a drink, thanks,' said Matt. He held his hand up and Tim tossed him one of the bottles they'd filled up back at the stream. Matt caught it, lifted it to his mouth and took a long, steady swig.

'Thanks,' he said. He went to hand the bottle to Tramper, but the big boy shook his head.

'Where's Tom?' James asked. 'I thought he was with you guys?'

Tim paused and glanced at his father, who looked back at him expressionlessly. Then he looked at James, arranging his face into what he hoped was a look of mild confusion.

'He wasn't with me,' said Tim. 'I went out to fill up, then Dad came and helped me.'

There was a moment of silence in the clearing. Matt was the first to speak.

'Mr Stevens, you didn't see him on the path? I thought you were going out looking for him?'

Don't question him, thought Tim. *For God's sake don't question him, or he'll make it worse for you.*

He glanced at his dad nervously, but Mr Stevens just smiled.

'Oh, he's probably just filling up at another place along the river,' he said. 'I didn't see him on the path, but there were plenty of places he could have broken off. It was only by accident that I stumbled across Timothy, really. I just wanted to loosen my legs up a bit before we set off again.'

James and Matt glanced at each other, and Tim could see the concern on their faces. Mr Stevens clearly saw it too.

'I wouldn't worry, boys,' he said. 'We've only been gone five minutes, I should think Tom will be back any second now. We'll just wait for him here.'

James nodded his head and stared off in the direction of the path they'd just come from, but Matt frowned and got to his feet.

'You can wait here if you want,' he said. 'But I'm going to go and check on him. I don't think people should be off on their own after what's happened with Gary. Come on, James.'

Tramper looked up at Matt and then glanced across at Mr Stevens, nervously.

There won't be a problem from him, Tim thought. *Matt might be a problem, but James shouldn't be one at all.* He glanced over at his dad, and wondered if he'd planned it this way. He'd spoken about how Tim had messed things up with Tom today and how he'd wanted to get them all in one go, but then maybe that was just one of his games. Maybe he didn't think he could handle all four of them but he didn't want to admit it, so he'd picked off the strongest two and left the weaker ones for the final night.

Tim stared at his dad, who was now smiling at Matt and nodding in an understanding way, and felt the familiar mixture of feelings – hate, revulsion, fear, guilt – rush through him.

I should have broken his skull with that rock while he was finishing off Tom, Tim thought. *I should have done it then, while he was occupied.*

'Absolutely, you're right of course,' Mr Stevens was saying to Matt. 'We should all be sticking together, good thinking. Why don't you and James go down that path and see if you can hurry him up a bit, and we'll wait here in case he comes back.'

'Okay, that sounds good.' Matt smiled and looked relieved. He nodded to Tramper and the two of them headed off in the direction of the path that Tim and his father had just come from.

When they were alone in the clearing, Mr Stevens looked at his son. His smile was gone. 'Let's get the stuff packed up now,' he said. 'That way we can hurry them along when they come back. This is the easy bit, now, because we don't even need to lie; the best bet we have of finding help really *will* be if we keep going along our planned route.'

He laughed then, a throaty unpleasant chuckle that made Tim think of a frog with something stuck in its throat, and Tim tried to imagine the sound the rock would have made if he'd brought it crushing down onto his dad's head. A thick, dull crunch, and then silence. No more bedtime stories; no more laughing; no more of that horrible mixture of feelings he felt every time his father looked at him.

Mr Stevens must have seen something in his son's eyes, because he suddenly stopped laughing. He took a step towards Tim and his eyes flashed yellow. They looked like the eyes of a very old and cunning animal.

'Don't forget to stick to the plan,' he said. 'You remember what happens to boys who don't listen, don't you, Timothy?'

For just a second his cheeks loosened and his mouth opened slightly, and Tim felt his stomach lurch with fear. Then he blinked and his dad was smiling normally again.

'Let's get these bags packed and get ready,' he said. 'It won't be much longer now.'

6

Tim's training started when he was nine years old.

Looking back he guessed it had *all* been training, in a way – not just what happened in the first half of 1998 but also the absences and the bedtime stories all those years before. Particularly the bedtime stories.

But the *real* training began when Tim was still in the first half of junior school.

Back in Year 3 he was a tall, skinny boy who stood almost a head taller than most of his classmates. In his first year he'd had some trouble with an older boy in Year 5, but he'd dealt with that one quickly.

The boy had tried to force him to trade GoGos – he'd wanted all of Tim's 12 GoGos for just two of his own – and when Tim had refused the boy had whispered that he'd get Tim after school if he didn't do it.

Tim didn't want to hurt the big kid, but he remembered his dad's story about the boy who didn't stick up for himself and what had happened to him – and he also remembered the look in his dad's eyes as he'd been telling the story – so instead of doing the trade he'd scratched his hand across the bigger boy's eyes. The boy had screamed and clutched his face, and as he bent over Tim had kicked him as hard as he could in the balls. He'd left the boy crying on the tarmac of the playground, and there had been no more talk of trades after that.

There hadn't been much talk between him and the other children at all after that, actually; they already kept their distance from Tim, and after the incident in the playground they steered well clear of him.

Tim didn't mind. He had his mum to talk to when he went home, and if his dad wasn't around then that meant there was no real reason for him to be scared of anything.

Then, towards the end of 1997 when Tim was wrapping up his first term in Year 4, his dad had come back.

Tim came home from school one day to find him sitting on the armchair in the lounge, staring impatiently at the door when Tim entered as though he'd been sitting there waiting for Tim all afternoon. Probably he had.

'Where's Mum?' muttered Tim.

'What, don't I even get a hello?'

'Hello.'

'She's upstairs having a lie down. Not feeling too well I don't think.'

'Oh.'

'Don't worry, though, I can look after you,' his dad paused, and that familiar empty smile appeared on his face. His *crocodile* smile. 'I'm home now, and we're going to spend some time together.'

Tim never asked his dad where he'd been when he went away. He'd found out early on that his father didn't like questions, so whenever he was around his dad he kept them to a minimum and tried to concentrate on listening instead. Listening was very important, because Mr Stevens didn't like to repeat himself.

Over the next few months, Tim listened plenty. He crouched at the top of the staircase when he heard his parents' voices in the lounge or the kitchen below, and at night he sometimes snuck over to the door of his bedroom to press his ear against the wood, desperately trying to catch what his mum and dad were saying to each other.

It was never easy, because Tim's mum was quiet by nature and his father never, ever raised his voice. Sometimes he heard his mum speaking in cracked whispers, like she had that time when Tim was younger and he drew all over the wallpaper of his bedroom during one of his rare tantrums; it was the voice she used when she was doing her best not to cry. Other times, when his dad was out of the house, he heard her sobbing softly in her bedroom.

Tim knew it was a bad thing to cry because of the stories his dad had told him, so he always ignored the sound when he heard it. He thought that maybe if he didn't actually see her crying then it wouldn't be real.

As the autumn term wound down to Christmas, Mr Stevens started coming to collect Tim from school. He was always charming and friendly to the teachers and the other parents, and the mums sometimes gathered around him in a group while he told little stories or jokes. They'd all laugh and grin round at each other and play with their hair, and Mr Stevens would stand there smiling and adjusting his glasses as if he was slightly embarrassed by the whole thing.

Pretty soon he was friendly with most of the mums and dads of the kids in his year, and Tim even found that some of his fellow classmates were starting to cautiously approach him in the playground to see if he wanted to join in their games of It and Stuck in the Mud.

Tim had no idea what his father did for work, but he once overheard his dad telling one of the other dads he was a *contractor*, whatever that meant, and Tim guessed he must have some sort of job because every day he left the house early and drove off in his dark blue BMW.

Tim would watch him from his bedroom window, and whenever the car was out of sight around the corner he'd always feel as though a small weight had been lifted off him.

One Saturday in late January of 1998, Tim was playing with his Pogs in the front garden when a shadow fell over him.

He looked up and saw his father, and immediately felt his cheeks redden as if he'd done something wrong. It was a mild day for mid-winter and Tim was bundled up warm in his coat and scarf, but he shivered nonetheless. He hoped his dad hadn't noticed.

'What have you got there?' said Mr Stevens.

Tim looked down at his Pogs as if seeing them for the first time. He'd been sorting the brightly coloured discs into different sets before his dad came out – first colour-coding them, then ranking them in order of his favourites to least favourites – but that suddenly seemed like stupid kids' stuff. He opened his mouth to say something, but his dad spoke before he had the chance.

'Your mother's out of the house tomorrow,' said Mr Stevens thoughtfully. 'She's not looking too well, and I've told her she should go into town for the day with one of her friends. Do her good to get out for a bit.'

He paused and Tim wondered if he should say anything. In the sky behind his dad's head the sun disappeared behind a small cloud, then peeked out the other side again moments later.

'We'll have the house to ourselves,' Mr Stevens continued. 'I thought it might be a good time to begin your training.'

Mr Stevens peered down at Tim, as if waiting to see if he was going to ask a question. Tim kept his mouth shut. After a moment Tim's father smiled and nodded, then turned and began walking back towards the house.

Tim took a breath and began packing his Pogs away.

The following morning, Tim found Mr Stevens waiting for him in the back garden. He was wearing a dark blue North Face jacket, gloves, a hat and brown corduroy trousers.

He looked Tim up and down, adjusted his glasses, then smiled.

'Good, you dressed warm like I told you,' he said. 'We're going to have to do a bit of waiting around, I'm afraid.'

He sat down in a garden chair and motioned for Tim to take the chair beside him. They were set up at the edge of the patio, facing out across the back garden. Mr Stevens waited until his son was sat next to him, and then motioned across the garden with his hand.

'What do you see?' he said.

The back garden of the house Tim had lived in his whole life was fairly unimpressive. It was modest, Tim supposed, with a poky wooden shed in the far-right corner and a flower bed over to the left. The middle section was a flat expanse of closely cropped grass that ran down to a fence at the back. There was a small wooden gate in that fence that led to a narrow path, which ran along the backs of the houses for the full length of their little street. If you cycled along it – as Tim often had in the past, first on his tricycle and then on his two-wheeled Raleigh Max mountain bike when he was big enough – you could see into the back gardens of all the neighbours' houses. They were much the same as Tim's garden – an assortment of bird tables, ponds, sheds and flower beds – but Mr Grealing at No. 64 also had a table tennis table in his, which Tim thought was pretty cool. Beyond the path that ran behind the back gardens was a thick line of trees, and behind them was a field that led on to an allotment.

The fences on either side of their little garden were tall and, in the case of the fence between their house and Mrs Peacock's on the right, overgrown with vines. It looked messy, Tim's mum sometimes said, but at least it gave them some privacy.

Mr Stevens cleared his throat, and Tim suddenly realised he'd been staring out at the garden for too long without saying anything.

'Um,' he said. He stared around again, frantically trying to work out the right answer, and then his eyes fell on something in the middle of the grass. Something that wasn't usually there. It was a small red dish, like a dog's bowl, and it was filled with something brown that looked like food.

'There's some dog food in the garden!' Tim said eagerly. 'Right there in the middle!'

Mr Stevens smiled thinly and Tim realised he'd got it wrong.

'Close, but not quite,' he said. 'It's a bowl of catnip, not dog food.'

Tim was about to ask what catnip was, but he stopped himself just in time.

'I've noticed there are a couple of strays around here that keep wandering into the garden,' Mr Stevens said easily. 'The neighbours two doors down have a large ginger tom, too, and he clearly thinks he owns the whole street, the way he struts around.'

Mr Stevens let out a low, throaty chuckle that made Tim's neck itch.

When he next spoke his voice was a barely audible mutter, and Tim thought at first he was talking to himself.

'We'll wait here for a while and see if any of our friends decide to show up,' he said. 'In this game, it's all about patience.'

Tim stared at him with no idea what he was talking about. The sun slipped out from behind a cloud and lit up the garden, and Tim suddenly noticed just how tired his father looked. His skin was a pale yellowy colour and the bags under his eyes were two purple bruises.

Had he always looked so exhausted?

'Shouldn't be too long,' Mr Stevens said again, softly. 'Not too much longer now.'

Tim felt a question bubbling up inside him, and before he could stop himself it was out.

'What are we waiting for, Dad?'

As soon as he'd spoken he felt a wave of fear and his hand shot up to his mouth as if to try to hold in what he'd just said, but Mr Stevens only smiled. A genuine one, Tim thought.

'We're going to make friends with one of the neighbourhood cats,' he said. 'There are enough of them out here, so it shouldn't be a problem.'

He reached out a hand and patted his son on the shoulder. Tim forced himself not to flinch.

The cat that hopped over the fence at the back wasn't the ginger tom from two doors down, and it wasn't a stray; it was a striped tabby that Tim recognised as belonging to Mr Talbot, the old man who lived on the other side of the road from them.

The cat paused at the far end of the garden for a moment, its tail flicking back and forth as it watched them through orange eyes. Tim felt his father tense in the seat next to him, and for some reason he didn't understand, he began to feel nervous. There was a heavy, unpleasant feeling in the pit of his stomach, like the feeling he used to get when he his father perched on the end of his bed to read him one of his stories.

'Come on, come on,' Mr Stevens muttered.

The tabby sat still for a moment longer, and then finally began to walk across the grass towards the bowl.

'They can smell it,' Mr Stevens whispered. Tim didn't look round at his father, but he knew from the sound of his voice that he was smiling. That crocodile smile that never quite reached his eyes.

As the cat approached the bowl, Tim had a sudden sense that something bad was about to happen. He couldn't say just why or what, but in that moment he knew that if he didn't do something the cat was going to be hurt in some way. He started to get up, then stopped when he felt his dad's hand clamp down on his shoulder like an iron vice.

Tim froze.

'No, don't move,' his dad whispered. 'She's going to come to us.'

Mr Stevens pursed his lips and began to make wet, kissing noises. The sound made Tim feel ill. The tabby had been sniffing around the bowl, but now it looked up and stared at them both with its large orange eyes. Tim willed the cat not to come, he concentrated every ounce of his brain on telling it to turn around and run off down the end of the garden, but it didn't work. The tabby took two tentative steps towards them, and then stopped again.

Mr Stevens reached into his right pocket and brought out a small brown biscuit in the shape of a fish. He tossed the biscuit onto the grass, a few metres in front of the cat, and then resumed those wet kissing sounds.

Tim's body was itching all over. He wanted to jump up and scare the cat away, but he knew if he did that his dad would be angry. Maybe he'd tell Tim another bedtime story, an even scarier one than all the others put together.

Or maybe he'd do something worse.

The tabby was only a metre from the patio now. It stopped one more time, staring up at Mr Stevens as if trying to guess what he had planned. Its tail flicked back and forth.

Run away, Tim thought. *Run away while you still can.*

If someone had asked him, Tim wouldn't have been able to explain why he felt something bad was going to happen – aside from the stories Tim's dad told and the fact he sometimes made Tim's mum cry, Tim had never seen him actually *hurt* anyone – but the feeling was there nonetheless. That deep, hard knot of dread, nestled far down in the base of his stomach like a lead weight.

Tim watched, frozen, as his father's hand disappeared into his right coat pocket again. He watched as the hand came out holding another of those little brown fish, pinched carefully between his thumb and forefinger. Mr Stevens lowered his hand down towards the patio, and a second later the tabby took its last two steps forward.

If he hadn't been so scared, Tim would have been almost in awe of how fast his father moved. As the tabby leaned forward to sniff the biscuit in his right hand, Mr Stevens' left hand shot down and gripped the cat hard by the scruff of its neck. It yowled and tried to jerk away, but Mr Stevens held it in a tight grip.

'Steady, steady,' Mr Stevens muttered. The cat tried to scratch at his right arm but he lifted it up so that its flailing paws couldn't reach. His mouth had fallen open slightly, and Tim could see thin rows of white teeth in the darkness behind his lips. For a second before it was over, Tim thought he saw something else in his dad's face. Some subtle change that he couldn't quite place. It might have been his cheeks, which suddenly seemed to droop down more than they usually did to give his skin a slack, flabby look, or it could have been his eyes. For just a moment his eyes had seemed more yellow than brown. Tim was reminded of how his dad looked when he used to perch at the end of

Tim's bed and tell him stories. How the bedside lamp had made his eyes appear yellow then, too.

Then Mr Stevens was dropping the brown biscuit and fastening his right hand over the cat's screeching head, and Tim's attention was drawn to what his hands were doing as they twisted first right and then left, sharply, like he was trying to twist the lid off a particularly stubborn jar, and suddenly the cat's body went limp and when Tim looked back at his father his face seemed normal again.

It must have been a trick of the light, Tim thought, and then he leaned forward and threw up his morning Cheerios onto the patio.

He stared down at the mess in front of him and felt the blood pounding in his neck, and he knew his dad would be angry with him, his dad hated mess and weakness, but when he worked up the courage to look at his father – who'd laid the cat's body onto his lap with something close to tenderness – he was surprised to see that Mr Stevens was smiling.

It might just have been the fact that the sun had slipped behind a cloud again, but Tim thought he also looked less tired than he had before.

The cat, Tim thought. *He just killed Mr Talbot's cat.*

He felt his stomach clenching and thought he was going to be sick again, but this time he managed to keep it down. His eyes drifted up to the fence at the bottom of the garden, the fence with the little wooden gate, and for a moment he imagined himself getting up and running. Running through that little gate and off down the road, away from his father.

I could just be one of those people that hates their parents, Tim thought. *Plenty of people are like that. Sally Graham at school always says she hates her mum, and Charlie Higgings hasn't seen his dad in years. It happens all the time, it—*

The thought cut off as Mr Stevens' hand touched Tim's arm. Slowly, Tim looked away from the gate and back at his father.

'I don't want you to worry,' said Mr Stevens. 'You didn't do anything wrong. The fact is this is just the start of your training, and it'll get easier the more we practise.'

Tim nodded because he didn't know what else to do. He didn't want to look at that cat again, so he kept his eyes on his father's face.

'You'll get used to it,' Mr Stevens smiled. 'I promise.'

Far up in the blue sky above them, the sun peeked out from behind its cloud. The light lit up the garden and reflected off Mr Stevens' glasses, which flashed like two rectangular discs.

7

Tim thought about the cat as he finished packing up his rucksack. Or rather, he thought about the *cats*. Had it been seven or eight of them in the end? Or more than that? Tim couldn't remember. He didn't really want to remember.

He could picture Mr Talbot's tabby clear as day because that had been the first, and he remembered the ginger stray they'd cornered in the alleyway between Charlotte Street and Hemingway Street, because that was the first one he'd done without his dad's help. His father had been smiling after that, *really* smiling, and despite the fact that Tim had felt like he wanted to throw up the whole time he'd been doing it he actually felt a strange, distant sense of pride when his dad ruffled his hair after they were finished.

He'd never ruffled Tim's hair before.

'Your mother doesn't think you're like me,' Mr Stevens had grinned. 'But I think she may be wrong about that.'

Sometimes after they'd killed a cat they'd leave it where they found it, but every now and then they'd cut bits off it or send the body back to its owner. Mr Stevens said it would throw people off the scent, because they'd link mutilation to a teenager with mental issues. He always made sure they left gaps between training sessions, too, and he drove them out to different parts of Yeovil so they wouldn't have to go back to the same places twice.

One day in April, Tim had been on his way to school when he'd caught sight of the local paper on a stand outside the newsagent's. The whole front page had been dedicated to Yeovil's 'cat serial killer'. Despite the anxiety he felt when looking at that headline and the heavy sense of dread and guilt that had been following him around for the last few months, Tim couldn't deny the small pinprick of excitement that went shooting through him. It was a secret he and his dad shared, after all. Just theirs.

Tim couldn't remember the exact moment when he realised his father wasn't human. It was certainly a long time before the final cat, when his dad got sick, but looking back he couldn't pin down a specific moment of realisation. Probably it just came as a gradual understanding, like so many things do at that age.

Either way, whenever his father killed a cat Tim was always careful to watch his face. He soon realised that the subtle change he'd seen in their back garden wasn't a one-off; in the moments building up to the kill and straight after it Mr Stevens' face would slacken and droop as though his skin had started to melt; his mouth would pucker open and his eyes would change from brown to yellow. It only ever lasted 10 seconds at most, though, and then the change would stop. The cat would be dead and his father's face would look normal again.

Tim used to pray that he'd never, ever see what his father looked like if the change went all the way through. And up until the last cat they killed – just before his father became ill and then disappeared for the next three years – Tim didn't have to.

Now, standing on the moor next to his rucksack in the wind and the light drizzle, Tim could see it all too clearly in his mind. His father's face drooping down and the mouth hanging open wider and wider; his yellow eyes lengthening and squeezing out at the sides, like the magnified eyes of some nightmare insect; his jaw stretching open to an impossible size, opening on a dark void ringed by multiple rows of tiny white teeth–

'He's not there!'

Tim was snapped out of his unpleasant daydream by the sound of a voice. Seconds later Matt and Tramper came bursting back into the clearing, their faces red and their eyes wide. James bent down and put his hands on his knees, breathing heavily, but Matt jogged over to Mr Stevens, who was busy adjusting the straps of his rucksack.

'He's not there,' Matt panted. He stopped a few feet away from Tim's dad and pulled in a deep breath.

'What do you mean he's not there?' Mr Stevens' face was a mask of surprised concern.

'We checked all down the path, both sides, and we were shouting his name. It's just like with Gary, he's gone, he's fucking disappeared.'

Tim flinched and glanced at his father, but Mr Stevens was frowning and looking at his watch. 'There's a storm due to come in later,' he muttered. He glanced from Matt to James, then back to Matt again. 'Are you sure you checked properly? He can't just have vanished, for goodness' sake.'

'Yes, we jogged down the path for 10 minutes and checked every side track that led to the river. We were shouting his name the whole time.'

James sat down heavily at the edge of the clearing and let out a shaky breath. Tim saw without much surprise that he'd started crying.

Mr Stevens frowned and ran a hand through his hair. He looked at his watch, then stooped to rummage in his rucksack. He brought out his map of Rutmoor in its plastic pouch, adjusted his glasses, then stooped to look at it.

Everyone watched him without saying anything.

After a minute or so, Mr Stevens frowned and looked at Matt. 'Okay, this is serious now boys. Unless this is all some clever joke you're all playing – and I really, really hope it isn't – then we have to start moving *now* so we can get some help. We've got two members of our party missing out on the moor somewhere and a storm is due to hit tonight. If we set off right now, we should be able to reach Creek Lane by nightfall. I've been there before and it's possible to get a phone signal, so I can call 999. Right, get your packs on and we'll move out.'

'Wait a second,' said Matt. 'What about Tom? He wandered off down that path five minutes ago and you're saying we should keep going without him?'

Mr Stevens paused, and for a second Tim thought he was going to do it right then and there. But when he reached out a hand towards Matt seconds later, it was only to place it on the boy's shoulder.

'Look, Matthew, I understand you want to help your friend,' he said. 'But you just told me yourself you've run for 10 minutes down that path shouting his name, and with no luck. Isn't that right?'

'I suppose, but maybe we didn't go far enough along, or...'

'If Tom's got himself lost or he's fallen down somewhere and hurt himself, we need a team out here looking for him as soon as we can,' said Mr Stevens. 'If we can make it to Creek Lane by nightfall we can get people out here tonight looking for him, storm or no storm. But if we go down that path now ourselves, we risk being caught out in the bad weather. And besides, there's Gary to think of, too.'

Matt paused and bit his lower lip. 'But when I last looked on the map, Creek Lane was still 10 miles away. Will we really make it there tonight?'

Tim, who had been watching the exchange between Matt and his father with a growing sense of dread, felt a sudden flicker of hope. Matt was clearly sharper than his father had given him credit for. He glanced at Mr Stevens, and saw without much surprise that the old crocodile smile was now covering his father's face. Mr Stevens lowered his voice but kept his smile fixed.

'Keep your voice down, please,' he said. 'Your friend over there is upset, and I don't want him to know how far we've got to go. The fact is it's going to be a struggle, you're right, but if we make good time we *will* be able to get there. And it's the best chance we've got of finding your friends.' Mr Stevens paused. 'You wouldn't want to be responsible if we were to waste time looking here, find nothing and then get ourselves caught in the storm with no way of getting help until tomorrow, would you?'

Matt didn't say anything for a while. He was staring down at his feet, biting his lip, and for a moment Tim thought he might be getting ready to disagree with Mr Stevens. He felt another brief flare of hope, which immediately guttered out when Matt looked up and shook his head.

'Okay, let's get moving,' Matt mumbled.

Mr Stevens nodded, stuffed the map in his bag, and hoisted the pack onto his back. Matt went over to James and helped the boy up to his feet. James wiped his eyes and his nose as Matt whispered something to him, and then they turned and watched as Mr Stevens looked at his watch again.

'Right, this way boys,' he said. 'Matthew, if you lead the way down this path here and you follow him, James, then Timothy and I will bring up the rear.' He paused and looked at them all. 'We'll get help and get everyone back safely, I promise.'

Matt took James by the arm and led him down the path that Mr Stevens was pointing to, out of the clearing. As they disappeared around the corner, Mr Stevens turned and winked at his son.

Tim nodded.

As his father turned and walked ahead of him out of the clearing, Tim thought once more about the rock by the river.

2015

Friday, Part One

When the horn beeps outside his house on Friday morning, he's already prepared. He says goodbye to his mum, hoists his rucksack onto his back, and carries his other bag – the important bag – over his shoulder.

Then he steps out the front door.

It's a clear, warm day, and he's glad he's only wearing his Helly Hansen base layer. He walks down the garden path and sees the familiar Peugeot 206, idling on the gravel pull-in just outside his front gate.

He raises his hand and waves at the muscular young man sat hunched behind the wheel. He still finds it hard to believe, sometimes, that the James Tramper of 2015 is the same James Tramper as the chubby, nervous boy that used to get picked on by Gary back in secondary school. 2015 Tramper is about six foot one, broad shouldered, and with arms thick from seven years of lifting weights in the gym. James says he got into it at uni – joined the gym with his housemates in Freshers' Week on a whim, and hasn't been a week without going since. Looking at him now, you can believe it.

As he approaches the car the passenger window rolls down.

'Hey Matt,' says Tramper.

Only now it's not Tramper or Trumper or Slim Jim, or any of the other stupid nicknames he had back at school. Now the guys at his office call him Trample. They say it with grins on their faces as they go to high five him, and James grins right back.

What a difference 13 years can make, Matt thinks, and he almost smiles.

'Hey, James.'

James pushes a button on the dash and the boot clicks. Matt walks round to the back of the car and opens it up, slinging his rucksack off his back and into the boot next to James'. He keeps his other bag in his hand and walks back to the passenger door.

Once he's in the seat next to James he leans over and hugs his friend.

'Man, you look tired,' says James. 'There's nothing to you, either. Are you sure you're eating enough?'

Matt laughs. 'You sound exactly like my mum.'

'How is she?' asks James, grinning back.

'Yeah, she's okay. Worried about me, as usual. She gave me a proper interrogation when she picked me up yesterday. Am I getting enough sleep, all that stuff.'

'You do look tired, though.'

'Been working long hours, I guess.'

For the last four or so years, since he finished a postgraduate course in journalism up in Sheffield, Matt has been in London working for various papers. He started out as a Junior Reporter for a local rag in Croydon, and he's gradually worked his way up the ladder. For the last couple of years he's been an investigative reporter for a large national. He likes the job a lot, but the hours aren't exactly sociable.

Then again, he thinks, glancing down at the brown bag in his lap. *It's not been the job that's caused you to lose sleep over the last year.*

James presses some buttons on the GPS stuck on the windscreen in front of him, then pulls away from Matt's house.

Matt glances back, and finds himself wondering if he'll ever see that house again. If he'll ever see his mum again.

We got lucky once, he thinks, *but maybe we won't be so lucky this time around*. He feels a sudden lurch of fear in his stomach which he does his best to ignore.

As the first 10 miles slip past, James and Matt make small talk. They catch up on James' career at PWC, Matt's job at the paper, girlfriends, friends, people from school and what they're doing now, and pretty much anything that saves them from talking about the thing they're going off to do. The thing they *have* to do.

After they run out of things to talk about, they sit in silence for a while.

It's James that finally breaks it.

'Are you sure?' he asks.

Matt glances over at him. He's looking straight ahead at the road in front, and his expression is impossible to read.

Matt pats the brown bag on his lap.

'Sure,' he says.

James nods, and they drive on in silence. As the road unfolds ahead of them Matt leans back against the headrest and stares out of the window. He feels the weight of the bag in his lap and finds his mind drifting back to the winter of last year. January 2014.

What was it he'd seen scrawled in that letter? The one he'd found in the study upstairs? *I know it's you.*

Yes, that was it.

I know it's you.

Matt closes his eyes.

The GPS says they'll reach Rutmoor just after midday.

2014

Matt turned the collar of his coat up against the rain.

He was striding down a long avenue lined with near-identical brick houses, screwing his face in the wind. Tree branches crashed together above him, shaking beneath a marble-grey January sky.

He felt the brown bag slung over his shoulder, unconsciously patted the front of it for the shape of his umbrella, then stopped himself when he realised he'd left it at home. That was okay, though. In fact he thought it might play in his favour.

A third of the way down the road Matt took shelter under a bus stop and wiped his eyes. He pulled his iPhone out of his pocket and bashed in the code. Opening his Notes app, he re-read the very top item for perhaps the fifth time since he'd got off the train half an hour before.

49, Willow Av.

He glanced up and stared through the murky, rain-soaked glass of the bus shelter at the house nearest to him. A little red door was just visible through the downpour, but Matt couldn't make out the number. Straightening his collar against his neck once more, he sighed and stepped out into the rain.

He found the right place a few moments later.

Number 49 looked exactly the same as every other house on the road. It was high and narrow – two tall floors and an attic space, from what Matt could tell – and stood separated from the buildings on either side by slim brick alleyways that ran down its length. A bay window at the front overlooked a tiny, neat garden and a driveway. Matt was pleased to see the latter was occupied; a small, blue Volkswagen was standing on the rain-soaked concrete.

Wiping more rain out of his eyes, Matt leaned forward and undid the latch on the tiny wooden gate in front of him. Pushing it aside he stepped over a puddle and made his way up the path towards the wooden front door. The wind howled overhead and the gate banged shut behind him, making him jump.

It's okay, he thought. *There's nothing to worry about in here.*

Still, the smile he forced onto his face as he reached out and rapped the metal door knocker felt hollow, and the sound that echoed away into the house caused his stomach to lurch. It was stupid, he thought. A couple of months ago he'd had to phone up the CEO of a large bank and tell the guy that the paper Matt worked for was planning to publish an article on his money laundering activities – *that* was the sort of thing you were meant to feel nervous about, not a house call with a middle-aged woman. But still…

Footsteps in the hall cut off Matt's train of thought. A shadow fell across the frosted glass square cut into the door, and he heard the sound of a bolt being drawn back. A second later there was the clink of a chain, and then a latch turned and the door swung inwards.

For a moment, Matt thought he'd got the wrong house after all.

The woman standing in front of him was the right height, but her hair was a glossy, reddish blonde and she looked younger than he'd been expecting. Her dark eyes were scanning his face, though, and after a second the smile she'd been wearing as she opened the door was replaced with a look of confusion. Her eyebrows drew together and old worry lines stood out on her forehead.

'Hello?' Her tone was light and airy, but her eyes continued to scan Matt's.

'Hello, Mrs Stevens?'

The name had the desired effect. The woman standing in the hallway took a step backwards and her eyes widened, and any residual doubt in Matt's mind was wiped away. He forced a frown onto his face.

'Sorry, have I got the wrong house? This is number 49, isn't it?'

The woman in the hallway had recovered. She smiled once more, but her eyes didn't leave Matt's face.

'No, I'm sorry, you are right, this is number 49. I don't go by the name Mrs Stevens anymore, though…' she tailed off, then cleared her throat. 'You're not selling anything are you? Only I've got a sign up that says I don't answer to sales people, and—'

'No, Mrs Stevens, it's me, Matt.' He arranged his face into a smile. 'Tim's old friend, remember?'

Her eyes widened once more, and for a fraction of a second – so quick it was barely even there – Matt thought he saw something like fear dart across her face. Then she was smiling again.

'Oh Matt, of course! I thought I recognised you but it's been such a long time, and I wasn't...' She trailed off again and her eyes flicked past him to the road behind, as though she was checking to make sure he was alone.

'Of course, no worries at all,' smiled Matt. 'Sorry to turn up like this out of the blue, only I was back home for the weekend and I thought I'd pop by to see if Tim was about.'

Mrs Stevens looked doubtfully at Matt's sopping hair and rain-soaked jeans. 'Oh, have you spoken to Tim then?'

'No, nothing like that,' said Matt. 'I haven't spoken to him in a little while, actually, but as I was down I thought I'd swing by to see if he was around. I know he sometimes comes home for the weekend, and I just...'

Matt forced himself to stop talking. Despite the cold and the rain, his back felt hot. He was rambling, speaking too much, and from the look on Mrs Stevens' face he was doing little to convince her. He took a breath, then counted to three in his head. Then he laughed.

'Sorry, I'm waffling,' he smiled. 'The truth is, I was feeling a bit bad. I haven't seen Tim in ages, and the last time he phoned me I missed his call. I've tried ringing him a couple of times since to arrange something, but I can never seem to get through. I knew it was a bit of a long shot, but I thought I'd pop round seeing as I was home for the weekend. I'm guessing I've missed him again, though?'

Mrs Stevens still wasn't smiling, but the look of doubt had gone from her face. 'I'm afraid he's not down this weekend, Matt, no. I think he's based up at some firm in Edinburgh at the moment, although he's so busy I lose track.'

Matt grinned. 'I know the feeling. Since everybody started work we don't seem to see each other half as much as we used to.'

Mrs Stevens smiled back, and Matt saw his opening.

'I'm really sorry to be a pain, but would you mind if I pop in quickly to use your bathroom?' He made a point of wiping more water from his face. 'I stupidly forgot my umbrella, and I can hardly see where I'm going.'

Mrs Stevens' eyes widened. 'Oh goodness, I'm so sorry! Yes of course, absolutely, I think I've got a spare towel you can use, and—' She paused for a second, then seemed to make a decision. 'And you should come in for a cup of tea at least, get yourself dry. It really is terrible out there.'

She stepped back and held open the door. Smiling, Matt followed her into the darkened hallway.

He could hear cups clinking from the kitchen.

Matt was sat in the lounge at the front of the house, staring around and trying to take in as much as he could. He was sitting on a large sofa that faced the door leading back into the hallway. On his left was the bay window, a shaft of light leaking through a gap in the curtains. A packed wooden bookcase stood to the left of the door, and on the right was a mantelpiece above an old fireplace. Matt's eyes searched the marble shelf for photos, but there weren't any.

He closed his eyes and tried to picture what he'd seen before Mrs Stevens ushered him through into the lounge. There was a long hallway that led back to what Matt assumed was the kitchen, and a staircase on the left that rose up into the shadows of the second floor. Matt imagined walking up that staircase, and what the layout might look like above him. Two bedrooms, or three? Maybe one at the back and one or two at the front, and in the middle a bathroom, surely...

Matt heard footsteps and opened his eyes. A second later, Mrs Stevens was standing in the doorway holding two steaming mugs. She moved into the room and placed them on a rectangular coffee table in front of Matt, a smile fixed on her face.

'So, how have you been, Matt?' She said, sitting down on a smaller sofa in front of the bay window. 'I was just having a think in the kitchen, and I seem to remember Tim telling me you were doing something like – PR, was it?'

'Journalism,' smiled Matt. He leaned forward and took a small sip of the scalding tea, then made to stand up. 'I'm really sorry to be a pain, Mrs Stevens, but—'

'Anne.' She cut across him, frowning. 'I don't go by Mrs Stevens anymore. It's Ms Sherling, now. But please, Matt, you can call me Anne.'

'Sorry, Anne,' he smiled, 'I don't suppose you'd mind if I pop to your bathroom quickly?'

'Oh yes, of course! I'm so sorry, I meant to get you a towel. Yes absolutely, please do, there are spares in the cupboard below the sink, you'll want something to dry your face at least...'

Matt was already up and halfway across the room. 'That's perfect, thank you!'

He walked back into the hallway once more and headed straight for the staircase. His heartbeat quickened in his chest, and that hot, prickly feeling had spread across his back again. His foot was on the first step when he heard movement behind him.

'You'll want the downstairs bathroom.'

Matt stopped and turned around, his hand on the bannister. Anne was standing in the lounge doorway, watching him.

'Sorry?'

'The downstairs bathroom. If you head through the kitchen and into the laundry room, it's the door on the right. The upstairs bath-room is having work done on it at the moment, I'm afraid.'

Shit, shit, shit.

Matt kept what he hoped was an indifferent grin on his face as he thanked her and stepped back into the hall. As he walked deeper into the house and through into the kitchen, he could feel her eyes on him.

Well, what do you expect? he thought. *She barely recognises you, hasn't seen you in about 10 years. And the last time she did—*

He shook the thought off as he headed through the laundry area and into the little bathroom. Locking the door behind him, he ran the tap and then glanced around. As promised there were towels lin-ing the cupboard beneath the sink, but apart from these, a toothbrush holder and a few bottles of shampoo and shower gel on the rim of a white shower/bath combo on the left, there was little in the room to hold his attention.

He glanced up at the mirror above the sink. The young man staring back at him looked older than someone in their mid-twenties should look. He already had a few grey hairs creeping in, and his forehead was mapped with frown-lines.

Noticing the hinge at the edge of the mirror, Matt leaned forward and opened what he now saw was a small medicine cabinet. A neat little row of bottles and cardboard packets lined the interior. He ran his eyes along the labels – Ibuprofen, contact lenses, Vicks Vaporub, Co-dydramol – and was about to shut the door when he spotted a cardboard packet half-hidden behind a bottle of perfume. He nudged the bottle aside and read the label: Citalopram.

Matt looked at it for a moment, then reached out to straighten the perfume and shut the door. He turned the tap off, dried his face on a hand towel and left the bathroom.

'So, have you seen much of Tim lately?'

Matt took another sip of his tea and placed it back on the table. Outside, the rain continued to hammer against the bay window. The noise of the wind thrashing through the trees hadn't stopped but it was softer in here, almost muted.

Anne watched him over the rim of her cup as she lifted it to her face. She really did look good, Matt thought. The last time he'd seen her she'd had flecks of grey in her hair and bags under her eyes. She'd walked with a bit of a shuffle, and hadn't met anyone's eyes when she spoke to them.

'I see him now and again,' she said. 'As I mentioned, though, he's so busy all the time.' She cleared her throat and put her mug back on the table. 'And you said you don't see him much?'

'No, nowhere near enough, really,' said Matt. 'I thought I would when I moved to London and Tim was based there too, but it's difficult. Such a big city and everyone working really long hours. And Tim's obviously away on work trips a lot of the time.'

Matt took another hasty sip of tea to fill the silence. His mind was racing. When he put his mug back on the table, he realised it was almost empty.

Outside, a large gust of wind shook the trees closest to the house. Rain hammered against the window.

'Did you need to borrow an umbrella?' said Anne suddenly. 'You can't go back out there in this weather, it's ridiculous.'

'Oh, no I should be fine, I—'

'Nonsense, you can't go back out with no cover! I'm sure I've got a spare.'

She got up and walked out into the hall, and Matt could feel his chance slipping away. He'd outstayed his welcome already, he could feel it. He got up to follow her, and as he walked past the wooden bookcase on his left his eyes fell on a small collection of DVDs grouped together on the bottom shelf.

'Oh, Mrs St– er, Anne – while I'm here, I just remembered that Tim still has a couple of films I lent him a while back.' He walked out into the hall and saw her halfway down, her head out of sight as she rummaged beneath the staircase. 'I don't suppose you'd mind if I pop upstairs and grab them, would you? I'll only be a minute.'

Matt watched her back as he spoke. He thought he saw it stiffen for a moment and was sure she'd say no, but when she next spoke her voice was calm.

'Oh, yes, I shouldn't think that'll be a problem,' she called. 'Tim's room's the one upstairs at the back, right above the kitchen. Do you need a hand?'

'No that's okay!' Matt was already at the foot of the staircase. 'I know what I'm looking for.'

Before she could say anything else he was off, taking the stairs two at a time, his heart thumping in his chest once more. His back was hot and sticky.

As he reached the top of the staircase, he forced himself to slow down. The lights were off and the upstairs hall was dimly lit, but Matt could make out the door directly in front of him that must be Tim's room. Climbing the last few steps he stared around himself. There were three other doors leading off the hallway. The one next to Tim's was ajar, and Matt could see a glimpse of white porcelain standing out in the grey murk through the crack. The upstairs bathroom. Behind him, in the shadows at the opposite end of the hallway, was another door that Matt assumed must be Anne's bedroom.

You can't risk it, he told himself. *She'll hear you, and there's no way you can blag that one.*

That left the final door, which stood just to the right of the bathroom in the middle of the hall. It was shut. Matt took a final step onto the landing. Moving forward he grabbed the handle of the door to Tim's room and opened it, trying to make as much noise as possible. As the door swung inwards he crept across the wooden hallway, this time treading softly and praying the floor wouldn't creak, and stood in front of the middle room, holding his breath.

The rain and the wind were even more distant up here. The inside of the house was silent, but Matt could still make out the sounds of Anne moving around on the floor below him. He reached out and slowly twisted the door handle.

The room beyond was small and cast in shadow. Opposite Matt, above a large, dark shape that he took to be a desk, was the only window. It led on to the small alley between Anne's house and the house next door, letting in minimal amounts of grey light and adding to the room's cramped feel.

Easing the door open wider, Matt crept over the threshold.

Don't fucking hang about, he thought to himself. *It doesn't take long to look for DVDs.*

With the door open wide, light from downstairs spilled through and gave Matt a clearer view of what was clearly a study. The left-hand wall was bare, and the right was lined with a tall wooden bookcase.

Matt's eyes scanned the titles; it was mainly novels, with a few non-fiction books with titles like *Keeping a Healthy Mind and Body* and *Being Your Best Self* tucked in a corner. A collection of National Geographic magazines ran along the top shelf. Matt took a step into the room, being careful to tread as lightly as possible on the wooden floor, and looked around.

Aside from the large desk and the bookcase, the study was empty.

Matt took two more steps across the room – a floorboard let out a small creak on his second, causing him to wince – and came to a stop by the desk. This, he thought, looked more promising. An old, chunky PC stood in one corner, but it had a layer of dust over the screen and Matt barely gave it a second glance. His eyes were more drawn to the cluster of notepads and books that littered the desk's wide wooden surface.

Piled on the left-hand side was a small stack of lined WHSmith writing pads. The cover of the top one was down so Matt couldn't read anything at a glance, but they all looked as though they'd been used. On the right was an even taller stack of red Moleskine notebooks.

And, directly in front of him, was an open, bound A4 notepad. A blue biro was lying next to the pad, and the lined page was crammed full of neat, slanted handwriting.

Taking out his phone, Matt swiped the screen and activated the little yellow light built into the back. The page in front of him lit up. Leaning forward and placing one sweaty palm on the edge of the wooden desk, Matt saw something that he at first mistook for a diary.

January 14th, 2014

Partials: One (recurring).

Complete: One (recurring).

The first is the same I've been having on and off for years, although last night it was a bit different. Well not different, maybe, but longer.

I open my eyes in bed and I feel like I need to pee. I lean over to the bedside table and check the time on my phone. It's around three or four in the morning, I can't remember exactly.

It's as I put my phone back down on the table and sit up that I notice him. George is sat in a chair at the end of the bed. I can't see his face because the room's too dark, but I know he's watching me.

Normally at this point I realise I'm dreaming and shut

my eyes and scream until I wake up, but this time, before I
get a chance, he's saying something to me.

'I was meant to find you, Anne,' he says. 'We'll always
be together.'

That's all I can remember. I tried to think back this
morning and work out if he's ever spoken to me in the
bedroom dream before, but I've had it so many times it's
hard to remember. I don't think so, though.

Matt paused and took a shaky breath. The mention of Mr Stevens' first
name made him feel faintly sick. His stomach rolled, as though some
large and twitchy animal had just woken up in there and was moving
around, searching for a way out. Matt took another long breath and
continued reading.

The second one's another I've had before, but less often and
certainly not for a long time.

I'm lying on my back in a field on Rutmoor. George
is lying next to me. It's night, and in the distance I can
hear the laughter of my friends and the deeper voices of
George's work colleagues, sort of jumbled together. They
sound blurred and distant.

I'm looking up at the stars, and I feel happy. George is
holding my hand.

'I love coming here,' he says. I turn my head so I can see
him properly but he's not looking at me, he's looking up at
the stars. The lights from our campsite in the next field over
are reflected in his glasses. He's got a frown on his face. 'It's
strange, but I feel closer to home when I'm out here.'

I reach out and take his hand and ask him where he's
from again. He came down from up north with his colleagues for a weekend trip, I think that's what he said, but
I want to know where he grew up. He doesn't answer,
though, and I don't think he's heard me. His eyes are fixed
on the night sky.

At this point the dream kind of skips forward, like when
you switch scenes on a DVD player, and it's still the same

night but now we're further away from the campsite. The sky above us is clear and by the light from the moon and the stars I can just about make out a footpath winding down into a sort of ravine, George leading me by the hand. I feel a bit scared. I try to listen out for the sounds of my friends laughing, but I can't hear them anymore.

I'm cold. The stars are spread out above us like diamonds in some vast, black ocean. The wind rushes through the heather on either side of the path as George leads me further down, down this steep winding track, and suddenly I realise his hand's around my wrist and he's holding me tight, almost pulling me.

I try to speak his name, but my mouth won't work.

The path winds through some bushes and all of a sudden the ground is harder beneath our feet and we're in a little clearing. When George stops and looks back at me his glasses are two hard, silver rectangles of light. I can't see his eyes.

'I love coming here,' he says again. His voice sounds hollow, dull. He turns away from me again and I realise he's looking at something. Even though I don't want to look, my feet are moving forward and the next thing I know I'm standing alongside him, staring into the clearing.

There's a huge crack running through the ground.

It's like those disaster films after an earthquake's hit and the earth's split apart. The crack in the clearing is about eight foot long and three foot across in the middle, at its widest point. It's like a great, black eye. Looking at it makes my stomach feel sick.

George starts to move forward. I want to resist, to pull back away from him and the gaping crevice he's pulling me towards, but my legs won't let me. I walk forward with him and suddenly we're standing at the edge of it, and when I look down into the blackness I realise there are stars in there too, there are tiny winking diamonds in that black cut just like there are in the sky. I feel dizzy and disoriented.

I can hear the wind, even louder now, and it's almost as if it's blowing up at me out of the ground, whistling up through that crack. George shuffles forward so his feet are hanging over the edge.

I don't remember anything after this point, so that must be the part when the dream ends or I wake up.

(One final note: it's funny, but even though I'm standing on the edge with him in this second dream and he's holding onto me and I'm terrified, I'm also fully aware that he's not going to pull me into the crevice with him. It's more like he's just showing it to me, so I know it's there.)

The writing ended a few lines from the bottom of the paper. Matt turned the page with fingers that shook ever so slightly. The next page was blank, and the one after that, and the next. He flicked through the pad, but the first page was the only one with any writing on it.

Matt could feel his heart hammering in his chest. His fingers were slick with sweat as he reopened the pad on the page with the writing and placed it back on the table, in roughly the same position he'd found it.

Somewhere in the house, a floorboard creaked.

Matt froze. He stood very still, locked in position, and strained his ears. Had that creak come from the staircase? He could no longer hear the sounds of Anne shuffling around on the floor beneath him. He couldn't hear a thing. From the small window above the desk came the soft sound of rain and wind.

After several more seconds of silence, Matt let out a breath he hadn't realised he'd been holding and continued to scan the desk with his eyes. He leaned over and grabbed the first WHSmith notepad on the pile. He flipped open the top and saw a shopping list. Discarding the pad on the table he grabbed the second one and flipped that open, dimly aware that he was running out of time.

The second notepad contained a few scribbled numbers and what looked like some calculations that Matt couldn't make sense of. The borders of the pages were lined with doodles. A tree grew up the right-hand side of one margin, its branches stretching among the scrawled numbers like grasping fingers. In the top left-hand corner of another page a large, dark eye stared out at him. Matt closed the notepad and discarded it.

He'd flipped the top page of the third notepad open and was about to put it straight down again when he stopped. The writing here was still unmistakably Anne's but it was harder to read, as if it had been scribbled down very quickly, and at first Matt hadn't noticed the name at the top of what appeared to be a letter.

He took a breath and brought the notepad closer to his face. Outside a stronger gust of wind kicked up, howling around the brick house.

Dear George,

I don't remember much, but I remember enough to know I hate you. I really, really fucking hate you. You've taken a large chunk of my life and turned it into a black hole.

I know it's you. You're the reason I feel tired all the time, the reason I jump every time the door goes. You're the reason I have to remember to take pills every day, and the reason I go and see Tricia once a week. You're the reason my son hardly ever comes to visit.

I don't remember much, but I know it's you. So here's what I do remember.

I remember I loved you once. You were kind when we first met, and the years before we were married we had fun together. We went places together, we were a normal couple. I think we were a normal couple. Even though the stuff that comes later is blurry I'm sure I remember most of our first few years together, and I trust myself on that.

I remember that something changed. I can't remember exactly when, or how it happened, but some time after our wedding – maybe it was around the time I got pregnant with Tim, or just after he was born – something changed. I think you changed.

When I think back to that time now it's funny, because I can't remember specific arguments or fights or even threats – Tricia believes you were abusive, I know that's what she thinks even though she's never said it out loud – but I remember feeling scared. It's like the anxiety I get in patches now; I remember feeling this constant background churning in my stomach, like something bad was about to happen even though I didn't know what it was.

I remember you went away. Not just for a few days, either, although you did that too sometimes, but for whole years. These are the patches I remember most clearly, because they were the times I started to feel better. It was like coming out of a fog; I'd suddenly find myself on my own again, not really sure how I got there, but I'd be aware that you'd gone and I'd be glad about it.

I'd get on with my life, and I hoped – although I don't think I ever really believed it – that you were never coming back.

I remember hating you when you did come back. I think at one point I tried to leave you – although this memory is very patchy and I'm not sure whether or not I invented it – but I think I remember you stopping me, telling me that Tim would be the one that'd end up hurt if I left. Tim would be the one that'd suffer.

Tricia's been a big help. I remembered even less when I first came to her. It's starting to come back now, though, just very slowly.

I used to feel numb and anxious, but now I feel angry as well as scared. Tricia says that's good.

This letter was her idea, actually. She says even if you're never actually going to give a letter to someone it sometimes helps to write one anyway, that way you can get everything out on paper. Organise all your thoughts. She says some people burn letters like this after they've finished writing them, but I don't think I will.

I think I'll keep this one as a reminder. It's a reminder

that the memories are out there, and they're coming back,
and the harder I work the better I'll—

A floorboard creaked directly behind him. Matt let out a small cry and
dropped the notepad back onto the desk. He spun around and saw
Anne standing in the doorway to the study, watching him.

'You didn't find the DVDs then?' Anne's face was a mask.

Matt stood looking back at her, his skin hot and prickly, not knowing what to say.

'I'm sorry, I—'

'You what? Got the wrong room, did you?'

Matt's heart was hammering somewhere up in his neck. He forced
himself to take a breath. 'No, I went into Tim's room but I couldn't
find the DVDs. I thought they might be in here, so I thought I'd pop
in quickly before I came back down. I'm sorry, I shouldn't have, I
know it...'

Matt trailed off, thinking. Had she seen him reading her notepad?
Anne continued to watch him, her face a blank. Matt took another
breath, and made a huge effort to keep his voice steady when he next
spoke.

'I'm really sorry, I should have shouted for you when I couldn't find
them, I know this looks like I'm snooping.' He forced himself to grin.
'I didn't want to drag you upstairs and cause more of a fuss, though,
especially after you've been so friendly, so I thought I'd just pop my
head around this door on my way down. You know, in case they
were here.'

'There's nothing of Tim's in here,' said Anne. Her eyes flicked past
Matt to the desk, then back again. 'The rain's slowed down a bit.
Maybe you'd better make a break for it now, before it picks up again.'

She turned and stepped from the room back into the hallway.
Without waiting to see if she'd glance back at him Matt spun on the
spot and gathered the three notepads into a hasty pile, returning them
to their stack on the left of the desk.

Then he left the room and joined Anne in the hallway.

They didn't speak as they descended the stairs. Anne waited for
Matt to go in front and he could feel her behind him as he walked,
her eyes on the back of his head.

When they were in the downstairs hall and back by the front door, he turned to her. He'd been building up to say something casual, possibly to thank her for the tea, but she cut across him before he had the chance.

'You know, when you knocked at the door earlier I thought you might be someone else.'

Matt opened his mouth to respond, then closed it again. Anne was looking past him, over his shoulder. Her eyes were distant and unfocused.

Matt thought of the notepads upstairs, and what he'd read in them. He wanted to ask her about them, but he couldn't.

'Did you think I was Tim?' he said eventually.

Anne blinked and looked back at him, as if only just remembering he was there. 'No. I told you, Tim's in Edinburgh.'

Matt nodded and stared down at the floor. He could still hear the rain crashing down outside the front door, but he didn't mind; suddenly he wanted nothing more than to get out of this house.

'Well, thanks for the tea and everything,' he said. 'Sorry for interrupting you, I should have called ahead first to make sure he was in.'

He smiled at Anne and turned to the front door. He'd just touched the handle when her voice rang out again behind him.

'You should visit my son.'

He turned back to her. Anne hadn't moved, but she was standing awkwardly in the hallway with her hands clasped in front of her.

'You should visit Tim,' she said again. 'I used to look after him, but I don't get to so much now he's away. I'm sure he'd like to see you.'

Matt smiled at her, nodded his head, then turned and left through the front door. The wind and rain buffeted him the moment he stepped outside.

As he turned the collar of his coat up and walked down the path to the road, he realised she'd never given him the umbrella.

Back on the bus and heading in the direction of the train station, Matt tried to collect his thoughts. It wasn't easy. Going into Mr Stevens' house he'd felt uncertain, not sure he was doing the right thing. Now he felt even less sure of himself.

The rain had eased up slightly but it was still falling steadily, hitting the bus window with a soft, constant patter. Matt's clothes felt damp against his skin.

He wished he'd thought to take a photo of the dream journal and the letter on his phone. He'd been in a rush, though, and the thought hadn't occurred at the time. It was sloppy.

Still, he could remember most of what he'd read. He'd keep it fixed in his mind until he was on the train, and then he'd make some notes on the pad of paper he kept in his bag.

There were two things in particular that had stuck in his head. The first was a line from the letter Anne had written. Four little words that she'd scrawled somewhere near the beginning.

I know it's you.

Thinking of those words made Matt feel a chill that was nothing to do with his damp skin.

The second thing he kept thinking of was from Anne's dream journal. An image from her first dream. Despite the strangeness of the second, longer dream she'd written about, it was the first one Matt found particularly disturbing. It was similar to a nightmare he'd had himself. One that had recurred on and off over the years.

Lying in bed, unable to move. Looking up and seeing someone sat watching you from across the other side of the room, their face cast in shadow.

Mr Stevens.

Matt drummed his fingers across the brown bag in his lap. His skin was turning cold beneath his wet clothes. He fidgeted in his seat, trying to get comfortable.

Outside, the rain continued to fall against the window in a steady stream.

Matt (2002)

1

The storm hit when they were only halfway to Creek Lane.

The first five miles had ended up taking them around six hours, because they'd had to skirt around two tors and the terrain in between had been terrible. Matt thought at least one whole mile had been nothing but tussocks, with no discernible path. James had fallen and twisted his leg during that stretch, and he'd been walking with a limp ever since.

As they'd been going around the second tor, James and Matt leading the way with drizzle blowing in their faces and Tramper's arm slung around Matt's neck for support, James had begun to cry. He was sobbing under his breath, trying to muffle the sound, but Matt could hear him whimpering below the noise of the wind.

The sound made him angry.

As the afternoon grew shorter and their progress became slower and slower, Matt had become convinced that Mr Stevens didn't know what he was doing. He had all the right equipment and he said all the right things, sure – shit, he even *looked* like a hiker – but Matt could tell he hadn't thought their route through at all. It was fucking ridiculous that they'd come this far out into the middle of nowhere, so far from any roads or help, when it was their first time on the moor.

Matt's mum and James' gran might think Mr Stevens was great, but Matt didn't see it. There was something about him, something in the condescending way he had of looking at people and the strict edge that sometimes crept into his voice, that Matt didn't like at all. He was like one of those teachers that's cruel in the classroom but can turn on the charm for parents' evening.

And now it was just after seven in the evening, they still had five miles to go, and the wind was picking up.

Matt had briefly left James half an hour before to go and speak to Mr Stevens. He told him that Tramper was injured and that he was worried they weren't going to make it to the road tonight, but Mr Stevens had brushed off his concerns with a wave of the hand.

'We've come over the hard bit,' he said, adjusting his glasses and smiling. 'The next five miles is flat, and there are plenty of paths.'

Matt thought he was right about the flatness and the paths, but not about the hard bit. Matt thought the hard bit was still to come.

Now, as Matt walked along a narrow footpath through an endless field of heather, watching Tramper shuffle along in front of him (he had Mr Stevens' walking pole to support his weight), he thought about Tom and Gary.

Gary, who'd been missing for almost a whole day now, and Tom, who'd gone off to get some water and seemingly vanished off the face of the earth. They weren't playing a joke, and surely – at least in Tom's case – they hadn't just wandered off. So where were they? The whole thing felt wrong. One person getting lost on the moor wasn't impossible – Matt knew it had happened before, probably on a number of occasions – but two in the space of half a day? It didn't make sense.

His eyes drifted up from the back of Tramper's sweat- and drizzle-soaked head to the cloudy sky above them. The day had started off okay, but big white clouds had filled the sky in the early afternoon, and now those clouds were stone grey in colour. And on the horizon, above the line of tors in the distance, were the storm clouds.

They were large and black, and the sky below them was smeared down to the earth in wet streaks of rain. *Real* rain, not like the drizzle that had been falling for the last few hours.

Matt glanced over his shoulder and saw Mr Stevens walking with his son. Tim's face was blank as he listened to his dad, who was stooping down to talk to him in a low whisper.

Mr Stevens suddenly glanced up and saw Matt looking at them. He raised his hand at Matt through the drizzle, and Matt turned away again.

He looked at his watch and saw that it was 19:30. That meant there were only two hours of light left in the day.

2

They were still three miles from Creek Lane when Mr Stevens finally admitted defeat.

They'd taken shelter beneath a large copse of trees just off from the footpath they'd been following, and by that point James was no longer making any effort to hide his tears. Matt had to practically carry him from the footpath to the trees, dragging him over the heather through the pouring rain as he sobbed and gripped Matt tightly around the shoulders.

When they reached shelter he'd tottered over to a large oak and crumpled to the floor, resting his back against the trunk with his head in his hands. Matt looked at his friend's shaking body and gritted his teeth.

When Mr Stevens and Tim joined them a few moments later, Matt marched over to them and pulled out his map.

'Look, we're still three miles out and it's getting dark.' He raised his voice partly in anger, partly so he could be heard over the rushing wind and the crashing branches of the trees above them. 'James can hardly walk and the rain's so bad I can't even *see* the path anymore.'

Mr Stevens wiped rainwater from his glasses and frowned. He was finally starting to look worried, Matt thought, but not nearly as worried as he should have looked.

Mr Stevens unslung his rucksack and pulled out his own map. He crouched down and placed it on the flat surface of his pack, then brought out a compass from the front pocket of his coat and laid it on the map. He frowned some more, stared around at the trees, and cleared his throat.

'Okay, I think we'll have to set up camp here,' he said at last. 'You're right, Matthew, we're not going to make it to Creek Lane in these conditions.'

He rummaged inside his pack, pulled out a ziplock bag with a phone in it, opened it and turned the phone on. He studied the screen as the boys looked on in silence, then shook his head and put the phone back in the bag.

'Nothing,' he muttered.

'You said we'd make it to Creek Lane before night fell,' said Matt. 'You said we'd be able to get help, and now we're stuck here.'

Mr Stevens returned the compass to his top pocket, then packed the map away slowly. He zipped up his bag and stood up, and there was something in his face that made Matt take a step back.

'I'm doing everything I can to get us help.' That strict edge had crept back into Mr Stevens' voice. He stared at Matt without blinking, his face an expressionless mask. 'I can't control the weather, and I can't help the fact that James has been injured.'

No, but you could have planned a route that didn't involve us walking 10 miles away from the nearest road, Matt thought, but he kept his mouth shut. There was something in Mr Stevens' eyes that suggested he wouldn't react well if Matt said what he was thinking out loud.

'We're in a bad situation,' Mr Stevens continued. 'And the important thing now is we bed down for the night, get some rest and keep warm. It's dry in here so we can make a fire, at least.'

Matt nodded and didn't say anything else. He glanced at Tim and saw the skinny boy watching him with something like concern on his face, but when Matt met his gaze Tim looked down at the ground.

The wind blew through the trees, causing the branches to sway and crash together. The clouds that Matt had seen on the horizon earlier were almost directly above them now, and even blacker than they'd looked from a distance.

Outside the copse of trees the rain hammered against the heather, hard enough to kick up a light mist of spray.

3

They sat around the campfire in silence, listening to the storm.

In the end they'd set up camp near the middle of the copse of trees, beneath the shelter of a giant oak. Rain hammered against the canopy above them, but only a spot or two managed to squeeze through the thick roof of branches. They'd built up their fire much larger than usual tonight to compensate for the storm, and the flames that twisted and shifted in front of Matt were huge and bright. The fire crackled and the wind moaned through the trees around them. Matt felt himself shiver with something other than the cold.

It was just after 10 now, and the last of the light was seeping out of the day. The trees around them were a network of grey and black shadows, dancing back and forth in the flickering light of the fire.

Matt looked around at his three companions.

James was slumped with his back against the base of the oak, his eyes half-closed and a streak of snot drying on his upper lip. Mr Stevens was sat to Matt's left, his face an expressionless blank as he poured bottled water into a small cooking tin. He dug in his rucksack and took out two Wayfarer meals, which he scrunched down side-by-side in the tin before positioning it over the fire on a clamp.

Tim was sat directly opposite Matt. His face looked extra pale in the glow of the fire. He kept biting his nails as he stared into the flames, and every now and then he'd steal a glance at Matt.

'We'll get some food down us and then we'll feel better,' said Mr Stevens. 'These two are for you, James and Matt. Tim and I will eat later.'

Tim paused in the act of biting a nail and glanced at his dad, before returning his gaze to the fire.

'I'm not hungry,' muttered James. Matt thought he'd drifted off to sleep, but when he looked again he saw his friend's eyes were now fully open.

Mr Stevens sighed. 'When you're anxious it's easy to feel like you can't eat, but believe me, your body needs it.' He looked over the fire at James and smiled. 'You've done a good job making it this far, James, and we're going to get you home first thing tomorrow morning.'

He paused and looked at his son, then over at Matt. 'Tomorrow morning. We'll get through tonight and then set off for Creek Lane first thing tomorrow morning. And as soon as we have a phone signal I'll make some calls and we'll get some people to help us look for Gareth and Thomas – assuming they're not already waiting for us when we get there, of course.'

Matt didn't say anything. He stared at the tin of water over the fire, watching the tiny bubbles form at the bottom and float to the surface. The flames flickered around the tin, dancing over its edges like grasping red fingers.

Mr Stevens cleared his throat. 'Timothy, hadn't you better get us some more firewood? I think we may be running a little low.'

'Sure, Dad.' Tim got to his feet like a zombie and began to move off into the trees.

'Timothy?'

He stopped at the sound of his father's voice.

'Yes, Dad?'

'Don't you think you ought to take Matthew with you? It'll be easier to carry the wood with two of you. We'll want to have enough to last the night.'

'But his food…'

Mr Stevens frowned. 'It won't be ready for another 10 minutes. Go on, off you go.'

Tim paused, chewing a fingernail, and for a moment Matt thought he was going to object some more. Mr Stevens obviously thought so too, because he was staring at his son with a fixed look. The tree branches groaned as a sharp gust of wind blew through their campsite, and the fire guttered.

'Sure, Dad,' said Tim. 'Come on, Matt, let's see what we can find.'

Matt climbed to his feet, wincing as his tired leg muscles groaned in protest.

James glanced up at him and gave a weak smile, which Matt returned as he walked past his friend.

It'll be a miracle if he can fucking stand tomorrow, thought Matt. *Let alone make it to Creek Lane.*

He followed Tim away from the campfire, into the darkness of the trees. Tim paused, felt in his jacket pocket, then pulled out a torch. He clicked the switch and a circle of yellow light appeared in front of them.

'Where shall we look for wood?' said Matt. He had to raise his voice over the sound of the wind so Tim could hear him.

Tim moved the torch beam left to right, then settled on a gap between two larger trees in front of them.

'Let's head down here for a bit,' he said. 'We gathered up most of the wood from around the campsite earlier, so we'll need to go in a bit further.' Tim kept his voice level when he spoke, hardly raising it at all, and Matt had to lean close to hear him. He could smell Tim's breath, drifting across to him in stale waves.

Shit, I probably don't smell much better myself, he thought.

They walked in silence for a minute or so. Matt glanced back the way they'd come a couple of times. At first he could see the campfire quite clearly through the trees, but the second time he looked it was more distant, like a candle on the far side of a dark room.

'Isn't this far enough?' Matt asked eventually.

Tim paused and shone his torch in a circle. They were even deeper in the copse, and the trees were thicker. Overheard the rain hammered down hard against the forest roof.

'Yep, this should do,' Tim said. His voice sounded quieter than it had before, and Matt thought he heard a shaky quality to it. As though Tim was trying to keep himself from crying. Matt reached out and put a hand on his shoulder, and Tim jumped.

'Are you okay?' he said.

Tim swung the beam of the torch round in his direction and Matt was temporarily blinded. He blinked and covered his eyes until Tim moved the beam away again. When he opened them and tried to look at Tim's face, his vision was obscured by the after-image of the light.

'There's something I need to tell you.' A large gust of wind blew through the trees and Matt leaned in close, struggling to hear.

'What?'

'I said there's something I need to tell you.'

Matt blinked his eyes and the after-image began to fade. When he opened them again and looked at Tim, he couldn't read the boy's expression.

'What do you need to tell me?' he said. 'What's going on?'

Tim continued to stare at him, his eyes unblinking, and Matt felt a sudden lurch of fear in the pit of his stomach. Images of Tom and Gary's faces drifted to the front of his mind, like objects floating to the surface of a pool.

'Is it about the others?' he said. 'What's happened, Tim?'

No reply. Just that unblinking stare.

'Tim, what the fuck is going on?'

Tim opened his mouth to say something, and that was when they heard the scream. In all his life, Matt had never heard a sound like it before. He hoped he'd never hear one like it again. It was a high-pitched, animal shriek of terror, a nightmare wail like the midnight screech of a fox in mortal pain, and for a brief second Matt thought it might actually be some injured creature out on the moor.

Then he realised the sound had come from the direction of their campsite. Tim's eyes widened in shock and his head flicked in the direction of the sound. He turned back to Matt, mouth slightly open, and then he looked back in the direction of the sound once more. He bit his lower lip.

'MATT!'

Tramper's terror-soaked voice cut through the wind like a blade. It was just the one word – one legible word before the voice descended into more of those animal screams – but it was enough to jolt Matt out of his shock and get him moving.

He turned and sprinted in the direction of the campsite.

'Matt, wait!'

Tim's voice was at his back, scared and desperate, but Matt ignored it and kept running. The beam from Tim's torch hovered in front of him, framing the trees, but as Matt moved off through the forest it quickly faded behind him. Matt was plunged into semi-darkness and forced himself to slow down, only slightly, to keep himself from running face-first into a trunk or tripping over a root that would send him sprawling.

He could still hear James screaming up ahead and he focused on the sound, running towards it with his hands stretched out in front of him. Twice he fell over in the dark and the second time a branch scraped a gash down his right cheek, but Matt ignored it and picked himself back up.

He could see their campsite up ahead in the darkness now, flickering through the trees like a distant candle flame as he dodged towards it. James' screams were louder.

Matt's night vision had been wrecked by Tim's torch. He shouldered into a tree, stumbled and just managed to keep his balance, then ran on. He wished faintly that he had his own torch with him to see by, but as the light from the campfire grew larger he began to make out the shapes of trees and bushes as they blurred past him.

He ran around a thick group of bushes, lost sight of the campfire, then came around the other side and saw it again. He dodged past a couple more trees and before he knew it he was skidding into the clearing where they'd set up camp. James' screams had stopped.

Matt almost tripped over a fallen pack on the ground, kept himself upright, and stared around. At first he couldn't see anyone. Wind roared through the trees overheard. Then he looked to his left and saw two giant shadows flickering on the trees trunks in the light from the fire. They were the shadows of two half-human shapes joined on top of each other, stretched and distorted in the flickering light, and as Matt took a step in their direction he heard a noise. It was a wheezing, half-choked cry, almost lost beneath the sound of the wind.

The noise was coming from the far side of a bush a few feet in front of Matt. Without thinking he jogged around it, then stopped dead when he saw what was on the other side.

At first his brain struggled to make sense of what he was seeing. He had a vague, half-glimpsed memory of a horror film he'd once stayed up late to watch on Channel 5, in which a giant slug-like creature had preyed on its victims by sliding over their bodies and digesting them whole. Matt felt something lurch in his stomach and then the memory was gone again, pushed from his mind by the sound of another wheezing half-scream.

James and Mr Stevens were a few metres in front of Matt. James was lying on his back and Mr Stevens was crouched on top of him, his arms locked straight and his hands wrapped around Tramper's neck in a death-grip. James was batting at Mr Stevens' locked arms like a puppy pawing weakly at a locked door. His face was a purple reddish colour. His eyes stared straight up at Mr Stevens, huge and empty, and spittle flew from his darkening lips.

Matt had heard of people who witnessed something shocking being rooted to the spot, but he'd always privately thought that was stupid. Cowards would stay still, but people who were brave – people like him – would immediately spring into action, wouldn't they? He'd always been certain of that as a kid. Now, looking on as James struggled beneath Mr Stevens' choking hands, he realised just how wrong he'd been.

He couldn't move. His feet stayed locked to the ground as his eyes drifted from James' blood-filled face to that of his attacker's. When Matt's eyes landed on Mr Stevens' face he heard himself let out a low moan. The sound seemed distant, somehow, as though it was coming from someone other than him.

Mr Stevens no longer looked human. His eyes were large and yellow. The skin of his cheeks drooped down and hung loose around his face like two swollen sacks. His mouth was open slightly, and Matt could see twin rows of needle-thin teeth shining in the light from the fire. As Matt watched, his mouth opened wider and wider, revealing more and more teeth in rows that didn't seem to end.

James let out another wheeze. It was much lower this time, and quieter. The sound of a dying animal.

As if from a great distance, Matt heard Tom's voice in his head. *He's going to die unless you do something*, the voice screamed. It was coming from a long way away, as if from the far end of a great tunnel. *He's going to die and then you're going to die too unless you MOVE.*

That last word was louder, and Matt felt his head clear. He turned to look at Tramper, and as he did so his friends' eyes rolled away from Mr Stevens' face and found Matt's. They were wide and staring and almost completely blank, but Matt saw something in them – some distant, minute flicker of recognition – that finally got him moving.

'GET OFF HIM!' he screamed. He ran towards the thing that had been Mr Stevens, meaning to dive and tackle it, but its head flicked towards him when he was still a few paces away and Matt changed his mind at the last minute. Instead of diving head on towards that open mouth and those rows of sharp teeth Matt threw his body weight to the right and lashed out with his left leg in a desperate kick. Matt felt his foot connect with the side of Mr Stevens' head as his right leg slipped out from under him and he went down.

He rolled over backwards, away from Mr Stevens, and sat up in a crouch.

Mr Stevens was on his knees next to James. His head was bowed as if in prayer, and one hand was clutching the side of his face. A low, stuttering sound was coming from him that didn't sound even remotely human. It made Matt think of hundreds of chattering frogs, or a field of crickets rubbing their legs together in unison.

'James.' He meant to shout but the word came out as a low croak instead. From where he was crouching he couldn't tell whether or not James was moving.

Matt stood and took a step forward. The trees roared and crashed around him. Droplets of rain blew down from the branches and splattered his skin. He took another step, then another. On the third step, when he was only a metre or so from James' body, Mr Stevens' lowered his hand. His head turned slowly and the croaking sound that was coming from his throat grew louder.

Matt froze. He glanced around himself for a weapon – some stick, or maybe a walking pole – but there was nothing. When he turned back, Mr Stevens was facing him.

The flesh around Mr Stevens' jaw was a sagging mass of skin. His mouth had stretched to twice its normal size, and Matt could now clearly see the endless rows of teeth emerging from his flabby gums. The skin on the lower half of his face was red and lined with veins.

All that was bad, but it was his eyes that made Matt take a step back. His ancient, yellow eyes. They were staring at Matt, unblinking, and Matt thought that if he stared into them for too long he might go mad.

Matt took another step back. The thing that had been Mr Stevens raised itself up onto its knees, and then slowly began to climb to its feet. The croaking sound grew louder still. Matt took one more step back, and felt the heat from the campfire at his back.

The next bit happened very fast.

The thing that had been Mr Stevens moved forward and Matt took a final step back, feeling his back bang into something hard as he did so. He half-turned and saw the clamp that was holding the little tin of Wayfarer meals. Half of the water had evaporated in the heat from the fire but the tin was still half-full, and the water was bubbling madly. The thing that had been Mr Stevens suddenly sprang forward, hands outstretch, and as Matt saw its movement from the corner of his eye he grabbed for the metal stand behind him and swung it round in a wild, desperate arch.

Matt felt the hot metal burning into his palms and he screamed, letting the clamp go and watching as the water from the tin flew straight into Mr Stevens' sagging face. The clamp's metal stand followed and struck Mr Stevens in the knee before bouncing off onto the grass. Mr Stevens screamed – a low, guttural shriek – and stumbled. He went down on one knee two paces in front of Matt, then collapsed to the ground, clutching his face. His skin looked like it was steaming. He kept both hands locked to his face as he continued to scream, his forehead pressed to the grass of the clearing.

Matt dodged past him and rushed over to James. He dropped to his knees and put a hand on his friends' chest. It didn't appear to be moving. James' eyes were closed. Matt forced himself to stop shaking and lowered his ear to Tramper's blue lips.

For a moment all he felt was the wind on his face. Matt stayed completely still, feeling the panic start to rise, and then after a very long couple of seconds he heard it. James' breath was weak, hardly a breath at all, but it was there. Matt breathed in deep himself and then leaned down until his lips were touching his friends'.

What would Gary say if he could see us now? he thought hysterically as he puffed air into James' lungs. He lifted his head, took another breath, then did the same again. He put a hand on James' chest and began to rub it back and forth without realising he was doing so.

'Come on, come on.'

After a moment he lowered his ear to James' mouth again. It could have been just his hopeful imagination, but he thought his friend's breathing sounded a little stronger.

'James?' he said. 'James, can you hear me?'

Tramper's eyelids fluttered.

'James?'

Matt leaned closer to his friend, watching his eyelids drift half open to show the whites, and as he bent lower still to whisper in James' ear he felt a hand close around his ankle.

Matt yelled and tried to yank his leg away. The grip was impossibly tight. He managed to turn away from Tramper, onto his back, but as he did so he was yanked across the grass. Matt looked at the thing that had hold of him and screamed.

Parts of Mr Stevens' face had melted. His skin was red and patchy in places, the skin of a burn victim, and in other areas it was missing completely. A large blotch on his forehead was gone and Matt could see something moving behind it, some writhing flesh-beneath-the-flesh that was the dirty green colour of rotten pond water. The purple bags beneath Mr Stevens' eyes drooped down like the lower half of his face, and his yellow eyeballs stood out like those of a corpse. His mouth gaped open and the bottom half of his jaw hung down as if it were on a hinge. Hundreds of teeth winked and glinted. Matt smelled death and rot on his breath.

Mr Stevens clambered higher up Matt's body like a lizard slithering over its prey. Matt tried to wriggle and shove him off, but Mr Stevens pinned his arms. He crawled up further, until he was sitting on Matt's stomach, and then his hands moved to grip Matt's throat.

Matt's breath wheezed out in a panicked rush. He grabbed at Mr Stevens' wrists, staring up in sick horror at his melted, writhing face, and as he tried uselessly to push Mr Stevens' hands away he caught movement out of the corner of his eye.

Matt saw a flash of brown in the light from the fire. Mr Stevens didn't even see it coming. He was focusing all of his energy on Matt's terrified face, and when the tree branch came whirring out of the darkness to strike the side of his head he didn't have time to react. The wood connected with his right temple and Matt felt the grip around his neck loosen.

Mr Stevens' yellow eyes rolled up in their sockets and his body went slack. He tumbled off Matt and collapsed in a heap on the grass.

Matt pulled in a deep breath, then another, and felt his eyesight waver. Sounds were coming at him from a long way away. Wind-blown droplets of rain pattered against his face and he opened his mouth, hoping to force some of the water down his sandpapery throat. His vision was a blur of grey shadows and flickering orange. Blood thumped in his ears. He tried to swallow and felt a muted, far-off pain.

Something moved above him.

Matt squinted his eyes and he just had time to make out Tim's shape before he lost consciousness.

4

His throat was burning.

'Matt. Matt!' Harsh whispers.

Matt felt something hard scrape his teeth, then felt a cooling rush against his tongue. Someone was trickling water into his mouth. He forced his eyes open and looked up into Tim's face. The boy looked as pale and scared as he had in the woods earlier, but there was now something else in his eyes that Matt couldn't quite place. Determination, maybe. Or resolve.

'You have to get up now. You have to get up and help me.'

Matt shut his eyes. All he wanted to do was sleep. He was tired and hurt and he just wanted to rest his eyes for a while, maybe—

Cold water splashed his face. Matt felt the shock of it go through him and he opened his eyes, breathing in deep and staring around him.

He hadn't moved. He was on his back in the same place in the clearing, and Tim was crouching over him and frowning. Matt looked to his left and saw that Mr Stevens was no longer lying beside him, and he felt a moment of panic before he saw that the body had just been dragged closer to the fire. He eyed it warily, watching for movement, but there was none.

Then he looked to his right, searching for James, and the panic returned. There was no sign of his friend. Matt tried to sit up further to look around, but Tim placed a hand on his chest.

'It's okay. He's okay. He's just behind you over there.'

Tim pointed and Matt rolled onto his side so he could follow his finger. James was just behind him and to the right. He was sitting with his back propped against a tree, just like he'd done earlier when they were sat around the campfire. His coat was unzipped slightly and Matt could see thick purple bruises snaking around his neck in the shape of fingers. He shuddered.

James' eyes were closed but Matt could see his chest moving. He rolled back over to look at Tim.

'What happened? What the fuck's going on?'

His voice came out in a dry rasp. Matt swallowed, then winced at the pain that went shooting through his throat.

Tim closed his eyes for a second, and when he opened them again Matt thought he looked years older. He glanced in the direction of his father's body, then back at Matt, and his face wasn't that of a teenage boy; it was the face of a tired old man.

'It's... I... I don't really know how to explain,' he mumbled. He looked down at the ground, then looked at Matt again. 'There's not time now, anyway. You need to get up and help me.'

'Help you with what?'

But Matt knew. He could see Mr Stevens' unmoving figure lying by the fire, and he'd seen the way Tim had looked at the body a moment before. He knew, but the thought of going through with it made him feel sick.

Tim stood up and took a step back, giving Matt space. After a moment he took a breath and pushed up into a sitting position. His head swam for a moment and he thought he might be sick, but then he closed his eyes and everything steadied. He turned onto his hands and knees, then pushed himself carefully to his feet.

When he turned back to Tim, the boy was standing by his father's body. His back was to the fire, the large flames dancing through the night air behind him, and his face was covered in shadow.

'Come on, quickly.'

Matt looked at Mr Stevens' body. Flecks of blood had spattered his walking coat, but aside from that his legs and torso looked like those of any normal man.

It was his face that gave the game away. Matt stared at it once, examining it for a couple of seconds, and then looked away again. The skin around the neck was a sagging mass of flesh. The left side of his head, where Tim had struck him with the branch, was a bloody pulp. Raw, blackened patches covered his forehead and cheeks where the boiling water had hit him.

His eyes were the worst, though. Those protruding, yellow eyes.

But could he really do what Tim wanted? Mr Stevens wasn't

human, that much was obvious, and what he'd just been trying to do to James…

Not to mention what he did to the others. The voice rose up in Matt's mind out of nowhere, and it took him completely by surprise. The others. A nasty, sick feeling began to stir in his stomach.

Gary. Tom. Surely he couldn't–

'Do it.'

The voice was quiet, almost a whisper, but firm enough to carry. Matt glanced round and saw James looking at him from his place by the tree. They made eye contact, and James nodded his head once. 'Hurry.'

Matt took a shaky breath and walked over to Tim.

'Quick, you grab his legs.' Tim's eyes were wide, but determined. As he bent to grip his father's arms, Matt saw his hands were shaking.

Even if he had nothing to do with Gary and Tom disappearing, he still tried to strangle my best friend, thought Matt. *Besides, Mr Stevens isn't a he. He's an* it.

Tim must have really built the fire right up while Matt was unconscious, because it was roaring now. He could feel the heat from it, blasting across his skin in waves. He took a breath and bent to grip Mr Stevens' ankles.

Tim looked at him. 'We've got to do this,' he said. Matt wasn't sure if he was talking to him or saying the words to himself. 'We've got to do this or he might come back. He might find a way to come back and get us.'

Matt glanced across the clearing at James. He hadn't moved, but his eyes were open and he was watching them. Matt looked back at Tim and nodded.

'Right,' said Tim. 'One, two, THREE.'

They swung their arms and let go at the same time. Mr Stevens' wasn't as heavy as Matt thought he'd be. His body sailed easily through the air and crashed into the centre of the fire. A cloud of sparks shot up. Wood and ash scattered. The flames licked around him, seeming to feel him out, and then his trousers caught. A few seconds later, his coat went up too.

Matt was about to turn away when he heard the croaking noise. It started off as a low buzz and at first he thought the fire was making the sound, but then it began to grow louder. Matt remembered the sound Mr Stevens had been making earlier as he strangled James. He stared at Tim in horror.

'I thought he was *dead*.'

Mr Stevens' body began to tremble. The trembling sound deepened to a dull, frantic roar. His yellow eyes rolled in their sockets, left and then right, until suddenly they fixed themselves on Matt. Something like recognition flickered in them.

Matt couldn't move. He thought he could hear someone shouting, possibly James, but it was as though he was trapped in a bubble. The thing in the fire was staring at him, and Matt couldn't look away. He wanted to turn and run, but he couldn't do that either.

The thing in the fire was moving now. The clucking, croaking noise in its throat was growing more urgent, more *insistent*, and as it twisted and writhed Matt saw that one of its hands was reaching out through the flames towards him. The skin on the hand was melting off, peeling away like thin strips of dried PVA glue.

It's going to pull me in with it, he thought vaguely. *It's going to drag me into the fire and we'll burn there together.*

The thing's eyes were locked on him. Matt could see timeless, never-ending years in those eyes. He could see a whole nightmare eternity.

Then the eyes moved. They flicked to Matt's right, looking past him and over his shoulder, and for a split second Matt thought he saw them widen in something like shock before he was being shoved to one side by a heavy hand.

Tim stood in front of the fire, looking down at the thing's burning body. He had a walking pole clutched in his right hand. As Matt looked on he raised the pole, holding it like they told you to hold the javelin on school sports days. For a second he held it in that position, staring down into the fire with a blank expression on his face. Then he lunged.

Matt was a few paces back from the fire now, but he saw it all. He saw the walking pole thrusting through the flames like a spear. He saw the thing in the fire try to twist in a last, hopeless effort to get away. He saw the pointy end of the pole pierce one of the thing's yellow eyes, then carry on travelling into its brain.

Black, bubbling liquid oozed out of the wound the pole had made. The thing's face broke open and the skin fell away like rolls of old parchment. Matt thought he caught a glimpse of something inside – some writhing, green mass – before the flames engulfed it and the head began to smoke and cook.

Tim stumbled back from the fire, then collapsed into a sitting position on the grass.

He closed his eyes and put his head in his hands.

5

Matt didn't realise he'd been sleeping until he opened his eyes and saw light filtering through the trees. It was morning. The worst of the storm had passed. The wind was still there, causing the branches to shift and whisper together, but it was softer now.

Matt sat up and looked around.

Tim had been keeping watch by the fire when Matt left him to lie down next to James, and he was still there now. The fire had died down overnight and was now nothing more than ash and embers. Tim was sleeping in a sitting position, a metre or so from the remains, with his chin touching his chest.

The remains.

Matt got to his feet and walked over to the fire, dreading what he might see as he stared into it. But there was nothing. Whatever Mr Stevens had been, the flames had swallowed him up and left hardly any trace at all.

Staring into the ash where the thing's head had been Matt saw a nest of sharp teeth, but that was it. The sight of those teeth made him feel ill. He looked down at Tim, still fast asleep, and the faces of Gary and Tom suddenly appeared in his mind.

'Hey!'

He bent down and shook Tim roughly by the shoulder. The boy stirred with a soft gasp and looked around.

'What is it? What's happened?' He got to his feet and stared into the pile of ash. Matt watched him carefully. Tim reached down and grabbed some shape in the ash, some long white thing, and for a second Matt thought it was a bone before Tim pulled it free and he saw it was the walking pole. Tim gripped the handle and stirred the ash and embers with the pole. He saw the teeth, prodded them with the pole's sharp end, and then nodded slowly.

'I burned the rest of his stuff in the fire last night,' he muttered. He patted the inside pocket of his coat absently. 'I've got his phone and the other stuff that wouldn't go.' Tim paused, frowning. His face was pale. 'I guess we'll have to find somewhere to bury the teeth.'

He dropped the pole back into the fire and collapsed onto the grass.

'Tim, I need you to tell me, right now, what the fuck happened here,' Matt said. He crouched down on the grass beside him. 'What's happened to Gary and Tom? Did that fucking *thing* get them? It did, didn't it?'

'Course it did.' The voice came from behind him and made Matt jump. He turned around and saw James climbing to his feet. 'It got them the same way it tried to get me last night.'

James limped slowly over to Matt and Tim, then carried on past them and stood staring into the fire.

'Tim, is that what happened?'

Tim stared into the distance for a long time without answering. Matt was about to repeat the question again, maybe give the boy a shake, when he finally nodded his head. Then he began to cry.

James turned around at the sound of the sobs. He looked at Matt, and the hardness that had crept into his face overnight broke. Now he only looked worried and scared. Matt shrugged his shoulders and turned back to Tim. For a second he felt like he might cry, too. He tried to think of something to say next, but Tim spoke again before he had the chance.

'I'm sorry,' he mumbled. 'I'm sorry, I'm sorry.'

His voice was thick with tears. He made no effort to hide his face, just sat there staring into the distance. 'It's my fault,' he said. 'I should have told you earlier. I— I tried to tell Tom, to warn him, and then I wanted to tell you, but—' He stopped and wiped his eyes. Then he turned to look at Matt.

'I was scared,' he whispered. 'I was scared of what he'd do to me if he found out.'

Tim started crying again, and this time he did hide his face. He placed both hands over his eyes and his body shook. After a while James came over from the fire and sat on the other side of him, and both boys put their hands on each of Tim's shoulders.

The three of them sat in silence as the grey morning light filtered in through the trees. A gentle breeze picked up in the clearing and began to carry away the fire's remains.

6

'Tim, was that thing really your dad?'

It was James who broke the silence. The three of them had been walking along a footpath in a line for the last hour, without speaking. Endless fields of heather disappeared into the distance on either side of them. The plants trembled in the wind, giving the illusion that they were walking across a vast, purple ocean. A line of tors was visible on the horizon ahead, made hazy blue in the morning light.

The question hung in the empty air for a long time, and at first Matt didn't think Tim would answer.

'I don't know,' he said finally. 'I honestly don't know what he was. My mum always said he was my dad, but then she was just as scared of him as I was. Maybe more scared.'

They kept walking without breaking stride. Matt was in the middle, with James limping up front with the aid of a walking pole and Tim behind him.

'But what *was* he?' said James. 'Where did he come from?'

This time the silence was even longer. When Tim next spoke, his voice shook ever so slightly.

'I don't think—' he paused, and Matt had the impression he was choosing his words carefully. '—I don't think he... I don't think he came from here.'

The pace of James' shambling walk slowed ever so slightly, but he didn't stop.

'Where did he come from then?'

Matt glanced back over his shoulder at Tim. The boy's eyes were fixed on the path in front of him, large and unfocused. As Matt watched he blinked and looked up at the cloud-covered sky above them, then flicked his gaze back down to meet Matt's.

'Somewhere else.'

Matt suddenly found it hard to meet Tim's eyes. He turned around and kept walking.

After a few moments, James' voice floated back again.

'You know, after Gary went missing and all his stuff was gone, a part of my mind kept telling me that the witch had got him. That Emily Brown woman *he* told us about. I knew it was stupid – I told myself witches aren't real – but Gary must have spooked me on Friday and I couldn't get it out of my head.' He paused. 'I even dreamed about her.'

Matt felt a light chill on his back. 'I dreamed about her, too,' he said. 'On Friday night, I had some nightmare where she was waving at me in the distance, like how she waved at that woman in the story.' He frowned. 'Why did he even tell us that story anyway, Tim? Was that just some bullshit to distract us or something?'

Matt could hear Tim's footsteps behind him on the path, slow and regular.

'I think—' Tim started, then paused for a moment. His voice was quiet, but it no longer shook. 'I think he liked to scare people. He'd probably heard the same rumours about the witch that Gary read about online, and I reckon he told us all that extra stuff to keep us on edge. I don't know how much of it he made up. I remember he used to tell me stories when I was a kid. Bad stories. They used to give me nightmares, too.'

Matt and James didn't say anything. The clouds above them drifted lazily across the sky, casting pockets of shadow on the purple fields.

'I don't remember him being around much when I was little,' Tim said, breaking the silence. 'He'd be away for a long time and then suddenly he'd show up again. I'd get back home from school one day and he'd just be there. He'd stay for a few weeks, or six months or maybe a year, and then he'd disappear again. Every time he went away I always prayed each night, before I went to sleep, that he'd be gone for good.'

The boys walked on in silence. Up ahead the clouds parted and the

sun broke through, coating the purple heather with a golden tinge. It
was James who spoke next.

'He is now.'

'What?'

'Gone for good.'

Tim didn't respond.

Matt shrugged his backpack higher on his shoulders and didn't say
anything either. He was exhausted, both mentally and physically, and
he was finding it hard to think. He knew he ought to feel sad about
Gary and Tom, but for some reason he just felt numb. It was as if
there were some huge wall at the back of his mind – a dam like the
ones him and James had tried to build when they were little – that was
holding all the fear and sadness back. Keeping it trapped in place.

For now, at least.

Matt looked at his watch and saw that it was just after nine. They'd
been walking for around an hour and a half now, and although their
pace had been slow Matt thought it wouldn't be long before they
reached Creek Lane. He had a Nokia 33/10 tucked in his inside coat
pocket which he meant to use when he got there. His mum had made
him take it. To use in case there's an emergency, she'd said, but it
hadn't registered any bars of signal since they were back at the campsite on Thursday. The thought of the phone and Creek Lane made
a question pop into Matt's head, one which filled him with a tired,
weary dread.

'What am I going to tell them?' he said. 'What am I going to say
when I phone up for help?'

'Tell them the truth.' Tim's voice was soft, but firm.

Matt thought about it for a while, then shook his head.

'I can't,' he said. 'What adult in the world is going to believe me if
I tell them what happened just now, with that– with that *thing*?'

'It doesn't matter,' said James. 'We'll back you up. They won't be
able to ignore all three of us.'

Matt shook his head. 'No, they'll think I'm prank calling them.
They won't believe a fucking word of it.' He paused. 'I'm not even
sure if *I* believe it yet.'

James started to protest, but Tim cut him off.

'He's right,' he said. 'I tried to tell someone about Dad when I was younger, back when we were living in Yeovil. It was just after he'd come back from being away, and he was trying to get me to... well, he was being really horrible to Mum and we were both scared of him, so I tried to tell a teacher at my school.'

'What happened?' asked James.

'I stayed behind after class and said I wanted to talk to her about my dad, and at first she looked really worried and she was being extra nice to me, but then when I started to tell her the truth – how he'd tell me these horrible stories before bed and how sometimes his eyes would turn yellow and I'd get really scared – she just burst out laughing.'

'She did *what*?'

'It's not so weird, when you think about.' Tim sounded impossibly tired. 'I was an eight-year-old boy who'd just told my teacher I was afraid of my dad's scary stories and that his eyes sometimes turned yellow at night. She thought my imagination had got the better of me, that was all. I couldn't make her understand what he was like, not really.'

Tim paused, and Matt heard him pull in a deep breath.

'If we phone up and tell them the truth about what happened – shit, if we tell our *parents* the truth – they'll probably react the same way. Only they won't laugh, because this time people are missing. This time they'll get angry, and if we stick to our story they'll make us tell it to lots of policemen and doctors and they'll all get angry too, and everyone will think we're either all lying or that we've all gone crazy.'

'But they'd *have* to believe us, wouldn't, they?' said James. Matt could hear the desperation creeping into his voice. 'If we all say it exactly like it is.'

'If we all say it exactly like it is,' said Tim, 'They'll probably lock us away. They'll shut us up and do tests on us and they won't let us out until we start saying something that they think sounds real.'

Matt wanted to protest – he wanted to believe that what Tim said wasn't true, they were talking about their parents and of *course* they'd believe their own children, they'd *have* to – but deep down he knew Tim was right. Because adults didn't believe kids, not when they came out with wild stories like this. They'd listen and they'd smile and nod, maybe even pretend they believed at first, but they never would.

'I know what we'll do,' said Matt suddenly. Up ahead, he thought he could see a distant line on the horizon where the purple heather finally ended. He thought it might be Creek Lane. Matt felt for the weight of the mobile phone in his inner pocket. 'I know what we'll tell them.'

They walked on through the heather, into the morning sunlight, as Matt explained his plan.

News Cuttings (2002)

From the Devonshire Herald, 19 August 2002

Two teenagers and one adult missing after sudden storm sweeps Rutmoor

Police have launched a search for two teenage boys and an adult who became separated from their walking group during a storm in Rutmoor National Park over the weekend.

Three 13-year-old boys, Matthew Fisher, Timothy Stevens, and James Tramper, were rescued by emergency services on Sunday afternoon after they called for help from Creek Lane using a mobile phone. All three were taken to Rutmoor Community Hospital where they were treated for shock, and James Tramper received additional treatment for exhaustion and a sprained ankle.

Two of their classmates, Thomas Carpenter and Gareth Roberts, and Timothy's father George Stevens, are still missing.

Police, together with the Rutmoor Search and Rescue Team, began a sweep of the area surrounding Creek Lane on Sunday afternoon.

'The people we're searching for became separated from their group during a storm that swept north Rutmoor on Saturday night,' said a spokesperson from Rutmoor Search and Rescue Team.

'We believe they're still in the surrounding area and we're doing everything we can to locate them as quickly as possible.'

From the Devonshire Herald, 20 August 2002

Massive search underway to locate three missing walkers

Police have expanded their search of Rutmoor National Park in an attempt to locate the whereabouts of two 13-year-old boys and one adult who have now been missing for over 48 hours.

The trio of walkers has not been seen since Saturday night, when they became separated from their walking group in the northern part of the moor during a storm.

Three of their companions, Matthew Fisher, Timothy Stevens and James Tramper, all 13, were rescued from Creek Lane on Sunday afternoon. They have all now been discharged from Rutmoor Community Hospital and are reunited with their families.

The search for Thomas Carpenter, Gareth Roberts and George Stevens, meanwhile, was expanded on Monday morning to include the entire expanse of north Rutmoor.

All four Rutmoor emergency rescue teams are involved, and volunteers from the local community have been called in to help.

'We have boat teams covering the water areas of the moor, and we've been widening our search area since Monday morning,' a spokesperson for Rutmoor Search and Rescue Team said. 'Hundreds of people are currently helping us look.

'We'd encourage anyone who thinks they may have seen any of these people to contact us as soon as possible.'

The *Devonshire Herald* reached out to the families of Matthew Fisher, Timothy Stevens, and James Tramper, but none were available for comment.

2015

Friday, Part Two

They pull in to the usual car park just after one.

James finds a parking space – it's not hard; even though it's a Friday, the car park is only half-full – and switches off the engine. He looks at Matt and nods, then pats a large hand firmly against Matt's shoulder.

They find him at the far end of the car park. He's wearing a North Face jacket and fiddling in his rucksack, and for a minute Matt thinks he looks just like his father. The thought makes him feel ill.

'Tim.'

When he looks up and shields his eyes from the sun – it's a surprisingly clear day for Rutmoor, and there are hardly any clouds in the sky – he sees them and grins.

'Bloody hell, there they are!'

Matt feels a smile forming on his face. He glances at James and sees that he's smiling, too. The three boys come together in the dusty car park, the same car park they've been meeting at on and off for the past decade or more, and they hug each other like old friends. Matt supposes they *are* old friends, in a weird way.

After a while they let each other go, and take a step back. Tim stares from James to Matt, that same grin on his face. He's grown into a tall, slender young man with thinning dark hair – a gaunt adult version of the 13-year-old boy they met back in Year 8.

'Jesus, this guy gets bigger every time I see him,' Tim laughs, staring at James and then tipping Matt a wink. 'Your arm's about the same width as my waist, James.'

James lets out a good-natured chuckle and pats Tim on the shoulder. It nearly sends him flying.

'It's good to see you guys again,' says Tim. For a second his grin fades and he looks serious. 'We shouldn't leave it so long next time.'

'It's— well, it's good to see you too,' James says. 'And you're right, we don't do it enough.'

'We've been chatting about a route in the car,' says Matt.

'Oh yeah?'

'Yeah, we were thinking of carving out west for a bit tomorrow, then heading up north.'

Tim stares at Matt for a moment. His smile is gone again, and he bites his bottom lip. After a while he sighs. 'You know, I thought you were going to suggest the old route.'

'No, not the old route,' Matt says quickly. 'Not exactly. But we thought, seeing as it's been a while, it might be good to visit some of the spots where— well, you know.'

'Tom and Gary.' It's almost a whisper. 'Yes, of course. And you're right, it would be. Good, I mean.'

Tim looks pale, and Matt's suddenly reminded of the white-faced teenager who followed them around Rutmoor like a ghost 13 years ago. The teenager who split his own father's head open with a walking pole, and then lied to go along with the story they made up afterwards like it was the most natural thing in the world.

Lying comes easily to some people.

Who was it who'd said that? Maybe James' grandmother. She'd had lots of little catchphrases when she was alive. Or perhaps it's a quote from some film he can't remember.

Matt realises the others are staring at him, and he clears his throat. 'Right, well, no time like the present.' He smiles. 'I say we grab our stuff and set out, we can catch up properly en route. Be good to make up some miles before it gets dark.'

They move off to James' car together to get their packs out of the boot. The sun is shining clear in the sky, and their shadows are nothing but short dark circles that puddle around their feet.

Friday, Part Three

It's the evening, and they're sat around the campfire.

They've made good progress, much better than Matt expected – the combination of their faster pace and the slight shortcut they've taken has put them way ahead of their 13-year-old selves – and Matt thinks they'll reach Hayworth Tor by around midday tomorrow. Maybe sooner.

He feels tired, but not too bad. Years of running have kept him in fairly good shape. He sits on his upturned rucksack a few feet from the fire, walking boots off so he can massage his feet. A metal tin of water simmers on a stand in front of him. He has no blisters today, which is a good sign. He's had his current pair of boots since sixth form – ever since he began training for the 13 Peaks Challenge, before ultimately deciding it wasn't for him – and they still fit like a glove.

He looks round the fire at the others. Tim is sat opposite him and James is on his right, back leaning against the trunk of a tree, and for a minute Matt gets a sense of déjà vu so strong it makes him feel dizzy. He has to look to his left, just to make sure Mr Stevens isn't sitting there too.

'Aching?' Tim's voice floats across the fire. Matt looks back at him and squints through the flames.

'What's that?'

'I said are you aching? You looked as though you were in pain for a moment there.'

Matt forces himself to grin. 'Believe it or not, I'm feeling surprisingly good today. Think I might even be in better shape than I was back at school.'

'It's all that reporting work,' James says. Matt looks at him and he smiles back, his face a mask. 'Keeps you on your toes, running from place to place, right?'

'Are you out in the field quite a bit then?' asks Tim. 'Going out to do proper reporting and stuff, not just stuck behind a desk?'

'Oh, they let me out now and then,' says Matt. 'I used to be in the office most of the time, but when I moved on to investigative stuff I started going out a bit more. You have to, really.'

'What, meeting people for interviews?'

'Yep, that sort of thing. Meeting people for interviews, chasing down a story. Following people around.' Matt grins. 'Proper MI5 stuff, you know.'

Tim laughs. 'Sounds a hell of a lot more exciting than my job.'

'I know I say this every time,' says James, 'But what exactly—'

'Do I do again?' Tim chuckles. 'Don't worry, I'm not even sure myself half the time. I work on different contracts so it varies but, basically, I'm an auditor. So, I'll go into different companies across the UK and make sure their finances and everything are in order.'

'So you must get to travel quite a bit too, then?' asks Matt.

'Yeah, that's one of the perks, in a way. I'm based in London but I can be away for weeks at a time. So last month I was in Liverpool, finishing up a project with a major gallery, and next month I'll be in Cardiff doing some stuff with a branch of the council.'

'Doesn't it get a bit tiring?'

'What's that?'

'All that travelling,' says Matt. 'Having to spend chunks of time in different places. Doesn't it make it hard to get settled?'

Tim has picked up a stick from the ground next to him, and as he stares into the fire, thinking, he breaks off bits of wood and throws them into the flames. After a few seconds he looks back at Matt.

'I actually quite like it,' he says. 'I get bored easily in one place, I think. It's good for me, seeing different cities. Sometimes I even think I might like to move abroad, even if it was only for a year or two.'

'Do you get back to Southampton much?' asks James. 'You know, to visit old uni friends.'

'Not if I can avoid it,' Tim laughs. 'No, I had enough of Southampton in the three years I was there, I think. Besides, most people I know from uni have moved on now.'

Tim throws another segment of stick into the fire, and Matt reaches out to take his water – now boiling nicely – off the heat.

'Do you ever think you'll get bored of coming back here?' He's pouring the water into a mug as he asks the question, but he keeps flicking glances at Tim through the rising steam.

Tim throws his last piece of wood into the fire and watches it burn. He nods his head, slowly, and for a second Matt isn't sure if he's heard the question.

'No, I wouldn't get bored,' Tim says at last. 'I think I'd always want to come back here, every once in a while.'

James looks from Tim to Matt, then back to Tim again. 'It's an important place, isn't it,' he says. 'For us.'

Tim nods. Matt isn't sure if it's just the light from the fire playing tricks, but for a second he thinks Tim might be about to cry.

'Sometimes,' Matt says carefully. 'I think about driving back down here myself. I've thought about doing it a couple of times, particularly on the years when we haven't been able to meet up.'

Tim's staring into the fire. He nods his head without saying anything.

'I thought about coming down last summer, actually,' says Matt.

Tim's eyes flick up from the fire and find Matt's face, then flick back to the flames again.

'Do you guys ever think about doing that? You know, just getting away from everything and coming down here for a day or two?'

James is nodding his head. 'Sometimes,' he says. 'Sometimes I feel like I should come down when we can't all make it. Just come down on my own. I don't like the thought of forgetting, I guess.'

'How about you, Tim?' says Matt.

'I don't think I could ever forget about it.' Tim has picked up another stick which he's breaking into pieces. His eyes are fixed on the fire like a man in a trance.

'But do you ever think about coming back?' says Matt. 'You know, on your own?'

Tim throws another piece of stick into the fire. After a long pause he clears his throat and looks up.

'No,' he says. 'No, I wouldn't want to come back here without you guys.' He pauses and lets out a dry, half-chuckle. 'I think I'd be too spooked.'

Matt shoots a glance at James, who meets his eyes for a second before looking down at the ground.

Matt takes a sip of his tea. It tastes too strong, but it's better than nothing. He puts the mug down on the ground beside him, and listens to the crackling of the fire.

After a moment he closes his eyes.

Saturday, Part One

They pass Hayworth Tor around midday, and reach the spot Matt has in mind around the middle of the afternoon.

It's just a clearing – one of what must be hundreds, if not thousands of clearings in Rutmoor – but Matt recognises it straight away. The sun is beating down overhead, and although there are some clouds off in the distance to the east, the majority of the sky is a clear blue. It shines down on the plush grass of the clearing, and Matt finds it hard to believe that this is the same place where he last saw Tom alive.

Tom, with his long legs and his good looks, who was always the leader of their little group. Matt supposes *he's* probably the leader now – he's the one that plans the get-togethers, and he's the one that organised this very special reunion on the 13th anniversary of that long-ago weekend in the summer of 2002.

I'm the leader, alright, Matt thinks. *I'm the leader and I need to think hard about what that means. What kind of responsibility it gives me.*

He feels a wave of uncertainty wash over him for a second, but then he closes his eyes and pictures the pages from his folder laid out on the bed he grew up in, the bed in his mum's house where he used to lie struggling to get to sleep as a teenager, and eventually the doubt passes. It always does.

'Shall we push on?' says Tim. He glances round at Matt and James and smiles, but Matt sees something else in his eyes. Something like discomfort, maybe. Or fear. 'If we pick up the pace a bit we should be able to make the far side of Garrett before nightfall, make camp there.'

James unslings his backpack and looks from Matt to Tim. 'Steady on, tough guy,' he says. 'I don't know about you but I need a drink at the very least. Five minutes to catch my breath wouldn't hurt, either.'

'I thought you were Mr Fitness,' Tim grins.

'Yeah, but I mainly do weights. All this cardio bollocks doesn't sit well with me.'

Matt, who's been drinking steadily from his Platypus for the last several miles, slurps the last bit of liquid and takes off his rucksack. He opens the top and pulls out the deflated bag.

'I need to fill up,' he says. 'Who wants to join me?'

'Yep, sounds good,' says James. 'Come on, Tim.'

Tim stands with his rucksack still on his shoulders, unmoving. 'I think I'm good,' he says.

'Yeah, well come and join us anyway,' says James.

'I think I'm alright.'

There's a moment of silence. Tim stares down at his walking boots.

James glances over at Matt, who nods his head, once, before taking a step towards Tim.

'You remember where we are, don't you mate?'

Tim looks up and stares around him, a slight frown on his face, but when he catches Matt's eye the frown disappears. Suddenly he just looks very tired. Older, too.

'Yeah, I know.'

'All the years we've been coming back to Rutmoor,' says Matt, 'And we've never once been back to this clearing. Not once.'

Tim sighs and shrugs. 'Too many bad memories,' he mutters.

'The whole place is bad memories,' says James.

Matt ignores him and continues looking at Tim. 'I want to go and fill up at the place where Tom died.' His voice sounds impossibly loud in the stillness of the clearing.

Tim looks up and meets Matt's gaze. The sun is behind him, and his face is half in shadow. After a few seconds, he nods.

'You're right,' he says. 'We've been everywhere else – Hayworth, Garrett, Creek Lane – so why not here as well? Let's go.'

He turns around and walks across the clearing without waiting for them to follow. Matt quickly does up his rucksack and nods for James to do the same, and they follow Tim to a footpath on the edge of the clearing.

Matt feels the sunlight beating down on the back of his head. He feels the sweat running down his neck, and hears the soft rustle of the bushes in the breeze blowing through the clearing.

As he enters the footpath ahead of James he fixes his eyes on Tim's rucksack, watching as it bobs along the trail ahead of him.

Saturday, Part Two

Matt focuses on the sound of the river.

It's calming, and it helps. With each step along the footpath he'd felt less and less sure of himself, and as soon as they left the track and caught sight of the water glinting in the sunlight he'd begun to feel a deep sense of unease building in his stomach. It was the same feeling he sometimes got at work before a call; not an interview – those barely phased him at all anymore – but a *big* call, like when he had to ring up and confront someone before going live with a story about them.

As Matt stares at the river – stares and listens to the sound of centuries-old water flowing over the rocks – the unease is still there, but he's able to block it out.

'This is it,' says Tim. He's a few feet in front of Matt and James, standing on the river bank. As Matt watches him he slings his bag off and takes out a water bottle. He walks over to the water's edge and lowers himself to a crouch. 'This is where it happened.' His voice is small and weak, and Matt can hardly hear him.

'Where what happened?' Matt says. 'I mean, what, exactly?'

Tim pauses in the act of lowering his bottle to the river. 'You know what happened,' he says quickly. 'My fucking *dad* happened. He came up and ambushed us, he—'

Tim's voice cracks and he stops talking. Matt sees him shaking his head, and then he lowers his bottle into the water's current.

James takes his bag off and walks towards the edge of the river. He dumps it a few feet behind Tim and then looks back at Matt, as if he's about to say something. Then he wipes the sweat from his forehead and looks down at the ground.

Matt takes a couple of steps forward. 'Why do you think they never got suspicious?' he asks.

Tim turns his head slightly but doesn't stop filling up his bottle. 'Who?'

'Oh, everyone, I guess. Our families, teachers, the police. All of them.' Matt pauses. 'Especially our families.'

'What do you mean, suspicious?'

'Well, all those years ago when the three of us walked out of Rutmoor, we told them that we didn't know anything. They asked us where Mr Stevens and Gary and Tom were, and we said we had no idea. We'd gotten separated, we said. Told them the others must still be out on the moor.' Matt pauses again and stares at the back of Tim's neck. 'It's a bit surprising how easily they accepted it, don't you think?'

Tim turns his head back to the river. He takes his bottle out of the water, peers into it, then dips it back in to top it up.

'I don't think it's that surprising,' he says. His voice is still quiet, but it's lost its shaky quality. 'We were just kids, and we stuck to a simple story.'

'I suppose.'

'And as for our families, they loved us. Everyone always wants to believe in the people they're closest to. That's natural.'

'Yeah,' says Matt. He glances at James, who's staring at him intently, and nods his head, once. 'Yeah, they do.'

James falls on Tim like a stone. One moment he's standing a few paces behind him, the next he's got a hand clamped on the back of Tim's neck. His other arm wraps around Tim's chest and he wrestles him to the ground. Tim lets out a startled grunt and drops his bottle into the river. It bobs in the current and catches the light as it floats away. For a second he struggles wildly, bucking his body back and forth – *he's fast*, Matt thinks – and James has difficulty holding on to him. Then James moves his hand from Tim's neck and wraps it around his shoulder, simultaneously pushing off from the ground with both his feet, and Tim collapses beneath the weight of his body.

'Hey!' Tim yells. 'Hey, hey!'

Tim's right arm is dangling over the small ledge of ground that juts above the river and he flails it back and forth, struggling for purchase. He finds none. James swings a leg over Tim's buttocks and straddles him, pinning him to the earth.

Matt sees all these things from a long way away, as if he's the observer in a dream. None of it feels real. He walks forward and kneels on the ground beside Tim's thrashing body.

'What the fuck are you doing, get off me!' Tim yells. 'What the fuck, James?'

'Shut up,' says Matt. 'Just shut your mouth and listen for a minute.'

There must be something in his voice that takes Tim by surprise, because he suddenly goes quiet and stops struggling.

'Jesus Matt. What the fuck?' He twists his head to the left and stares up at Matt with one eye. Matt isn't sure if it's just a trick of the sunlight, but that eye looks yellow to him.

He looks down at Tim's helpless, pinned body, and he feels a mixture of disgust and pity pulse through him. Sadness, too. Maybe that most of all.

'We know what you've been doing,' Matt says. He looks for a reaction on Tim's face, but sees none. Tim squints his eye and spits dirt from the side of his mouth.

'What the hell is that supposed to mean? James, can you get the fuck off me now please?'

James' eyes are wide, but his mouth is a firm line. 'I'm afraid not, mate,' he says. 'Not just yet.'

'Look, is this some kind of wind-up? Because if it is I thought we were too old for this kind of crap now.'

'It's not a wind-up,' says Matt.

'Then what the fuck?'

'You know.'

'No, Matt, I really fucking don't. I know I'm dirty and pissed off, but that's about it.'

'You said you wouldn't come down to Rutmoor on your own without us.'

'Yeah, and what's your point?'

'You lied.'

'Eh?'

'Last year, you did come down. And don't try to deny it, because I had a tracking device on your car. I've got your whole route, including the dates and times, saved on my laptop.'

Now Matt sees something in Tim's face. A narrowing of the eye, maybe a slight tensing of the jaw. It's gone as quickly as it comes, but it was there. Part of Matt's job as an investigative journalist is to find out whether or not people are telling the truth, and he's learned to look out for the signs.

'You put a tracking device on my car?' Tim's voice is neutral. His face is an expressionless mask.

'I had to,' says Matt. 'I had to know for sure.'

'Matt, this is ridiculous.'

'I had to know for sure, and once I got that GPS tracker back I did. Of course that wasn't quite enough; I ended up coming down here myself and speaking to some people anyway, just to be on the safe side. You're careful, but you're not careful enough. I spoke to three different people who were able to give me a description that matched yours. That, coupled with everything I suspected from before…'

'Matt, please, please listen to me.' Tim's voice is high and thin, and Matt can hear real fear in it now. 'Whatever you think I've done, it's not true. Yes, okay, I did come down here last summer. You got me. It's the first time I've been down on my own, and to be honest I felt embarrassed admitting it to you guys. But I felt like I needed to come.'

'Why?'

'I just needed—' Tim's voice cracks and he closes his eyes for a second, breathing rapidly. 'I just needed to see the place where it all happened, to have some alone time here. I still get nightmares about that weekend, and I thought—'

'You're lying. I can tell you're lying.' Matt's heart is thumping hard in his chest. Despite the litres of water he's drunk over the last several miles, his mouth feels dry. 'Your dad would be proud of you, you know that?'

'DON'T YOU FUCKING MENTION HIM!' Tim screams the words and James flinches but manages to keep his balance. Tim's face has contorted into a sudden mask of rage, and as Matt sees the way his lips pull back over his teeth – as he takes in the now unmistakably yellow tint in Tim's eyes – the main thing he feels isn't disgust or pity or sadness. It's relief.

'You're more like him than I suspected.'

Tim's yellowing eye rolls around and finds Matt's. For a second he stares at Matt in defiant anger, but then he drops his gaze to the ground and his face creases up. He closes his eyes and starts to cry. This time Matt thinks the tears are genuine.

'That boy who disappeared last year on Rutmoor was 13, Tim. He was the same age as us.' Now Matt feels like *he* might cry. He bites his lip to hold the tears back. 'And he wasn't the only one, was he? In Southampton… those twin girls…'

Tim's face is red and his eyes are screwed up. His mouth is wide open as he sobs silently into the ground, lines of spit falling from his mouth to mix with the dirt. His whole body shakes.

'I'm sorry. I'm sorry, I'm sorry.' He repeats the words again and again, like a mantra.

Snot runs from his nose. Tears slip from his closed eyes and trickle down his cheeks into his open mouth.

Matt stares at him for a second or two longer, then bites his lip again. He gets to his feet.

'Not as sorry as I am.'

Matt takes two steps forward and jumps down into the river. His feet sink into its soft bed and the freezing water comes up to his thighs. Then he turns and grabs Tim. He takes Tim's flailing arm in one hand and the hood of his coat in the other and nods to James, who stands up and grabs Tim's other arm.

'NO!' Tim screams. The sound is high-pitched and deafening. 'NO, NO!'

James jumps down into the river with Matt and they yank Tim forward. He spills over the bank and lands on his belly in the water, kicking and writhing. He comes up, spluttering, and as Matt tightens his grip on the back of his hood Tim manages to twist his head and find Matt's eyes with his own.

'Wait, wait!'

Matt pauses, keeping his grip on Tim's hood, and looks at him. There is no longer any trace of yellow in Tim's eyes. For a split second Matt feels a final wave of doubt, but then he remembers the missing teenager on Rutmoor and the stories of decapitated dogs in Southampton; he remembers the failed abduction attempt in Christchurch – he actually managed to track down the parents of the eight-year-old boy who was nearly taken and arrange to speak to him, and the kid had given him an almost spookily accurate description of Tim – and he remembers the twin girls. Yes, they're the ones he thinks of most. The drowned twin girls. The papers didn't publish a description of the bodies, but Matt read the police report. He doesn't even want to think about how much those little girls suffered before they died.

'It's not my fault,' Tim says, and for a moment Matt thinks he's read his mind. 'It's not my fault Matt, you have to understand that, please. *He's* in me, Matt. I don't want to be like this but he's fucking *in* me.'

He kneels there in the river, water dripping down his face to mix with the snot and tears and his fringe hanging in his eyes, and for a second Matt remembers the younger Tim. The quiet, 13-year-old boy who walked in his father's shadow on that long-ago weekend. The tears sting his eyes so suddenly they take him by surprise.

'You have to help me, Matt,' Tim pleads. 'Help me, you have to help me get rid of him. You have to help me.'

Matt shuts his eyes against the tears, opens them, then puts his hand on the back of Tim's head.

'Okay,' he says. His voice cracks, but only a little. 'Okay, I'll help you.'

He tightens his grip and shoves Tim's head under the water. James goes tense and tightens his own hold on Tim's arm. He doesn't look at Matt. Tim's body thrashes back and forth in the water. Matt has to shift his weight a couple of times and at one point he thinks he's going to lose his balance, but he holds on.

He can hear Tim's garbled screams coming from beneath the water, but they're distant. They'll stop soon.

You have to do this, he thinks. *And not just for the other children he'll hurt. You have to do it for that boy who disappeared last year. You have to do it for the Plumber twins. You have to do it for Tom and for Gary, and for all the others who aren't here anymore.*

The sun beats down on the river and makes Matt squint. The bushes by the footpath rustle in a thin breeze. The river rushes along, unstoppable, its shushing noise drowning out the dwindling sounds of Tim's screams. The whole thing takes longer than he expected it would. He wants to be sure.

When it's done and they are, he lets go of the body without looking at James. It floats up to the surface, a black shape against the blue of the water, and begins to drift off down the current.

The two men watch it go without saying anything.

When it's finally out of sight, they turn away and wade back to the bank. They climb ashore, pick up their rucksacks and tighten the straps, then head back along the footpath in silence.

Acknowledgements

Without the help, hard work and support of a number of people, this book wouldn't exist.

The handful of friends, family and friends of friends who read the book when it was still in its early stages. You know who you are, and your feedback helped make *The Moor* better.

My agent, Zoë Apostolides, for believing in the book.

Kwaku Osei-Afrifa, who first commissioned it; Annabel Wright and Leonora Craig Cohen, who guided me through the editorial process; and all the brilliant people at Unbound who helped it along the way.

My developmental editor, Michael Rowley, whose insightful suggestions improved the story.

My family and friends, whose excitement and interest in the project made me want to make it the best it could be.

All the awesome people who pledged.

My partner, Keely, whose support has been invaluable. I love you, sweetheart.

Patrons

Sandra Armor
David Bailey
Duncan Bailey
Irene Baldoni
Nicholas Batchelor
Damon Beres
Christiane Brossi
Madeleine Bruce
Charlotte Catling
Ellie Champion
Scott Claessens
Stephen Coyle
Michelle DiPietro
Emma Gilbertson
Amy Hall
Liz Hall
Angie Han
Baylea Hart
Jack Hickish
Bob Hickish
Rachael Hogg
Tim Holmes
A L
Anthony Lee
Sophie Lees
Vicky Leta
Rachel Marinos
Natalie Martin
Joshua Mckay
Kathleen McKee
Jen Menin
Gianluca Mezzofiore

Mia Olorunfemi
Philip Omar
Jilian Polentarutti
Sarah Powell
Jo Price
Michael Pursey
Rebecca Rosenberg
Guido Rößling
Stella Rowlands
Erin S
Stan Schroeder
Rosie Smith
Jack Staddon
Ciaran Sundstrem
Sarah Twomey
Amy Victoria
Aliza Weinberger